# THE EMPEROR OF
# THE ANCIENT WORD

Borgo Press Books by DARRELL SCHWEITZER

# THE EMPEROR OF THE ANCIENT WORD

## AND OTHER FANTASTIC STORIES

## DARRELL SCHWEITZER

THE BORGO PRESS

MMXIII

# THE EMPEROR OF THE ANCIENT WORD

FIRST EDITION

Published by Wildside Press LLC

www.wildsidebooks.com

# DEDICATION

For Mattie, Once Again

# CONTENTS

# INTRODUCTORY NOTE

I've come to the conclusion that unless one can write them as engagingly as Harlan Ellison does, long introductions to collections of one's own stories are usually not a good idea. Here are some of my best stories from the past ten years or so, which I hope you will enjoy. That's really all I have to say. If you are going to enjoy them, you might as well get past the introduction quickly and begin.

Pay no attention to the man behind the curtain.

—Darrell Schweitzer
Philadelphia
March 2013

# AT THE TOP OF
# THE BLACK STAIRS

It was a stirring of dust that roused King Vardabates back from the sleep of death. He was himself dust then, oblivious in the Land Beneath the World, but a voice seemed to blow upon the dust, like breath, and the voiced called out his name and bade him come forth, and he had neither strength nor will to resist. And so, as if a faint breeze had arisen on a hot, still summer's day (although in the Land Below the World there are never any breezes), the dust arose into the air, less substantial than smoke, but assuming a shape of a sort.

And King Vardabates awoke from a featureless dream, into the dream of memory. He did not recall, at first, that he had ever worn a crown or commanded armies, or the splendor of his processions or the magnificence of his palace, which still stands in Bersion, beyond the Merimdean Sea.

No, his first memory was of a sunrise, glimpsed through the window when he was an infant, and then there was the feel of hot stones beneath his bare feet, when he ventured out into a courtyard in the hot sun, and was scolded by his nurse for being dirty.

Remembering that, he took a step forward, and felt nothing, and drifted life a cloud of dust on a wind that was impossible in the Land Below the World.

Still the voice called out to him, not in any language the king had spoken in life, but in the universal speech of the dead, "Arise, Vardabates, arise. I, Urcilak, summon thee."

Now his passage over the flat, grey plains left a kind of track, not in the dust itself, but in the memories of ghosts, aroused by motion, the slow regathering of his mind, like a cloud that has been dispersed, coming together again. These others reached up, to touch him, insubstantial as he might be, that they might cling to something, and whisper their memories, that those memories might not be utterly forgotten: a song, a storm at sea, a night of love or rage, the terror of battle, the relief and joy of homecoming.

Now the eyes of Vardabates opened, and he gazed across the featureless, horizonless landscape, and up at the grey sky and the few pale stars, and he remembered another sky, far darker, where this was the color of thick smoke, and other stars, vivid and brilliant where these few were like failing embers.

By the time he reached the base of that vast, black tower, which reaches up out of the Land Beneath the World, into the World itself, he was able to touch the cold stone and feel it, to place his foot upon the first of the black stone steps within and rise to the second. Now all around him whispered a wind, descending the staircase from far above, the voices of the newly dead, pouring down out of the World, shouting out the last of their sorrows, their rage, the shock of departure from life, or even their grateful acceptance of same. In his ears, King Vardabates heard them, inasmuch as he had ears, and he heard among the babble of voices some speech he recognized, from his own country, which he had heard before.

And the voice called him again, saying, "Vardabates, King, come forth," and he had the strength to push against the current of the wind within the tower, to rise up, up, and around, as the stairway spiraled. The name *Urcilak* remained with him, like a thorn in his flesh, tearing, but he could not place it, could not find its meaning or significance. The pain of it kept him going.

It was only as he reached the top of the black stairs, with the wind of descending spirits swirling around his ankles, that he knew who he was, that he remembered his crown, and there came to him another name, Andrathemne, whom he had loved.

Now he stood on the threshold before a low, vaulted room at the top of the tower, where two shrouded figures sat at table, playing a game on a board. He saw that both figures were hard and skeletal, that there was only dread in their features, and he knew that these two were Time and Death. Yet, because they were engrossed in their game, and had set aside the accoutrements of their offices—a scythe leaned against the wall, and an hourglass and a sack of seed rested on a window ledge—he did not know which figure was which.

Because he had been, because he *was* a king who had led armies, he boldly approached to observe their game.

On the board were figures carven of bone, like unto ships or castles or cities, or even in the shapes of individual men and women. One of the players held what might have been a king in his thin hand, in the midst of a long pause.

Now King Vardabates thought to simply slip past these two, occupied as they were, and escape out the door behind them as a truant child might; but he knew he was a king now, and kings have honor and should not be sneaks.

When he spoke up, groping for words in the tongue of living men, he felt as a child again, inarticulately explaining himself before two powerful masters who were not inclined to hear.

"I am....I have to get by. I'm summoned.... Someone *knows my name*."

Now one of the figures turned toward him, its face pale and pitted, yet gleaming like a newly-risen moon. It leaned down and whispered into his ear.

"We know. Go, and take our message into the world of living men." And the other whispered the message at some length, and now King Vardabates was much closer to being actually alive, for he was afraid.

Then he hurried from the room, out the door, and climbed up that long, dark slope down which the ghosts of the dead come streaming, before they reach the black tower. Indeed, now, it was as if he struggled against a torrent. Now the voices of the newly-dead shouted all around him, and their hands clutched at him, trying to drag him with him, outraged that he should be able to defy the order of things, and return where they could not.

As his feet found purchase in that hillside and he leaned into the wind, it seemed that he came together, bone unto his bone, and the dry earth became his flesh. Yet there was no breath in him, and he was not alive; yet animate, more substantial now, he made his way up, and clutched with his hands the edge of that stone wall which guards the borderlands of the afterworld.

At once an alarm was sounded, and borderers came racing to confront him, living men, weary priest-soldiers in tarnished armor, whose task it was to drive back such invaders as himself, that the dreams of men might be untroubled.

Yet when he had climbed over the wall, and spoken the message he had been given (by Time or Death, one or the other, he knew not which) the borderers fell in behind him and became his honor guard. Thus King Vardabates returned to the world of men, by moonlight, beneath a dark sky and brilliant stars. In the moonlight he was barely visible, like a gleam off polished metal glimpsed through the corner of the eye. His footsteps were silent, yet he stirred the dust of the roads along which he marched. There were still ghosts around him, like swirling sand stirred up by the tread of an army. In the night, in the moon-light, the ghosts spoke with voices like the distant tinkle and clanging of metal, before the wind which drove them toward the wall, the dark slope, and the open door of the black tower swept them away and on their way.

And the ghosts cried out to him, "Remember...remember me...."

From this apparition, as it passed, prophets prophesied doom or the return of glorious things, depending on their nature and wont; and the king remembered, not the names of the many ghosts, but some things, the name Andrathemne, whom he had loved, and *Urcilak*, whom he did not.

He felt the road beneath him now, and the night air, and when the procession reached the river Arrax, he heard the waters laughing. He heard too, the shouts and songs of the boatmen on the river, and he felt the dreams of men drifting there, like mist among the ghosts.

A ferryman, terrified, carried them all to the other side in a barge. They passed through villages and towns. People saw them and cried out, or turned away, or were troubled in their dreams if they were asleep. When the sun rose, and throughout the day, the shape of the king was no more than a wisp of dust hung in the air by a trick of the wind, but still it was there, like something glimpsed dimly out of the corner of the eye; and the borderers could not quite remember why they had deserted their posts or where they were bound, and they milled about in confusion. Then evening came, and the moon rose, and King Vardabates was among them, a mighty figure in gleaming armor and splendid raiment, grown stronger from the touch of the earth and the mist from the river and the passing dreams of living men (which he had troubled). Now the shore of the Merimdean Sea was before them, and the risen moon gleamed upon the waters, making a road of light. King Vardabates and his entourage (including many ghosts, and witches and wizards, who had joined him as their souls roamed abroad, like leaves drawn along by a strong current of wind) crossed the sea in a mighty war galley, ablaze with lights, and when they had come to Bersion, and to the immense palace of the great kings of Bersion (many towered it was, and gleaming, carven, so men said, all out of a *single piece* of white marble, around which the whole world was formed even as silt gathered around a boulder in a stream). Now the gate of that palace opened up, and the galley sailed into a harbor within. Above, higher and higher until they blended with the stars, the battlements and towers of Bersion and lighted windows gleamed in the night, until even King Vardabates and his entourage and the thousands of richly-robed and plumed courtiers who had come to greet him seemed as mites of some kind, insects crawling on the floor of a vast cavern.

Dragons, curled and resting in the battlements, gazed down on the scene with lazy indifference, though it was a splendid sight.

One last time the voice touched the king's ear, saying, "Vardabates, I have summoned thee."

The king answered, "I have come."

Then he and the borderers and others of his entourage, and the thousand courtiers who had come to greet him, accompanied by drummers drumming and trumpeters blaring away, strode into the palace which has once been his. All of them flowed like a river, like a tide, the storm-wind which is the breath of Fate (or Time, or of the gods), and memories poured back into the king's mind, and he knew all his past glories, all his conquests and triumphs, all the treasures he had amassed; and it seemed, as he ascended to his golden throne, and put on again his gorgeous robe of state, and sat upon his throne with scepter in one hand and the globe of kingship (which represents the world of men) in the other, that the golden age had again returned, that the mightiest king of all had returned to his glory, that Death itself had been defeated, and the trumpeters might blast the news of this to the stars, into the very ears of the gods.

The dragons, disturbed in their rest among the rooftops, fluttered off into the night.

\* \* \* \* \* \* \*

But it was not to be. Vardabates, though he had been a harsh man when living, though he has spilled whole seas of blood in the course of his conquests and the amassing of his treasure, though he had been an awesome and terrible figure to his enemies, as dreadful as the lightning, did have a certain sense of honor, of duty, of the fulfillment of promises.

Therefore he delivered the message which had been given to him to deliver.

He opened his mouth, and there poured out something like impossibly ethereal black dust, which no man could touch or smell or wipe off the surface of a glass, but which dimmed the blazing lights and muted the trumpets.

He spoke in the language of the dead, addressing first his queen, who was not named Ardathemne and whom he did not love; for Queen *Buran* was cold-hearted women who loved only power and schemed against all. It was she who had conspired with *Urcilak*, the sorcerer, to poison the king by means of a tiny, silver serpent that wriggled into his ear as he slept and which troubled his dreams, speaking of his wife's unfaithfulness as it gnawed away at his brain.

To the Queen, first, Vardabates spoke, and at once her beauty and majesty left her, and she went away to live for many years, alone in a cell of her own choosing, until she was but a withered husk, unable to recall her name or her crimes, yet finding no release.

As the king spoke, the dust which was his breath spread to blot out the brilliant stars and the moon.

Vardabates spoke to Urcilak, whose scheme had been first to murder the king, then call him back and capture his soul in a bottle that he might wield power over all the lands forever. But *no*, the King said, conveying the message of the one who has whispered to him (whether Time or Death), *this was folly, and before Urcilak went completely mad, but long before his death, he should direct that his own soul be captured in a bottle, the bottle sealed, and hurled into the sea. Not that there was any release for him, either.*

And the ghosts and witches and demons which had accompanied the king this far now scattered in fright.

Then the king spoke to his beloved Ardathemne, who was his daughter, whom Queen Buran had given to an evil courtier, who had raped and defiled her, murdered her children for sorcery and locked her up in a tomb. His words passed through the air like dust and found her in her tomb, and whispered, *Comfort, child, for my master will find you soon*, meaning either that Death would claim her, or that Time, sowing years upon her from out of his bag of seed, would soon take away her pain.

As the king spoke of the greatness of the realm, and the glory of conquest, of the riches he amassed, then the black dust which issued from his mouth (and covered the moon and shut out the stars) now settled upon the fields of the land, killing cattle and smothering the firstborn of every household. Still the message (from Death or Time, one or the other) was incomplete, and still the king spoke, until the rivers silted up with dust and even the Merimdean Sea withdrew far from Bersion; until each courtier saw that his own splendid robes were as moldy cerements, that all their ambitions would be worn away by Time as the wind polishes a carven stone face smooth again. To poets, he spoke of silence, to the prophets (according to their inclination and wont) either of the doom of all things or of the ending of days.

Still his message was not complete, as the darkness poured out of him and the souls of the dead streamed away from the king and his throne, pouring, swirling out of the palace, down steps and out of windows, from off the battlements; streaming across the empty lands to froth like a tide over the wall which guards the frontier of the world; thence down, down the black slope and through the door of the black tower, swirling again around the ankles of the two who sat at the table engrossed in their game before plunging, at last, screaming, howling, their voices fading to a susurrus of wind as they descended the black, twisting stairway up which none by King Vardabates had ever returned.

And the king spoke until the great palace in which he sat was wiped smooth, then made craggy again, like a mountain, and the Varadbates sat on his throne in the heart of that mountain, speaking still to trouble the dreams of men, forgotten alike by history, legend, myth, and the gods, who, all this while stared down vacuously from behind the screen of stars in the night sky and did and said nothing; for even they could not defy the one who had given Vardabates the message and even they dreaded to hear it.

They knew it would reach them eventually.

At the very last, Vardabates poured out all his own memories, all his loves and hates, all he had ever treasured or feared, even that moment on the hot stones before the nurse scolded him for being dirty.

A single tear formed and streamed slowly down the king's cheek.

And in the black tower, at the top of the stairs, the player who had held his piece amid a pause for so long (whether Time or Death, none can say) made a sudden move and cried out, "Ha! The victory is mine!"

# THE HERO SPOKE

*We regret our lies most of all.*
                              —*The Book of Mirrors*

So he spoke, opening up the hoard of his words. They flowed forth, like spilled gold.

"Lies," he said, "all lies."

He was a young man, I could tell, under the grime and the scars. When he took off his helmet and placed it in his lap, I saw a smooth face, barely able to sustain a beard.

Weeping, he denied everything.

"None of it is true," he said. "I am not the one you think I am. I didn't do the things I myself have claimed to have done. This helmet is not mine. It belongs to another, who will surely come to claim it and his vengeance."

The helmet was of tarnished bronze, with a T-shaped split for the eyes and nose, a huge black, horsehair crest on top. Indeed, the helmet of a champion. It gleamed dully in the firelight.

We two sat in the dark, beneath the brilliant stars, at a cross-roads.

"Tell the story then, as a story, as a lie."

He wept, and spoke:

"It's not true," he said, "that I journeyed in the company of a genuine hero, whose name is immortal, though I am unworthy to repeat it. Call him my Master, then."

"Hypothetically," I said, "part of the lie."

"Yes."

"We sat around a campfire, much like this one. Imagine that much. In the dark and cold. The great man hunched by the fire, while I tended to what needed to be tended to. And his words, like thunder in my mind. *Of course you will sing my praises, boy,* he said. He spoke without any boastfulness, merely stating a fact as obvious as the weather. Of course I would sing his praises, though he shouldn't have called me a boy. Anyone who has spent five summers fighting alongside one such as he has the right to be called a man, but heroes have no time for such details. It is the way of things.

"So we paused to rest beneath the strange, faint stars—not the stars of Earth at all, but those stars which rise out of the mist as you descend the final slope toward the river, on the border of the Land of the Dead. Wizards have names for those stars. I do not.

"We had come through the country of the centaurs. We had battled dragons, men, and winged demons. We had cut down countless foes, trampling thousands into the mud and dust. Now, here, on the last night, beneath those stars, high up the bank above the Dark River, he seemed to recede into his helmet and his armor, to become all the less a man, more a purely heroic force, the crest of his helmet giving him the appearance of a fierce and predatory bird, an avenger of the gods. It was the supreme honor of my life to be with him that night, as he recounted the story thus far, numbering our deeds that they might be more easily remembered.

"I was to be the *first* to remember them, the *first* to put them into the form of telling, into words which would be improved upon by others. Let me begin the process that would continue on even as I myself would be forgotten, like a vast river flowing from an unknown source.

"We sharpened our weapons, and then we slept. Before I faded away completely I tried to compose a few heroic lines, but the music did not come to me. Never mind. I, like my Master, was beyond all such things now. Let others, who did not witness, refine the telling.

"After a time, we awoke, in the dark, for the sun did not rise here. Beneath those scant stars, we made our way down the bank.

"I heard water flowing gently nearby. The River. Our goal. Did I truly hear it, or dream it? Were we transported in our dreams at the very end, or did we rise up and walk the final distance?

"There, at the very lip of the waters, we slew our horses, in final sacrifice, as was required of us, and we poured out the blood on the barren earth, and we saw, clearly before us, as if a curtain had parted, the great River of the Dead and the Land of the Dead beyond it. We walked along that penultimate shore, pouring out libations of blood from our cupped hands, and it seemed that the spirits rose up around us like cold mist, whispering in our ears, pleas, curses, sometimes just names.

"We accosted the Ferryman, where his boat was tied up at a little dock. We held out our hands and let him lick the blood off them like a dog. This was sufficient payment for our passage, though I could tell from his hungry eyes, from the way his shrunken face swayed lustfully, that he greatly desired the living blood within our veins.

"But he would not have that. My Master drew his sword and as if to whack the vile creature's head clean off. He pointed to the boat and to the further shore, and the Ferryman laughed, like the wind wheezing through rattling bones.

"So we set forth, until the nearer shore was lost behind us in darkness and the hills on the far side loomed huge and black, blotting out even those few stars of the Deathlands. No one spoke. The Ferryman strained at his oar.

"I heard the angry voice of a rival I had once slain in a duel, buzzing in my ear like an insect, then fading away to a remembrance, then gone.

"On the further shore, as we disembarked, the Ferryman groveled before us, both pleading and demanding at the same time, as we had known he would. At a signal from my Master, I drew my sword and he his, and we struck off the Ferryman's head and broke his bones, and ground him into the dust of the Deathlands, lest he raise the alarm at our coming.

"Then we pressed on, against the black wind, against the impenetrable night which would have devoured us. We leaned into our shields, while the Deathlands, alarm or no, threw up against us every terror, every danger and pain and dread we had ever known. All our slain foes fought us once again, and yet my great and perfect Master did not waver, and when once I stumbled, he bore me up.

"I *worshipped* him then. He, truly, more than any other, deserved to be celebrated in epic and song, my own humble efforts at first, then those of the great bards to come after.

"Yet I cannot speak his name."

\* \* \* \* \* \* \*

The teller stopped telling the tale, holding his tear-streaked face in his hands, perhaps to add verisimilitude to an otherwise unconvincing pack of lies, for heroes do not weep, but liars often do.

Idly, I picked up his helmet out of his lap to examine it. I even made to try it on.

But he screamed, and snatched it back, leaping to his feet and drawing his battered sword. I myself did not rise. I saw only madness in his eyes, gleaming there in the firelight. I think he would have cut my head off in another second, but I bade, him, in a soothing voice, to sit down again and continue telling lies, and I promised not to believe a word of it.

\* \* \* \* \* \* \*

"It's all a muddle," he said. "It makes no sense. How then was I ever supposed to tell the story, and *why* did my Master command me to rehearse the tale of our deeds? *Why* did I struggle toward the composition of heroic lines, if I was never supposed to return from the mission, if *he intended to betray me?* Heroes do not commit treachery. It is impossible. I can't go on—"

"I believe you can," I said, "though I believe nothing else."

\* \* \* \* \* \* \*

"This, then, is untrue:

"We came at last to that great palace of bone, which rises like a mountain into the black sky, where dwells the King of Death with all his secret treasures. We stood before the massive gates whereon are carven a record of all the sins and folly of mankind. The lights in the windows far above us glowed a pale green, like baleful eyes, when we pounded on that gate with the pommels of our swords.

"All, thus far, according to plan.

"*But the gate would not open*, and I stood there, looking at my Master, and he at me, and I thought, for the very first time, that my Master was at a loss as to what to do, that he had no further stratagem.

"He put his hand gently on my shoulder, and rehearsed again, in synoptic form yet more eloquently than I ever could—words made golden by the mere fact that *he*, the inestimable Hero, was speaking thus—the tale our deeds, praising as he did my own role in the consummation of things, the unravellings of Fate or the doom of the gods or whatever one should call it.

"'That is for a poet to decide,' he said.

"'Shall not I, then?'

"He shook his head sadly. 'I'm afraid not.'

"He explained to me, solemnly, but with deliberation, that it was, alas, the inherent nature of our mission that only *one* of us was to return from it, either the Hero was to accomplish the thing or the Companion who would witness it, but not both, because someone's blood, *living blood*, must be shed before these gates if ever they were to open, so that *someone* might storm the very citadel of King Death and learn his secrets, to demand an explanation and remedy for the world's pain, for the benefit of mankind.

"'It's very important,' he said.

"'What about the song of your praise, which I am supposed to compose?' I asked.

"'Merely a ruse,' he said, 'to get you to come along. I'll try to remember some of it. I regret this. It is truly regrettable.'

\* \* \* \* \* \* \*

"I can't—!" The teller broke off his narration once again. He wept like a child who has been beaten, just then, though he had the form of a man, and, wearing his crested helmet now, had assumed the aspect of an avenger of the gods.

"Say on—"

"In the lie of the man who was lying, the liar told untruths, that my Master might resort to such tactics. Since he could not, he could not be my Master, therefore this is not the tale of him, and I, who went into the Land of the Dead at his side, cannot be telling it. There can only be silence now."

"How did it all turn out?"

"I don't know."

"Make something up."

\* \* \* \* \* \* \*

"Truly regrettable, I agreed, and I wept for my Master as I drew my sword stealthily in the dark and ran him through, slipping the sword up past his groin, under his breastplate. With a hard, upward jerk I gutted him like a fish.

"He looked down at me in amazement, and sputtered something, but only blood and foam poured out of his mouth and out of the immense wound beneath his breastplate.

"His blood splashed upon the ground before the Bone Gates. I touched the carvings and smeared blood on them, and the carven figures wriggled beneath my hands like a netful of fish, reconfiguring themselves to record even this latest folly of mankind.

"Yet it wasn't a folly.

"I tell you I slew him because I *loved* him, because only by this means could he die with his soul *entirely pure*, the tale his deeds untainted by treachery.

"And the gates of the Palace of the King of Death swung wide, and it was I who stormed in, leaning into my shield against the black wind, against all the terrors the place might hold.

"It was I who burst into the inner hall, to confront the Dark Lord on his dark throne, only to discover that throne empty.

"Nothing there. Only dust and the echoes of my footsteps, as I climbed the steps before the great seat and took into my hands the very bronze, plumed helmet into which my Master's face had vanished entirely when I left his corpse crumpled by the gate.

"Yet. There. The helmet, in my hand.

"It was the final step that completes a dance. I sat upon the throne. I put the bronze helmet on my own head. I receded into it, so that whoever I had been faded away.

"Before my eyes, the walls of the bone palace thinned into mist, and I saw the stars beyond, and beyond the stars the wild, mad faces of the gods of war and of pain and of nightmares rising out of the universal darkness like an inevitable tide.

"And I gained the secret my Master and I had come for. It was mine now, for I was the Hero. I had stolen his name. I felt the terror and despair of all those he had slain in the course of his wars, for how can there be a Hero without violence, and what is the Hero but Death, an ender of lives?

"This palace was my own."

\* \* \* \* \* \* \*

"Or it would be, if you were telling the truth," I said. "Of course you are not."

Weeping still, he rose, helmet upon his head and covered his face, sword in hand. I could not see his eyes.

"The Hero must rise up and go into the world of living men, and there commit deeds of unspeakable atrocity so that men will admire him; and this must continue until he can recruit some companion, who would love him so much, so desire that the tale of his deeds remain pure, that the Hero might gain release."

He raised his sword. I thought he was going to kill me.

I said, "It might work that way...in the story. Which isn't true. Which is over."

"For the Hero, perhaps. But no one loves a liar. No one will ever give *him* release."

He vanished into the night then, and I almost thought I had dreamed the entire episode, but for the war and plague, fire and death that followed in his wake like a tide over the subsequent weeks and months and years, for which such a farrago of lies can hardly be sufficient explanation.

That morning, I took up my own sword and put on my own helmet and set out after him.

# TOM O'BEDLAM AND
# THE MYSTERY OF LOVE

*Love is madness and madness is love, and never the
twain shall part.*

—*Anonymous the Elder*

Winter. London. Fifteen Hundred and Something-Something. In his bed at Whitehall, King Henry VIII dreamed of love, of lovely maidens who became his numerous queens, some of them now minus their heads...which sometimes happened in the entanglements of love, a way of cutting through the Gordian knot of the heartstrings, so to speak.... He dreamed of dancing, of songs, of roistering, of maidens and meat-pies.

Courtiers, with their heads in their hands, serenaded him with lines he'd stolen from another but of which he was nevertheless inordinately proud, *"Alas, my love, you do me wrong....."*

He sniffled. He started to sneeze.

* * * * * * *

Tom O'Bedlam dreamed. Nick the Lunatic dreamed with him, his bosom and boon companion, whom Tom had redeemed long since from the labors of Reason, from the ardors, the cruelty, the slavery of Sanity. This same Nicholas, who had once been gaoler in Bedlam before Tom spoke to him with the true Voice of the place and set him free, which is to say mad; AHEM! *This very Nicholas* walked with Tom O'Bedlam in the dream they both dreamed together, in the cold and the dark of the night.

They passed a troop of the Watch, pikes and armor gleaming in the pale moonlight; but sober watchers do not affect to see madmen, particularly madmen abroad in dreams; therefore, dreaming, Tom and Nick went on their way without any interference.

Dreaming still, they reached the countryside, drifting down empty lanes, past trees naked of all but their last leaf. And that last leaf rattled mournfully, one leaf per tree, as it was the custom among trees in winter to retain but one.

Tom and Nick jangled their bells, mournfully, by moonlit midnight, as was their custom to reply; but they felt, the both of them, a certain emptiness, a melancholy, and remarked on it without words, for two madmen dreaming the same dream surely do not have to trouble themselves to *speak.*

*Alas, for great loss.*

*Something burning where the heart is broken, where joy is stolen away, like the last spark sputtering when the fireplace is swept clean.*

*Aye, and swept clean of all hope, but beautiful in its tragedy, its sorrows like intricately-carven black onyx.*

*Is there any other kind?*

*You got me.*

They passed through a forest of branchless trees, the naked trunks like enormous, tangled blades of silver grass. A wind rustled through the forest, sighing far away.

The forest gave way to open country, but like none Tom had ever seen. The ground was white in the moonlight, but not covered with snow; more leathery than earthen. It had a distinct bounce to it.

Nick did a handstand, bells jangling. He clapped the sides of his soleless shoes and wiggled his dirty toes, then flung himself high into the air as if from a trampoline...high, high...until great black, winged things began to circle him hungrily, eclipsing the Moon as they passed.

He called out to Tom, who leapt up to catch Nick as he

tumbled and caught him by the ankles and hauled him down, out of the clutches of the fiery-eyed, softly buzzing flyers with their gleaming-metal talons; down, down—

They bounced for several miles, soaring over another stand of forest, coming to rest before what seemed a vast mountain with two oval caves in it, side by side. Here yawned the very Abyss, the darkness which swallows up even madmen.

Fortunately more of the silvery strands grew thickly about. Tom and Nick clung to them, at the very edge of the abyss, to avoid falling him.

And standing there, gazing into the depths, Tom O'Bedlam had a vision, as if he were dreaming his own dream *within* the dream and had now awakened from it.

He understood, as only a madman could.

It was this: he and Nick had become as *lice.* They had travelled for what seemed like hours across an enormous *face,* through the forest of the *beard,* escaping the flying peril of the *gnats* (or perhaps flies) until they found themselves deposited at the very lip of *No! No! That wasn't it. Abysses may have lips but nostrils don't!*

He and Nick clung desperately to a giant's nose-hairs as their presence had unfortunate consequences.

"AH—AH—AH—!"

Now the wind roared more profoundly than all the world's hurricanes—profound, yes, though it didn't actually say anything; for the hurricane is the philosopher among storms, Tom always said, or one day would, or so said in his dreams (some confusion on this point), and its profundity is so profound that even the hurricane cannot fathom it—

"AH—AH—AH—!!"

—the one certainty being the thunder of its blast, as the eye of the storm passed, or in this case perhaps you might say it was the nose of the storm; and the winds reversed themselves and Tom and Nick lost their grip and went tumbling into an abyss vaster than any that yawns between the grave and the world, between the world and the stars—

"CHOOO!!!"

* * * * * *

Burning the midnight oil that would never expire, because this midnight would never pass, Peter the Poet paced petulantly in his drafty garret. He sat down at his desk again.

His fancies raged. But words would not come.

His quill scratched across the page:

> *Alas, my love, you do me wrong,*
> *to cast me off discourteously....*

Rubbish, he knew. Anybody could do better than that, even, he fancied, a pair of lice crawling up someone's nose.

* * * * * *

King Henry sneezed and awoke briefly. He thought of love. His royal wrath roused. He considered shouting for the headsman and finding someone's head to lop off, just for the exercise, but, no, 'twas late, 'twas cold, and he could do it in the morning. For now he turned and sank back into the deep recesses of the royal bed, and dreamed of meat-pies, and so does not figure largely in our narrative.

> *"And I have loved you so long,*
> *delighting in your company...."*

* * * * * *

Tom O'Bedlam sneezed and awoke. Nick lay beside him, still asleep, sniffling, but not for long, as the not-so-kindly innkeeper, who hadn't so much allowed them to stay through the miserable cold of the night as failed to eject them because he was himself entirely too drunk (and customers lay snoring across the tables and benches of the common room; here and there somebody sneeze; a belch; flies or fleas or gnats hovered); verily, i'faith, this same innkeeper, arisen early, unsteady on his feet with an ugly expression on his face, approached them in his thundering, clumping boots with a bucket of slops in hand that he *might* manage to heave out into the street and then again maybe not, as he would have to step over the recumbent Tom and Nick to make his way to the door—

"Nick," Tom said, nudging him.

Nick sneezed and swatted a louse off his cheek.

"Nick, we have to go."

The innkeeper loomed clumpingly.

Nick swatted again.

Just in, as he thought to phrase it, the nick of time, Tom hauled his companion up and out the door and into the street. The innkeeper slipped or tripped, or out of sheer spite threw the slops after them. Foul liquid landed with a splat in the snow.

\* \* \* \* \* \* \*

Still Peter the Poet gazed out his window into the darkness, which he fancied to be the darkness of his own melancholy.

The words would not come.

He scratched more rubbish on the page.

> *I have been ready at your hand,*
> *to grant whatever you would crave.....*

He watched the Moon set. He watched it rise. The night would never end.

\* \* \* \* \* \* \*

"Is it morning, Tom?"

"It should be, yes."

"But, look—"

Tom looked. The full Moon was setting in the west, but to the east another Moon was rising where the Sun should be. Birds in the eaves of the houses around them twittered and began to sing, then hesitated, uncertain of what to do next.

"That's not right, Tom," said Nick.

"No, 'tisn't."

They had to scramble aside as a troop of guards with pikes and armor, with banners flying, with moonlight gleaming off their silver helmets, came tramping down the street, screeching "Make way! Make way for our great lady!"

They bore their lady in a sedan chair. She gazed out through the curtain, resplendent in her fiery, jewels gleaming, regarding the two madmen through a glass of some sort, which only magnified her hideous face, which was that of a naked skull.

Her guardsmen screeched because their heads were not those of men, but of ravens and crows.

"That's not right either," said Nick.

"No, 'tisn't."

They stared after the company as it passed.

And so the day passed too, though it was a misuse of the term to call it a day, as there was no daylight in it, as the Moon passed again across the sky amid stars which seemed subtly out of place. And the Moon made to set, and yet *another* rose in the east; and the cold of the night continued; and though Tom and Nick half-heartedly capered at times, and did their tricks in the cold and the snow—Nick lit a candle at both ends and swallowed it, and spat it up again, still burning—no one gave them any pennies for their pains. There were only ghosts abroad, and ghouls, skeletons, the King of Faerie with his rout, the occasional furtive wizard, the former Lord Chancellor of England in all his state (but minus head) and frequent lunatics—there being such a surfeit of Moons that for the moonstruck it was a very special occasion indeed.

\* \* \* \* \* \* \*

Yet the respectable folk of England were still in their beds, still asleep, in the night that would not end.

Peter the Poet paced, not asleep at all.

King Henry dreamed of meat-pies.

\* \* \* \* \* \* \*

Tom and Nick came upon a man who sat calmly on a low wall. As they approached he rolled his eyes and shook his head, made a gobbling noise, and fell over backwards into a snowy rubbish heap.

Tom looked down over the wall.

"Never mind the formalities. Can't ye tell we're as mad as thou art—?"

"Forsooth," said Nick. "Or possibly fivesooth."

But the other merely groped among the rubbish, crooned, and said, "Do not wake me from this wondrous dream, for I lie in the arms of a beautiful maiden!"

Nick regarded him, then turned away.

"Is it sooth he says?"

"No, 'tisn't."

"You keep saying that."

"That's because a madman must be obsessed, Nicholas. Therefore he hath tics and twinges and odd tatters of phrase, which he repeateth anon and anon, as, well, one whose wits are diseas'd—"

"Oh, aye."

"You ought to do it more yourself. Keep your madness in good trim, for Madness, though the most natural and unpracticed thing in the world, requires practice, which is a paradox, as 'twas told to me by a pair o'doxies once in a particularly friendly fashion—"

But before Tom could continue his discourse, lunatic as it might be, Nick tried to remind him that none of this would matter a jot if they both froze to death in the dark.

"That nears dangerously close to common sense," said Tom.

"Stop it."

But even as he spoke there came One with hooded robe and scythe and hourglass.

*"Do I not know you two?"*

Tom shook his head and jingled his bells.

*"We've met before, perhaps?"*

Tom and Nick shook their heads in unison.

*"Let me look it up."* Bony fingers flipped through a notebook made of tiny tombstones, which clapped thunder as the pages turned.

But Tom reached over and flipped the pages back, with a thunder, a crackle, and a crack, losing the place.

*"This gets so confusing sometimes."*

"Aye," said Tom. "It does at that."

\* \* \* \* \* \* \*

Tom and Nick ran. Nick continued his discourse on how the world was ending, the sunrise would never come, there would be no more pennies, warm cups of ale, or inn floors to sleep on. He started to sob. His tears froze and fell down like sparkling diamonds. He stopped to scoop some of them up, wondering if he might be able to use a few to buy ale and mutton.

Tom turned to him and shook him.

"Nick. You're almost making *sense*, a fearful thing from a madman."

"Saint Fibberdeygibbet preserve us! What shall we do?"

"I think we should sleep on it."

"Are we not already dreaming? That makes no sense at all!"

"Exactly."

So they lay down in the street, in the snow and mud, and again slept, and again dreamed, though they were never sure they had ever awakened. A coach ran over them almost at once, but it was a phantom coach, drawn by flaming, headless horses, conveying a bishop of London speedily to Hell (or possibly a bishop of Hell speedily to London), and so it hardly disturbed their rest.

\* \* \* \* \* \* \*

Meanwhile the poet rose from his desk and paced the room, mournfully, yet again. His fancies gathered all around him, thick as gnats, or fleas, or flies...he would decide which later on...and he imagined himself no more than vermin, crawling on the face of mankind...and all ladies gazed upon him as if they were foul specters, or he was...and he yearned for someone who could understand the burning yearning he had in his breast... *that* phrase, he knew, would have to go into the rubbish heap, as soon as he found the words, as soon as inspiration returned....

\* \* \* \* \* \* \*

Tom O'Bedlam slept, and dreamed that he rode in a phantom coach drawn by flaming, headless horses (there were a lot of them on the streets this night; business was booming for spectral conveyances of all sorts) and that a queen in all her finery sat across from him.

The coach sped; it jostled and swayed as it rattled over the rough streets.

The queen's head, which had been in her lap, bounced to the floor at Tom's feet.

"Oh dear," she said. "You must excuse me."

Gently, Tom placed the queen's head back in her lap. There was no room to bow, but he swept his hat from his head in a gallant gesture, bells jingling.

"Are you a Fool?" she asked.

"Are they the ones who say 'i'faith' and 'hey, nonny-nonny,' and call everybody 'nuncle?'"

"Yes. My husband had one like that."

"Tiresome lot. No, I, Your Highness, am a madman."

Her Highness found that to be something of a relief. It was a relief, too, to have a sympathetic ear to talk to, as she recounted how the King and wronged her, jilted her, and lopped her head off for good measure, which didn't even let enjoy the afterlife, because of the constant, tedious obligation to rise from her grave and haunt him.

"We ghosts wail and sing a lot," she said. "Not that it does much good. No matter how off-key we are, *I think he likes it*."

Tom commiserated. He did remark, incidentally, on how the sun did not rise and the world seemed to have come to an end, but only incidentally, remaining focussed on what really mattered, which is to say the lady's sorrows, lost love, broken hearts, and the miscarriage of romance.

"Ah me," the ex-queen sighed. The coach bumped. This time her head bounced into Tom's lap.

"Ah, you...by the way, while you're here...are these *your* fancies that fill and haunt the night, that forbid the sun to rise...?"

She groped forward and took her head back.

"You have been a friend to me, sir. I would grant you any favor I have within my power...but, alas, my powers have been much curtailed by, by...you know." She hefted her head and gestured with it. "All I can offer you is the advice, that, being a madman, you alone understand the mystery that is love, and that if you find the one who is most wounded in love, and somehow heal that wound, then the world will go on as before...though I can't see why even a madman would want that."

"You'd have to be mad to understand, Majesty. Being dead isn't enough."

"Ah, yes, of course—"

Just then the coach hit a particularly large bump, the door flew open, and Tom tumbled out into a snowbank.

He sat up, sputtering, awake (relatively speaking), though some distance from where he had lain down with Nick.

On his way there he passed a line of monks who chanted solemnly and hit themselves on the forehead with wooden tablets. He passed pure maidens, gallant highwaymen, dashing pirates, honest politicians, and other such persons as inhabit dreams.

He came again upon the One with the scythe, hood, and hourglass, who hissed at him, *"Ssayyy...don't we havvv an appp-pointmenttt?"*

He spun the hourglass with his finger and hurried on.

Above him, there were now *eight* moons in the sky. A ninth seemed to have become stuck somehow on the spire of St. Paul's, like an apple on the tip of a knife. The Man in this particular Moon complained vehemently. His dog barked. He dropped his lantern into the street, where it exploded into glittering shards, each of which, Tom knew, was filled with enchantment and could lead someone on a magical, romantic quest, or provide some great and impossible revelation, or boon—but he didn't have time for that.

The air was thick with melancholy. Gloom hung over the city like a damp fog, dimming the outlines of the rooftops to a dull blur. In the houses as he passed, he heard sleepers cry out and sob in their dreams, dreams which might never, ever end at the rate things were going.

He found Nick lying in the street. Several pigs nuzzled around him. But sufficient Melancholy had puddled there (a foul, dark fluid, like slops) that they were the most sorrowful pigs Tom had ever seem. They merely gazed at him reproachfully as he shooed them away.

He shook his friend. "Nick! Nick!"

"Oh alas," said Nick, awakening. "I was dreaming of meat pies. I almost had a bite when—"

"Come on!"

"Come whither?"

"Hither. Thither."

"Blither."

"Oh, yes. Do so Nicholas. Absolutely. Your madness is like a rare sapling, gently nurtured, which now grows into a vast forest that shall not be cut down in a single night."

"But what if that night never ends, Tom?"

Tom told him what the headless queen had suggested.

"Now *you're* almost making sense, Tom. Beware! Beware!"

Nick jangled his bells in warning.

Tom urged him to consider the source. Such advice might have been sound, but *how* it had been obtained put it safely within the allowable bounds of madness.

\* \* \* \* \* \* \*

Now all they had to do was find the one so wounded in love that all the rest had followed.

It wasn't hard.

They went where the fancies were thickest, where the melancholy filled the streets like black syrup, rising above the windows, splashing over walls, while Tom and Nick swam in it amid bobbing skulls thick as foam on a stormy ocean.

They glimpsed the hooded One with the scythe again, who was standing in an upper window, surveying all that passed below, looking rather pleased with himself.

But when that One saw Tom and Nick paddling by in a washtub, he shouted something and ran downstairs.

But Tom looked ahead, not behind. He saw that he and Nick had come to a forest of gallows, from which skeletons hung, all singing as the wind passed through their bones.

*I have both wagered life and land*
*Your love and goodwill for to have....*

They beheld knights on quests, always failing, maidens pining away at tombs which bore the effigies of those same knights. A dragon, quite pleased with itself indeed, gobbled down the maidens one by one.

There were ten moons in the sky, eleven. They bumped into one another. The various Men in the Moons quarrelled furiously.

The skeletons sang:

*I brought thee kerchers to thy head*
*That were wrought fine and gallantly....*

Nick tugged on Tom's sleeve. "What's a kercher?"
"Rubbish!" someone shouted from a loft, high overhead.
"I think we have arrived," said Tom.

\* \* \* \* \* \* \*

Introductions were in order.
"Peter the Poet, I'm Completely Mad. Completely Mad, this is Nick the Lunatic."
"Actually his name is Tom O'Bedlam," said Nick.
"Ah me!" said the Poet, half in a swoon, hand to his forehead.
"Poets do that a lot," said Tom to Nick. "It's part of the trade."
"Sort of like being mad."
"Yes! Exactly!" said Peter the Poet. "Even more so because I am *in love!*" He paced back and forth, gesticulating, waving pen and paper in the air. Tom and Nick stretched and bent, trying to read what was written, but the page never stood still long enough. Meanwhile Peter explained how he had been smitten, indeed, with the madness of love, which burned him, from which his life bled as if from a wound, as fortune's wheel turned but would not favor him, as his fancies raged forth into the night on the holy quest of love (several hundred metaphors followed; we need not list them all), how he had given his heart away—
Indeed, this was so. He undid his doublet, unlaced his shirt and showed them the hole in his breast where his heart used to be.
"Good place to store cheese," Nick remarked.
And in a great storm of words then, in thunder and fury, in drizzling melancholy the Poet told the whole soppy, sorry story, which had no end, and could only be interrupted to further explain that a Poet's fancies come from the heart, and if he has already given his heart away, and does not possess it, those fancies must arise in some place other than the residence where

the poet resides; *ergo* a problem of uncontrollable proportions, which the Poet can hardly be expected to do anything about; ahem, since he, therefore, struggling with the Muse, with inspiration, can hardly be expected to recapture and rein in his fancies because what he writes *has no heart in it* and the result is likely to come out more like:

> *Thy gown was of the grassy green,*
> *Thy sleeves of satin hanging by,*
> *Which made thee be our harvest queen.*
> *And yet thou wouldst not love me.*

"Doesn't even rhyme," said Nick.

"It could be worse," said Peter the Poet bitterly. "It could be *Hey nonny-nonny.*"

"I shudder to think," said Nick.

"Does she have a name?" Tom asked.

"Who?" said Peter.

"Your lady-love. Now I too have some experience in the madness of love, for I was wounded in love myself, when I loved a giantess who was unfortunately moonstruck when she stood up too tall one night and the Moon hit her on the head and knocked her over the edge of the world—'twas a sad thing, but not entirely tragic, for still she tumbles in the abyss, among the stars, and she rather enjoys herself—I hear from her on occasion, as she dreams of me, or sings love-songs in her dreams, though she has fallen so far now that sometimes they take years to reach me—but as I was saying, ahem, it is my experience that in these cases the beloved usually has a *name*...."

"It's Rosalind," said the Poet.

"Ah."

"At least that's her poetical name. I spied her from afar. I fell instantly, madly in love—something you can appreciate, I am sure—and I declared her my Rosalind. I set her on a pedestal, as my inspiration, my Muse. I gave her my heart, as you've seen, but still she loves me not, and my poetry cannot speak of the sorrows I suffer—"

"But you haven't actually ever *spoken* to her, have you, much less inquired of her name?"

"What else can she be but my Rosalind?"

"Her name might be Ethel," said Nick.

"You haven't actually—?"

"I poured my love into a poem, and thus I gave her my heart. It melted into the paper like butter into toast. I followed her to where she lived, and slid the poem under the door—"

"Where for all you know the scullery-maid found it, and used it to wipe her nose when she sneezed."

"All gooey with melted butter?" asked Nick.

*"Alas, for unrequited love!"* said the Poet. "Now sorrows and fancies pour from my heart, which is somewhere else, so what can I hope to do about it?"

"I think I know," said Tom.

\* \* \* \* \* \*

And One who bore a scythe and hourglass, and had to hold both rather uncomfortably under his bony arms as he paged through his notebook, stood on the doorstep of the house where the Poet lived in the loft. There were by now twenty-seven moons in the sky, but the night was still somehow dark, the light itself steely, gleaming of death, the air chill, Doom and Gloom and Melancholy flowing by in the street like a vast river from an overturned witch's cauldron. (In fact every witch in the kingdom rushed out with a jar or a jug to get a sample.)

*At last* he found the page in his notebook. *Yes,* he did know these two, who were due and overdue and had evaded the ravages and reapings of himself and all his kind. These two had escaped all the tyranny of Time, for entirely too long.

*Now* would be a reckoning.

He passed through the door of the house and began to ascend the stairs to the loft, his scythe scraping awkwardly as he held notebook in one hand, hourglass in the other, and in situations like this wished for a third.

Just then Tom, Nick, and Peter the Poet came padding or clattering down the stairs (depending on condition of footwear) and nearly collided with the One who ascended.

The Poet let out a frightened cry. Nick just tugged on Tom's sleeve as if to say, *Do something*, and Tom, calmly, with the assuredness of madness, snatched the gravestone notebook out of the apparition's hand, flipped through it back and forth, laughed at a few things he saw in there, sighed at a few others, and said, "Oh, alas, I have lost your place."

While the hooded One was still sputtering "Stop that!" and trying to find his place again, Tom said, "May I borrow this?" and took the hourglass. He popped off the top, wet his finger with his tongue, and reached in to draw out a few of the Sands of Time on his fingertip.

He touched his finger to his tongue, then turned to Nick and Peter and touched their tongues also.

\* \* \* \* \* \* \*

It was a beautiful spring day, the sky so bright it was almost booming, *"Hey! Look how bright I am!"* Birds sang, not one of them with a *hey-nonny-nonny* either. The air was filled with the scents of flowers wafting as such scents traditionally do (as a poet would describe it); and on such a day, Tom, Nick, and Peter the Poet came to a country fair. There, amid the bustling country folk, among the motley of jesters and clowns, the fantastic costumes of the players (who noisily out-Heroded Herod), the puppets, the banners, and funny hats with exotic feathers, *there*, shining before them all like a beacon, her beauty parting the mass of confusion as a the staff of Moses parted the Red Sea, stood none other than Rosalind.

"That's her," said Peter the Poet.

Thus she had appeared to his eyes when first he saw her.

"I am without words," said the Poet, enraptured once again.

So it was Tom who went up to the lady, bowed low and

gallantly, did several somersaults, stood on his hands with his toes waving in the air, while he said, "Your pardon, gentle maid, but if you will take the word of a poor madman, there is a poet yonder who is mad for love with you—"

But the lady merely shrugged and said, "Why of course? I *am* of radiant beauty, am I not? Poets appreciate that sort of thing."

She laughed. Tom fell over onto his feet. He found himself with Nick and Peter, back in London. The sky darkened and was once again filled with dripping melancholy and intermittent droplets of *ennui*, which rattled off windowpanes like sleet.

"That didn't accomplish very much," said Nick.

"I feel a *hey nonny-nonny* coming on," said the Poet.

Again, Tom held up his finger and touched their tongues.

\* \* \* \* \* \*

The Hooded One flipped through his notebook furiously. These things had to be done according to protocol. He would have to be patient. But not *too* patient.

\* \* \* \* \* \*

Now it was past high summer, with just a touch of autumn in the air, night-time but a proper night-time, with only one moon (a crescent) in the sky, and the Hunter rising to gaze over the horizon onto the fields and towns of England.

Tom, Nick, and the Poet came to a cottage. They knocked on the door and a plump, middle-aged woman met them.

Tom introduced himself, did a few handstands, pulled an egg out of his ear (which hatched in his hand; he gave the woman the resultant chicken) and explained why they had come.

"Ah, madmen," she said. "Of course. Enter."

"I'm not mad," said Peter. "I'm a poet."

"The same."

They entered in, and before Peter could launch into another of his flowing, poetical, and very long speeches, the lady broke in and said, "My name really is Rosalind, which is but happen-stance. You, young man, are too wild-eyed for me, too like these other madmen. You speak of love. I remember love in all its rages. I think of it sometimes, on quiet evenings by the fire. But my life is not like that now. I count the days. I count sheep. I go to market on market day. The seasons follow one another the way they should. I am content. I might have cared for love once, but not now. Why bother?"

She served them warm ale and bread. They sat by the fire for a while, but said little.

Peter the Poet began to weep. Then he stood up, and swept his arm back as if he were about to declaim.

"Quick!" said Nick in alarm. "It might be one of those *hey nonny-nonnies—*!"

Tom bowed politely to the lady and touched Peter's tongue with the last grains of the Sands of Time, then Nick's, then his own.

\* \* \* \* \* \* \*

The Hooded One had it *figured out.* All he had to do, ulti-mately, was *wait.* Time, after all, was on his side. They were relatives. They saw each other occasionally at parties and family reunions.

Yes, wait. He reset his hourglass and thumbed his scythe-blade with a bare, pale bone.

\* \* \* \* \* \* \*

In London again, in the snow, Tom, Nick, and the Poet walked along the dark streets. There was no moon at all in the sky this night, only stars, but there were lights in windows, wreaths on doors, and groups of people singing carols. It must have been close to Christmas. From the taverns came the sounds more singing, and of much roistering.

Nick held up his foot. His bottomless shoes flopped around

his ankles. He wiggled purplish toes.

"Couldn't we go in and roister for a while? I'm getting cold."

"Not yet," said Tom. "Not quite yet."

They came to another house, in the city, and climbed a long, dark flight of stairs, the bells on their caps jingling softly, the Poet's boots scraping.

Gently, Tom pushed open a creaking door, revealing a room where an old woman lay in a bed under thin, ragged blankets, by the light of a single sputtering candle.

She sighed as they entered, *"Alas, my love, you do me wrong...."*

"I beg your pardon," said Peter the Poet.

"Had I known when I was young what I know now," she said, "I would have found a time and place for love. It is the one thing which is both constant and most fleeting. We clutch it like gold, but it trickles away like water. A poet told me that once. I never met him, but he wrote many things, in notes and poems he slipped under my door. I guess he was too shy. I never found out who he was. I could have loved him."

"Oh, alas!" said Peter, sinking to his knees at her bedside.

"Yes, alas," said the old woman. She fumbled in a drawer by her bedside. She unfolded a piece of paper, and, though it was too dark to read in that room, he recited what was written thereon, for she had memorized it long, long before.

> *"Well, I pray to God on high,*
> *That thou my constancy mayst see,*
> *And that yet once before I die,*
> *Thou will vouchsafe to love me."*

Her hand went limp. She let the paper fall onto the bed-clothes.

"Not very good," she said, "but written with real feeling. That's what matters."

There on the paper was something that shone like a brilliant jewel, like a star fallen to earth and captured in the hand, a thing as delicate as a snowflake, but all of fire. It was his soul, his heart, the very source of his inspiration, which he had given away in hopeless love so long ago.

First he reached under his clothing, removing a bit of cheese from where his heart used to be, putting the cheese into a pocket. Then gently, reverently, he took up the glowing thing and replaced it within himself, where it belonged.

Now his fancies were under control.

He looked at the lady sadly, but hardly weeping, and began thinking of the words to a sonnet he would write about this night, something elegant in form, like a deftly carven jewel.

*"Now I've got you!!"* hissed the Hooded One, stepping out of the shadows, bones rattling, swinging his scythe wide. *"I've figured it out! All I had to do was wait! Ha!"*

"And you shall have to wait a little longer," said Tom O'Bedlam, "as anyone who is completely insane can understand readily enough."

He tapped the hourglass and sent it spinning, end over end. But as the lid had not been secured properly after Tom had opened it during their previous encounter, the Sands of Time spilled out all over the room, and there was much confusion.

*"That's not fair!"*

\* \* \* \* \* \* \*

Tumbling, then, back through the days of their lives and the days they had never lived, Tom, Nick, Peter the Poet, and Rosalind found themselves once more in a London street, under the bright sky of summer (which is somewhat less obstreperous than many spring skies you could meet). It was an ordinary day. People went about their business. There was talk that the King was going to chop off another queen's head, or maybe had invented a new kind of meat-pie. No one seemed entirely sure. Rumor, painted in tongues, wagged idly.

The poet got out pen and paper, sat on a wall. Beyond the wall lay a lunatic who had shaped a lady out of rubbish; but she had come to life and the two made passionate love, each of them perfect in the other's eyes.

The poet started to write a sonnet.

Tom, with the insight that comes only to the mad, stayed his hand, and said, "Have you considered becoming an accountant? Lots of lovely numbers in neat rows. Steady wages. No heartbreak or raging metaphors."

(The lunatic behind the wall and his lady-love began to sing, something with *Hey nonny-nonny* in it every other line. It was time for Tom and the others to move on.)

* * * * * * *

The ending was this: Peter married Rosalind, after a proposal that added up their accounts neatly and showed how one side balanced the other. They lived quietly and happily together for a long time. If theirs was not a fiery, all-consuming passion, it was just as well, for such love is only for madmen, as Tom O'Bedlam knew so well. It deprives one of reason by its very nature, but even so, you have to have a knack for it, as you do for really inspired madness.

He explained as much to the Man in the Moon (there was only one) at night when he climbed to the top of the spire of old St. Paul's and helped free the Moon, which had gotten stuck up there, like an apple on the end of a knife.

# THE FIRE EGGS

Uncle Rob's voice was breaking up, either from emotion or a bad transmission or a combination of both. I tapped the enhancer key and he came through a little better.

"It's your Aunt Louise. She's worse."

"She's already dying," I said without thinking, and just barely stopped myself before blurting out, *so how could she be any worse?* Even over the phone, at that distance, I knew I had caused my uncle pain. "I'm sorry, I—"

How hideously selfish we can be at such moments.

But the moment passed. Rob was beyond grief, I think, into some sort of acceptance of the fact that his Louise was doing to die soon of one of those new and untreatable cancer-like diseases that were going around.

Then he told me.

"She's talking to the Fire Eggs, Glenn."

"Jesus—" to use a slightly obsolete expression. Of course lots of people had talked to the luminous, two-and-a-half meter high ovoids since they first appeared all over the world in the course of half an hour on January 23rd, 2004, anchoring themselves in the air precisely 1.3 meters above the ground. Sure, lots of people claimed the Eggs *answered back* by some means which evaded all recording devices but was an article of faith among believers. More than one religion had started that way. There were dozens of bestselling books from the revelations. Countless millions had merely surrendered to the inexplicable and were comforted.

But not Louise. She and Rob were *both* too supremely rational for that, even Louise, who liked to tweak his pride by pretending to believe in astrology or psychic healing. It was just a game with her. Or had been.

Uncle Rob had once told me that he regarded true mental decay, meaning organic senility, as the worst of all possible fates. "If I get like that, shoot me," he said, and he wasn't joking.

And now Louise was talking to the Fire Eggs.

She'd once compared them to lava lamps, from the way they glow in the night, the darker colors rising and swirling and flowing within the almost translucent skin to no discernible purpose. She was old enough to remember lava lamps. She explained to me what they were and what they were for, which was, in essence, nothing. Purely aesthetic objects.

\* \* \* \* \* \* \*

But I am ahead of myself. The first theory to explain the presence of Fire Eggs was that they were bombs, the initial barrage in an invasion from space. I *am* old enough to remember that. I was almost six in 2004, the night of the Arrival, when the things popped into existence with muted thunderclaps (though some reported a crackling sound). There was panic then, the roadways clogged with carloads of people trying to flee somewhere where there weren't any Fire Eggs, all devolving into one huge, continent-wide traffic jam when it became clear that there *was* no such place.

My own family never got that far. My father bundled us all into the car, backed out of the garage with a roar, and then made the discovery shared by so many others that first night,that a Fire Egg could not be removed from where it had situated itself by any human agency. We crashed into the one which blocked our driveway. I remember the trunk of the car flying open, my mother screaming, my father screaming back.

Later, I saw that the rear of the car was crumpled like a soda can. That night, we all sat up bleary-eyed in front of the television, slowly concluding that the world's governments and scientists were just as helpless as we were.

We also learned that it had been worse elsewhere. Innumerable traffic accidents. In the London underground, a train hit one of the things in the tunnel just north of Charing Cross. The first car disintegrated, the second accordioned, and almost a hundred people were killed.

Another one, on a runway in South Africa, had destroyed an airliner, which "fortunately" was empty at the time, but for the crew, who died.

My father made a noise of disgust and shut off the TV.

I remember that we prayed together that night, something we didn't often do. I think my parents, like a lot of people just then, were waiting for, expecting imminent death.

But nothing happened. Days, weeks, months passed. Life settled down, nervously. If the Fire Eggs are bombs, they're still ticking away, silently, thirty-five years later.

\* \* \* \* \* \* \*

So I dropped down from orbit, invoking the compassionate leave clause in my contract in ways I never would have gotten away with if I were not tenured, and as I drove from the airport I did something very few members of my generation have ever bothered to do and certainly none of my students would ever have tried.

I counted the Fire Eggs, the ones hovering above lawns, others in abandoned stretches of roadway off to my right or left. There was a larger accumulation near the city limits, which might have made some sort of sense, but then they were so thick in an empty field that they reminded me of a herd of sheep mindlessly grazing on the gently sloping hillside.

But I couldn't count them any more than anybody really knew how many had been served by that fast-food restaurant, the one with the Golden Eggs; but of course those were man-made imitations, since, as was apparent from innumerable tests, not to mention attempts to adorn them with graffiti or redecorate them as conceptual art, nothing of terrestrial origin would adhere to a Fire Egg. Indeed, you really couldn't touch them. There was some kind of electrical barrier which made the surface totally frictionless.

I gave up counting somewhere in the low thousands. Of course there were no such easy answers, though numerologists and even serious mathematicians had done their best.

The next theory was that Fire Eggs were alien probes. All the religions were based on that one, The Church of Somebody Watching. This was not wholly without merit, or even benefit. There had been no wars since the Fire Eggs arrived. Maybe they'd put mankind on good behavior.

* * * * * * *

Uncle Rob's house looked pretty much as it always had, the towering tulip-poplars along the driveway now leafless and waiting for winter, the house's split-level "ranch" design a left-over from the previous century, even a decorative "mailbox" out front, for all nobody had actually received mail that way in years; and of course the Fire Eggs on the front lawn, arranged by random chance into a neat semi-circle. We'd named them once, years after they'd arrived, when few people were afraid of them anymore and Fire Eggs had become just part of the landscape and Uncle Rob's last book, *What to Name Your Fire Egg* had enjoyed a modest success. We called ours Eenie, Meenie, Moe, and Shemp. They glowed as they always did in the evening twilight, completely unchanged. The one on the far right was Shemp.

And there was Uncle Rob in the driveway, who was very much changed, not merely showing his years, but worn out, defeated. Here was a man who had been a world-famous celebrity before his retirement, the ebullient apostle of rationality to the world, his generation's successor to Carl Sagan, and he had four utterly defiant enigmas practically on his doorstep and

Louise was dying and she'd started talking to them.

"I'm glad you could come," was all he said. He insisted on taking my bag, a leftover courtesy from a time long ago, when there were no Fire Eggs.

* * * * * *

My students could never remember such a time. Many couldn't even imagine it. A landscape without Fire Eggs wasn't real to them. Art gallery attendance dropped off, first from disinterest, then from security problems as every now and then someone tried to "improve" various famous canvases by painting Fire Eggs onto them. It was a compulsion for a while in the 2020's, a kind of mania, which spawned several cults of its own.

Then came the fads, the t-shirts with the Mona Lisa Fire Egg, *Starry Night* with Fire Eggs hovering somewhat unrealistically up in the sky, *The Last Supper* with a Fire Egg on either side of Christ.

I've even seen a redigitalized version of *Casablanca*, still in black and white to satisfy the purists, but with the occasional Fire Egg added to the background in some of the scenes.

I did my graduate thesis on the retro-impact of Fire Eggs on the arts. You know, Hamlet addressing his famous soliloquy to an Egg.

* * * * * *

Uncle Rob, Aunt Louise, and I had a very uncomfortable dinner together. It was a shock that she came downstairs to see me at all. I had envisioned her bedridden, with tubes and drips, surrounded by monitors. I *knew* they'd sent her home to die, so I was shocked, not just mildly surprised, when she descended the stairs in her bathrobe and slippers. She flashed me her patented mischievous smile and a wink, and sashayed down, swinging her hips and bathrobe belt in time like a showgirl.

Then she stumbled and I could see the pain on her face. Uncle Rob and I caught her by either arm and eased her into a chair.

"Take it easy," he whispered. "Just take it easy. Glenn is here. You'll be all right."

"I can see for myself that he's here and you don't really believe I will be all right. Stop lying."

"Louise, please—"

She was still able to eat a little, or at least go through the motions for my benefit. We three went through the motions of a nice friendly meal, doting uncle and aunt and favorite nephew, the Fire Eggs on the lawn glowing through the curtains of the front picture window like Christmas lights glimpsed through snow.

"How was your conference, Glenn?" Louise said.

"I, ah...had to leave early. I missed most of it."

"Oh."

"And what's...with you?"

\* \* \* \* \* \* \*

One of the other things I investigated in the course of becoming one of the leading academic experts on Fire Eggs was what I labelled the Nuke Rumor. During the period in which the world's governments had assigned their top scientists the task of Finding Out What Those Things Are At All Costs, after the attempts to probe, scan, drill through, transmit into, or otherwise penetrate the Eggs had failed, so the story goes, somebody somewhere—always in a nasty, remote place where They Have No Respect For Human Life—set off a nuclear device under a Fire Egg. It made a huge crater, destroyed much of the countryside, killed thousands directly and thousands more from the subsequent radiation, but the *Egg* was utterly unperturbed. The world held its breath, waiting for retaliation.

And nothing happened.

As I first heard the story, it happened in China, but a colleague at Beijing University I knew on the Worldnet assured me no, it was in India. In India they said it was in the Pan-Arabic Union and the Arabs said it was the Russians and the Russians said the French; and I was able to follow the story all the way back to Wyoming, where people were sure the blast had wiped out some luckless desert town and the CIA had covered the whole thing up.

"I think the aliens are trying to exterminate us with boredom," some late-night comedian quipped. "I mean, who the hell *cares* anymore?"

* * * * * * *

"I've been having dreams," Louise said.

*"Please—"* Rob whispered.

She reached over and patted his hand. "Now you hush. This is what you called the boy all the way down from his conference to listen to, so he might as well hear it. You can't fool me, Robert. You never could."

"Just...dreams?" I said.

"You know the kind where you know you're dreaming, and you say to yourself, *this isn't right*, but you go on dreaming anyway? It was like that. I fell asleep in front of the TV and woke up inside my dream, and it was *The Smothers Brothers* on the screen, and I was a girl again. Then somebody turned it off and the room filled up with my friends from school—and I knew a lot of them had to be dead by now, so they couldn't be here—but they were all young ago too, and dressed in bell-bottoms and beads, and barefoot with their toenails painted, the whole works. You know, like hippies, which is what we pretended to be. Somebody put on a Jefferson Airplane record and it was going on about sister lovers and how in time there'd be others. And there were Fire Eggs with us, there in my own living room—here, in *this* house, not where my parents lived when I was a girl—one Egg for each of us, and they seemed to radiate warmth and love. Fred Hemmings, Fat Freddie we called him, tried to get his Egg to take a toke of pot, and it seemed *so* funny that I was still laughing when I woke up, and you know, *there were ashes on the rug!*"

Aunt Louise laughed softly, and for a while seemed lost in a world of her own, and Rob and I exchanged wordless glances which said, *I don't get it* and *You wouldn't want to, believe me.*

"It was just a dream, Aunt Louise. I'm glad it made you happy."

"I didn't use to have dreams like that."

"Maybe now—"

"Yes, maybe now it's time. I can hear my dreams now."

"Hear them?"

She sat for a time, oblivious to us both, and she seemed to be listening to her dreams from long ago, which had Fire Eggs in them.

As always, nothing happened. The four Fire Eggs glowed softly on the lawn and the world was still.

\* \* \* \* \* \* \*

Uncle Rob took me aside into the kitchen.

"If this weren't so awful, I suppose you'd find it academically interesting."

"Is there anything I can actually *do?* Why exactly did you ask me to come here?"

"She's going away, Glenn."

"Don't mince words. She's dying. You know that. I know that. *She* knows that. It is not news. If there is anything I can do to provide comfort, Uncle Rob, or otherwise help you cope, please tell me. Right now I feel about as useless as an ornamental mailbox."

"Or a Fire Egg, doing nothing."

"Maybe they're *supposed* to do nothing. For thirty-five years, they've just sat there. We've waited for them to speak, to open up, to explode, to vanish and leave gifts behind, to *hatch*, for Christ's sake. But they will not hatch, which may be the whole point."

"Always you change the subject, Glenn. I suppose it is helpful to have a questing mind, but you are changing the subject."

"Not entirely. Please. Hear me out. Maybe they're like the plastic sunken ships and mermaids and stuff we put into the fishbowl. They're decorations, and make little sense to the goldfish. Most of the goldfish, after a while, just keep on swimming, but maybe a few, the sensitive ones, respond in some way. That's what the objects are for. That's why they're passive. They're waiting for just the right people to respond."

Uncle Rob began to cry. He held onto my shoulder. I was afraid he was going to fall over. I just stood there, wondering exactly what I'd said wrong, but he explained soon enough. "You're talking crap, Glenn. You know it. You're an educated man. Before I retired, I was the world's top science guru. We're goddamn *experts*, both of us. Our job is to know. When we're up against something we *can't* know, it just tears us down. We've both been skeptics. We've both published articles debunking all the crazy stories and rumors about the Fire Eggs. You were the one who pointed out that the stories of people being taken inside were just a continuation of the UFO mythology of the last century. We kept ourselves clean of mysticism. We were *rational*. Now this. Louise wants me to believe that as she approaches the threshold of death she can hear things from the beyond, and the beyond is inside those Fire Eggs, as if whoever sent them is building a gateway to Heaven—"

"I thought it was a stairway."

"What?"

"One of her old songs."

"Can't we at least retain a little *dignity?* That's what you're here for, Glenn. I want you to help her retain a little dignity."

\* \* \* \* \* \* \*

The presence of Fire Eggs actually stimulated the moribund space programs of the world, a bit cautiously at first, as if everybody were afraid that They would swoop down and crush us if we started pressing out into the universe. This was called the Tripwire Theory, the Fire Eggs as alarm device, ready to start screaming if the goldfish tried to climb out of the bowl. But, as always, nothing happened. The Eggs remained inert. No pattern was ever detected in their subtle, shifting interior light. There was no interference as robots, then live astronauts, then a combination of the two proved definitively that there were no Fire Eggs on the Moon or on Mercury, or Venus, or Mars, or on the rocky or ice satellites of the gas planets. The results from Pluto, I understand, are still being evaluated, but meanwhile the first interstellar probes have been launched, and some people began to look out into the universe again for an answer, rather into their own navels. They began to regard the Fire Egg problem as one that could be solved.

The optimists said that was the whole purpose of the Fire Eggs being here in the first place.

* * * * * * *

I looked back into the dining room.

"She's gone."

"Another damn thing after another I have to put up with," said Uncle Rob, opening a closet, getting out a coat, handing me mine. "She wanders sometimes. But she never goes very far."

I put on my coat. "In her condition? Should she be out at all?"

"No. But her mind is sick too, not just her body."

I didn't ask any more. There was no sense making him review the endless futilities, the grinding, subtle agonies he'd gone through as each and every medical option had been exhausted. She couldn't be put in an institution. There was no money for that. All his was gone. The various plans had long since run out of coverage. Besides, the legalistic wisdom went, what actual harm was there in an old lady wandering around the neighborhood talking to the Fire Eggs? Which is a bureaucratic euphemism for *nobody gives a shit.*

"Come on," I said, nudging Uncle Rob toward the door. "I'll

help you find her."

* * * * * * *

If they'd appeared precisely in the year 2000, things would have been really crazy, but in any case the Fire Eggs rekindled millennialist fears. Clergymen denounced them as tools or emissaries of Satan and searched the scriptures, particularly *Revelations*, to come up with a variety of imaginative answers. There had been a time when Uncle Rob and I had enjoyed deflating this sort of thing. "The Beast of the Apocalypse does not lay eggs," I had concluded an article, and Rob had used that line on his TV show and gotten a lot of applause.

But the Spiritualists took over anyway. Fire Eggs were Chariots of the Dead, they told us, come to carry us into the next life. They were also alive, like angels. They knew our innermost secrets. They could speak to us through mediums, or in dreams.

* * * * * * *

Rob and I found Louise on the front lawn, sitting cross-legged on the icy ground in her bathrobe, gazing up at the Fire Eggs. It was almost winter. The night air was clear, sharp.

"Come on." She patted the ground beside her. "There's plenty of room." "Louise, please go back inside," Rob said.

"Tush! No, you sit. You have to see this."

"Let me at least get you a coat."

"No, you sit."

Rob and I sat.

"Just look at them for a while," she said, meaning the Fire Eggs. "I think that it's important there's one for each of us."

"But there are four, Aunt Louise."

She smiled and laughed and punched me lightly on the shoulder and said, "Well isn't that lovely? There's room for one more. Ask your wife to join us, Glenn."

"I'm not married, Aunt Louise."

She pretended to frown, then smiled again. "Don't worry. You will be." "Did...*they* tell you that?" She ignored me. To both of us she said, "I want you to just sit here with me and look and listen. Aren't they *beautiful?*" I regarded Eenie, Meenie, Moe, and Shemp, and they looked as they always had. I suppose in other circumstances they could indeed have seemed beautiful, but just now they were not.

I started to say something, but then Louise put her dry, bony hand over my mouth and whispered, "Quiet! They're singing! Can't you hear it? Isn't it heavenly?"

I only heard the faint whine and whoosh of a police skimmer drifting along the block behind us. Otherwise the night was still.

Uncle Rob began sobbing.

"I can't stand any more of this," he said, and got up and went toward the door. "Can't we have a little dignity?"

I hauled Louise to her feet and said, "You've got to come inside, *now.*" But she looked up at me with such a hurt expression that I let go of her. She wobbled. I caught hold of her. "Yes," she said, "let me have a little dignity." I think she was completely lucid at that moment. I think she knew exactly what she was doing. She sat down again.

I turned to Uncle Rob. "You go on in. We'll stay out here a while longer." So we sat in the cold, autumn air, in front of the Fire Eggs, like couch potatoes in front of a four-panel TV. No, that's not right. It doesn't describe what Louise did at all. She listened raptly, *rapturously,* to voices I could not hear, to something which, perhaps, only dying people *can* hear as they slide out of this life. She turned from one Fire Egg to the next, to the next, as if all of them were conversing together. She reached out to touch them, hesitantly, like one of the apes in the ancient flat-video classic, *2001: A Space Odyssey,* but of course she could not touch them, and her fingers slid away as if her hand couldn't quite locate the points of space where the Fire Eggs were.

At times she answered back, and sang something, as if accompanying old voices, but I think it was some rock-and-roll song from her psychedelic childhood, not an ethereal hymn from the Hereafter.

Or maybe the Hereafter just likes Jefferson Airplane. Or the Fire Eggs do. I would like to be able to say that I achieved some epiphany myself, that I saw the Fire Eggs in a new way, as if the scales had fallen from my eyes and I saw truly for the first time. I would like to say that I heard something, that I received some revelation.

But I only watched the pale reds and oranges drifting within the creamy, luminous white. I only saw the Fire Eggs, as every human being on Earth sees Fire Eggs every day of his or her life.

I only heard the police skimmer slide around the block. Maybe one of the cops was staring at us through the darkened windows. Maybe not. The skimmer didn't stop.

And I looked up and saw the autumn stars, as inscrutable as the Fire Eggs, never twinkling, almost as if I were looking at them from space.

Louise died during the night. She started drooling blood, but she looked content where she was, and it wouldn't have made any difference anyway, which may be a euphemism for something too painful to put into words.

I just stayed there with her. After a while, her breathing had a gurgling sound to it, and she leaned over into my lap. I could see by the light of the Fire Eggs that she was bleeding from the bowels and the whole back of her bathrobe was stained dark. But she didn't want to leave. She had what I suppose someone else might have called a beatific expression on her face. She reached up toward the Fire Eggs once more, groping in the air.

And then I rocked her to sleep, by the light of the unblinking stars and of the Fire Eggs.

* * * * * * *

Somehow I fell asleep too. At dawn, Uncle Rob shook me awake. I got up stiffly, but I'd been dressed warmly enough that I was all right.

He couldn't bring himself to say anything, but the look in his eyes told me everything.

I didn't have to ask. I didn't have to search. Aunt Louise was gone, bloody bathrobe and all.

Of course any number of disappearances and murders had been attributed to the Fire Eggs in the past, as had so much else. "The Fire Egg ate my homework" was an old joke. "The Fire Egg ate Aunt Louise" didn't go over well with the authorities, so there *was* an investigation, which concluded, for lack of any real evidence, that, despite what the two of us claimed, Louise had wandered off in the night and died of exposure or her disease, and finding her body would only be a matter of time.

* * * * * * *

"I'll tell you what the fucking things are," said Uncle Rob. "They're pest-disposal units. They're roach motels. They're here to kill us, then to clean the place out to make room for somebody else. Maybe the poison tastes good to the roach and it dies happy, but does it make any difference?"

"I don't know, Uncle. I really don't."

The night before I was to leave, he went out on the lawn and lay down underneath one of the Fire Eggs and blew his brains out with a pistol. I heard the shot. I saw him lying there.

I just waited. I wanted to see what would happen. But I fell asleep again, or somehow failed to perceive the passing of time, and when I came to myself again, he was gone. The pistol was left behind.

* * * * * * *

It was Aunt Louise who first named them Fire Eggs. Not everybody knows that. Uncle Rob used the term on his television show, and it caught on. He gave her credit, over and over again, but no one listened and the whole world believes he was the one who coined it.

That's what his obituaries said, too.

* * * * * * *

I think that we're wrong to wait for something to happen.
I think it's been happening all along.

# THE DEAD KID

## I.

It's been a lot of years, but I think I'm still afraid of Luke Bradley, because of what he showed me.

I knew him in the first grade, and he was a tough guy even then, the sort of kid who would sit on a tack and insist it didn't hurt, and then make *you* sit on the same tack (which definitely *did* hurt) because you were afraid of what he'd do if you didn't. Once he found a bald-faced hornet nest on tree branch, broke it off, and ran yelling down the street, waving the branch around and around until finally the nest fell off and the hornets came out like a *cloud*. Nobody knew what happened after that because the rest of us had run away.

We didn't see Luke in school for a couple days afterwards, so I suppose he got stung rather badly. When he did show up he was his old self and beat up three other boys in one afternoon. Two of them needed stitches.

When I was about eight, the word went around the neighborhood that Luke Bradley had been eaten by a werewolf. "Come on," said Tommy Hitchens, Luke's current sidekick. "I'll show you what's left of him. Up in a tree."

I didn't believe any werewolf would have been a match for Luke Bradley, but I went. When Tommy pointed out the alleged remains of the corpse up in the tree, I could tell even from a distance that I was looking at a t-shirt and a pair of blue-jeans stuffed with newspapers.

I said so and Tommy flattened me with a deft right hook, which broke my nose, and my glasses.

The next day, Luke was in school as usual, though I had a splint on my nose. When he saw me, he called me a "pussy" and kicked me in the balls.

Already he was huge, probably a couple of years older than the rest of the class. Though he never admitted it, everybody knew he'd been held back in every grade at least once, even kindergarten.

But he wasn't stupid. He was *crazy.* That was the fascination of hanging out with him, even if you could get hurt in his company. He did *wild* things that no one else dared even think about. There was the stunt with the hornet nest, or the time he picked up fresh dogshit in both his bare hands and claimed he was going to *eat* it right in front of us before everybody got grossed out and ran because we were afraid he was going to make *us* eat it. Maybe he really did. He was just someone for whom the rules, *all* the rules, simply did not apply. That he was usually in detention, and had been picked up by the police several times only added to his mystique.

And in the summer when I was twelve, Luke Bradley showed me the dead kid.

Things had progressed quite a bit since then. No one quite believed all the stories of Luke's exploits, though he would beat the crap out of you if you questioned them to his face. Had he really stolen a car? Did he really hang onto the outside of a P&W light-rail train and ride all the way into Philadelphia without getting caught?

Nobody knew, but when he said to me and to my ten-year-old brother Albert, "Hey you two scuzzes"—*scuzz* being his favorite word of the moment—"there's a *dead kid* in Cabbage Creek Woods. Wanna see?" It wasn't really a question.

Albert tried to turn away, and said, "David, I don't think we should," but I knew what was good for us.

"Yeah," I said. "Sure we want to see."

Luke was already more than a head taller than either of us

and fifty pounds heavier. He was cultivating the "hood" image from some hand-me-down memory of James Dean or Elvis, with his hair up in a greasy swirl and a black leather jacket worn even on hot days when he kept his shirt unbuttoned so he could show off that he already had chest hair.

A cigarette dangled from his lips. He blew smoke in my face. I strained not to cough.

"Well come on, then," he said. "It's really cool."

So we followed him, along with a kid called Animal, and another called Spike—the beginnings of Luke's "gang," with which he said he was going to make himself famous one day. My little brother tagged after us, reluctantly at first, but then as fascinated as I was to be initiated into this innermost, forbidden secret of the older, badder set.

Luke had quite a sense of showmanship. He led us under bushes, crawling through natural tunnels under vines and dead trees where, when we were smaller, we'd had our own secret hideouts, as, I suppose, all children do. Luke and his crowd were getting too big for that sort of thing, but they went crashing through the underbrush like bears. I was small and skinny enough. David was young enough. In fact it was all we could do to keep up.

With a great flourish, Luke raised a vine curtain and we emerged into the now half-abandoned Radnor Golf Course. It was an early Saturday morning. Mist was still rising from the poorly tended greens. I saw one golfer, far away. Otherwise we had the world to ourselves.

We ran across the golf course, then across Lancaster Pike, then up the hill and back into the woods on the other side.

I only thought for a minute, *Hey wait a minute, we're going to see a corpse, a kid like us, only dead*...but, as I said, for Luke Bradley or even with him, all rules were suspended, and I knew better than try to ask what the kid died of, because we'd see soon enough.

In the woods again, by secret and hidden ways, we came to the old "fort," which had probably been occupied by generations of boys by then, though of course right now it "belonged" to the Luke Bradley Gang.

I don't know who built the fort or why. It was a rectangle of raised earth and piled stone, with logs laid across for a roof, and vines growing thickly over the whole thing so that from a distance it just looked like a hillock or knoll. That was part of its secret. You had to know it was there.

And only Luke could let you in.

He raised another curtain of vines, and with a sweep of his hand and a bow said, "Welcome to my house, you assholes."

Spike and Animal laughed while Albert and I got down on our hands and knees and crawled inside.

Immediately I almost gagged on the awful smell, like rotten garbage and worse. Albert started to cough. I though he was going to throw up. But before I could say or do anything, Luke and his two henchmen had come in after us, and we all crowded around a pit in the middle of the dirt floor which didn't use to be there. Now there was a four-foot drop, a roughly square cavity, and in the middle of that, a cardboard box which was clearly the source of the unbelievable stench.

Luke got out a flashlight, then reached down and opened the box.

"It's a dead kid. I found him in the woods in this box. He's mine."

I couldn't help but look. It was indeed a dead kid, an emaciated, pale thing, naked but for what might have been the remains of filthy underpants, lying on its side in a fetal position, little claw-like hands bunched up under its chin.

"A dead kid," said Luke. "Really cool."

Then Albert really was throwing up and screaming at the same time, and scrambling to get *out* of there, only Animal and then Spike had him by the back of his shirt the way you pick up a kitten by the scruff of its neck, and they passed him back to Luke, who held his head in his hands and forced him down into that pit, saying, "Now look at it you fucking pussy faggot, this because it's really cool."

Albert was sobbing and sniffling when Luke let him go, but he didn't try to run, nor did I, even when Luke got a stick and poked the dead kid with it.

"This is the best part," he said.

We didn't run away then because we *had* to watch just to convince ourselves that we weren't crazy, because of what we were seeing.

Luke poked and the dead kid *moved*, spasming at first, then grabbing at the stick feebly, and finally crawling around inside the box like a slow, clumsy animal, just barely able to turn, scratching at the cardboard with bony fingertips.

"What *is* he?" I had to ask.

"A *zombie*," said Luke.

"Aren't zombies supposed to be black?"

"You mean like a nigger?" That was another of Luke's favorite words this year. He called everybody "nigger" no matter what color they were.

"Well, you know. Voodoo. In Haiti and all that."

As we spoke the dead kid reared up and almost got out of the box. Luke poked him in the forehead with his stick and knocked him down.

"I suppose if we let him *rot* long enough he'll be black enough even for *you*."

The dead kid stared up at us and made a bleating sound. The worst thing of all was that he didn't have any eyes, only huge sockets and an oozy mess inside them.

Albert was sobbing for his mommy by then, and after a while of poking and prodding the dead kid, Luke and his friends got tired of this sport. Luke turned to me and said, "You can go now, but you know if you or your piss-pants brother tell about this, I'll kill you both and put you in there for the dead kid to *eat*."

# II.

I can't remember much of what Albert and I did for the rest of that day. We ran through the woods, tripped, fell flat on our faces in a stream. Then later we were walking along the old railroad embankment turning over ties to look for snakes, and all the while Albert was babbling on about the dead kid and how we had to do something. I just let him talk until he got it all out of him, and when we went home for dinner and were very quiet when Mom and our stepdad Steve tried to find out what we had been doing all day.

"Just playing," I said. "In the woods."

"It's good for them to be outdoors," Steve said to Mom. "Too many kids spent all their time in front of the TV watching *unwholesome* junk these days. I'm glad our kids are *normal.*"

But Albert ended up screaming in his sleep for weeks and wetting his bed, and things were anything but normal that summer. He was the one with the obvious problems. He was the one who ended up going to a "specialist," and whatever he said in therapy must not have been believed, because the police didn't go tearing up Cabbage Creek Woods, Luke Bradley and his Neanderthals were not arrested, and I was more or less left alone.

In fact, I had more unsupervised time than usual. And I used it to work out problems of my own, like I hated school and I hated Stepdad Steve for the sanctimonious prig he was. I decided, with the full wisdom of my twelve years and some months, that if I was to survive in this rough, tough, evil world, I was going to have to become tough myself, *bad*, and very likely evil.

I decided that Luke Bradley had the answers.

So I sought him out. It wasn't hard. He had a knack for being in the right place at the right time when you're ready to sell your soul, just like the Devil.

I met him in town, in front of the Wayne Toy Town, where

I used to go to buy model kits and stuff. I still liked building models, and doing scientific puzzles, though I would never admit it to Luke Bradley.

So I just froze when I saw him there.

"Well, well," he said. "If it ain't the little pussy scuzz." He blew smoke from the perennial cigarette.

"Hello, Luke," I said. I nodded to his companions, who included Spike, Animal, and a virtually hairless, pale gorilla who went by the unlikely name of Corky. As I spoke, I slipped my latest purchase into my shoulder bag and hoped he didn't notice.

Corky grabbed me by the back of the neck and said, "Whaddaya want me to do with him?"

But before Luke could respond, I said, "Hey, have you still got the dead kid at the fort?"

They all hesitated. They weren't expecting that.

"Well he's *cool*," I said. "I want to see him again."

"Okay," said Luke.

We didn't have any other way to get there, so we walked, about an hour, to Cabbage Creek Woods. Luke dispensed with ceremony. We just crawled into the fort and gathered around the pit.

The smell, if anything, was worse.

This time, the dead kid was already moving around inside the box. When Luke opened the cardboard flaps, the dead kid stood up, with his horrible, pus-filled eye-sockets staring. He made that bleating, groaning sound again. He clawed at the edge of the box.

"Really cool," I forced myself to say, swallowing hard.

"I can make him do tricks," said Luke. "Watch this."

I watched as he shoved his finger *through* the skin under the dead kid's chin and lifted him up like a hooked fish out of the pit. The dead kid scrambled over the edge of the box, then crouched down on the dirt floor at the edge of the pit, staring into space.

Luke passed his hand slowly in front of the dead kid's face. He snapped his fingers. The dead kid didn't respond. Luke smacked him on the side of the head. The dead kid whimpered a little, and made that bleating sound.

"Everybody outside," Luke said.

So we all crawled out, and then Luke reached back inside with a stick and touched the dead kid, who came out too, clinging to the stick, trying to chew on it, but not quite coordinated enough, so that he just snapped his teeth in the air and rubbed the side of his face along the stick.

I could see him clearly now. He really *was* rotten, with bone sticking out at his knees and elbows, only scraggly patches of dark hair left on his head, every rib showing in hideous relief on his bare back, and *holes* through his skin between some of them.

"Look!" said Luke. "Look at him dance!" He swirled the stick around and around, and the dead kid clung to it, staggering around in a circle.

Corky spoke up. "Ya think if'n he gets dizzy he'll puke?"

Luke yanked the stick out of the dead kid's hands, then hit him hard with it across the back with a *thwack!* The dead kid dropped to all fours and just stayed there, his head hanging down.

"Can't puke. Got no guts left!" They all laughed at that. I didn't quite get the joke.

But despite everything, I *tried* to get the joke, despite even the incongruity that I really was, like it or not, a more or less "normal" kid and right now I had a model kit for a plastic Fokker Triplane in my schoolbag. I still wanted to measure up to Luke Bradley, for all I was more afraid of him than I had ever been. I figured you had to be afraid of what you did and who you hung out with if you were going to be really *bad*. You did what Luke did. That was what transgression was all about.

So I unzipped my fly and pissed on the dead kid. He made that bleating sound. The others chuckled nervously. Luke grinned.

"Pretty cool, Davey, my boy. Pretty cool."

Then Luke started to play the role of wise elder brother. He put his arm around my shoulders. He took me a little ways apart from the others and said, "I like you. I think you got something special in there." He rapped on my head with his knuckles, hard, but I didn't flinch away.

Then he led me back to the others and said, "I think we're gonna make David here a member of the gang."

So we all sat down in the clearing with the dead kid in our circle, as if he were one of the gang too. Luke got out an old briefcase from inside the fort and produced some very crumpled nudie magazines and passed them around and we all looked at the pictures. He even made a big, funny show of opening out a foldout for the dead kid to admire.

He smoked and passed cigarettes out to all of us. I'd never had one before and it made me feel sick, but Luke told me to hold the smoke in, then breathe it out slowly.

I was amazed and appalled when, right in front of everyone he unzipped his pants and started to jerk off. The others did it too, making a point of trying to squirt on the dead kid.

Luke looked at me. "Come on, join in with the other gentlemen." The other "gentlemen" brayed like jackasses.

I couldn't move then. I really wanted to be like them, but I knew I wasn't going to measure up. All I could hope for now was to put up a good front so maybe they'd decide I wasn't a pussy after all and maybe let me go after they beat me up a little bit. I could hope for that much.

But Luke had other ideas. He put his hand on the back of my neck. It could have been a friendly gesture, or if he squeezed, he could have snapped my head off for all I could have done anything about it.

"Now David," he said, "I don't care if you've even *got* a dick, any more than I care if *he* does." He jerked his thumb at the dead kid. "But if you want to join our gang, if you want to be cool, you have to meet certain standards."

He flicked a switchblade open right in front of my face. I thought he was going to cut my nose with it, but with a sudden motion he slashed the dead kid's nose right off. It flew into the air. Corky caught it, then threw it away in mindless disgust.

The dead kid whimpered. His face was a black, oozing mess.

Then Luke took hold of my right hand and slashed the back of it. I let out a yell, and tried to stop the bleeding with my other hand.

"No," Luke said. "Let him lick it. He needs a little blood now and then to keep him healthy."

I screamed then, and sobbed, and whimpered the way Albert had that first time, but Luke held onto me with a grip so strong that *I* was the one who wriggled like a fish on a line, and he held my cut hand out to the dead kid.

I couldn't look, but something soft and wet touched my hand, and I could only think, Oh God, what kind of infection or disease am I going to get from this?

"Okay David," Luke said then. "You're doing just fine, but there is one more test. You have to *spend the whole night* in the fort with the dead kid. We've all done it. Now it's your turn."

They didn't wait for my answer, but, laughing, hauled me back inside the fort. Then Luke had the dead kid hooked under the chin again, and lowered him down into his box in the pit.

The others crawled back outside. Before he left, Luke turned to me, "You have to stay here until tomorrow morning. You know what I'll do to you if you pussy out."

So I spent the rest of the afternoon, and the evening, inside that fort with the dead kid scratching around in his box. It was already dark in the fort. I couldn't tell what time it was. I couldn't think very clearly at all. I wondered if anyone was looking for me. I lay very still. I didn't want to be found, especially not by the dead kid, who, for all I knew, could crawl out of the box and the pit if he really wanted to and maybe rip my throat out and drink my blood.

My hand hurt horribly. It seemed to be swelling. I was sure it was already rotten. The air was thick and foul.

But I stayed where I was, because I was afraid, because I was weak with nausea, but also, incredibly, because somehow, somewhere, deep down inside myself I still wanted to show how *tough* I was, to be like Luke Bradley, to be as amazing and crazy as he was. I knew that I *wasn't* cut out for this, and that's why I wanted it—to be *bad*, so no one would ever beat me up again and if I hated my stepdad or my teachers I could just tell them to go fuck off, as Luke would do.

Hours passed, and still the dead kid circled around and around inside his cardboard box, sliding against the sides. He made that bleating, coughing sound, as if he were trying to talk and didn't have any tongue left. For a time I thought there was almost some sense in it, some pattern. He was *clicking* like a cricket. This went on for hours. Maybe I even slept for a while, and fell into a kind of dream in which I was sinking slowly down into incredibly foul-smelling muck and there were thousands of bald-faced hornets swarming over me, all of them with little Luke Bradley faces saying, "Cool...really cool...," until their voices blended together and became a buzzing, then became wind in the trees, then the roar of a P&W light-rail train rushing off toward Philadelphia; and the dead kid and I were hanging onto the outside of the car, swinging wildly. My arm hit a pole and snapped right off, and black ooze was pouring out of my shoulder, and the hornets swarmed over me, eating me up but by bit.

Once, I am certain, the dead kid *did* reach up and touch me, very gently, running his dry, sharp fingertip down the side of my cheek, cutting me, then withdrawing with a little bit of blood and tears on his fingertip, to drink.

But, strangest of all, I wasn't afraid of him then. It came to me, then, that we too had more in common than not. We were both afraid and in pain and lost in the dark.

### III.

Then somehow it was morning. The sunlight blinded me when Luke opened the vine curtain over the door.

"Hey. You were really brave. I'm impressed, Davey."

I let him lead me out of the fort, taking comfort in his chum/

big-brother manner. But I was too much in shock to say anything.

"You passed the test. You're one of us," he said. "Welcome to the gang. Now there is one last thing for you to do. Not a test. You've passed all the tests. It's just something we do to celebrate."

His goons had gathered once more in the clearing outside the fort.

One of them was holding a can of gasoline.

I stood there, swaying, about to faint, unable to figure out what the gasoline was for.

Luke brought the dead kid outside.

Corky poured gasoline over the dead kid, who just bleated a little and waved his hands in the air.

Luke handed me a cigarette lighter. He flicked it until there was a flame.

"Go on," he said. "It'll be cool."

But I couldn't. I was too scared, too sick. I just dropped to my knees, then onto all fours and started puking.

So Luke lit the dead kid on fire and the others hooted and clapped as the dead kid went up like a torch, staggering and dancing around the clearing, trailing black, oily smoke. Then he fell down and seemed to shrivel up into a pile of blackened, smoldering sticks.

Luke forced me over to where the dead kid had fallen and made me touch what was left with my swollen hand.

And the dead kid *moved.* He made that bleating sound. He whimpered.

"You see? You can't kill him because he's already dead."

They were all laughing, but I just puked again, and finally Luke hauled me to my feet by both shoulders, turned me around, and shoved me away staggering into the woods.

"Come back when you stop throwing up," he said.

# IV.

Somehow I found my way home, and when I did, Mom just stared at me in horror and said, "My God, what's that awful smell?" But Stepdad Steve shook me and demanded to know where I had been and what I'd been doing? Did I know the police were looking for me? Did I care? (No, and no.) He took me into the bathroom, washed and bandaged my hand, then held me so I couldn't turn away and said, "Have you been taking drugs?"

That was so stupid I started to laugh, and he *smacked* me across the face, something he rarely did, but this time, I think, he was determined to beat the truth out of me, and Mommy, dearest Mommy didn't raise a finger to stop him as he laid on with his hand, then his belt, and I was shrieking my head off.

All they got out of me was the admission that I had been with Luke Bradley and his friends.

"I *don't* want you to associate with *those* boys any further. They're unwholesome."

He didn't know a tenth of it, and I started to laugh again, like I was drunk or something, and he was about to hit me again when Mom finally made him stop.

She told me to change my clothes and take a bath and then go to my room. I wasn't allowed out except for meals and to go to the bathroom.

That was fine with me. I didn't *want* to come out. I wanted to bury myself in there, to be quiet and dead, like the dead kid in his box.

But when I fell asleep, I was screaming in a dream, and I woke up screaming, in the dark, because it was night again.

Mom looked in briefly, but didn't say anything. The expression on her face was more of disgust than concern, as if she really wanted to say, *Serves him damn right but, Oh God, another crazy kid we'll have to send to the so, so expensive psychiatrist and I'd rather spend the money on a new mink coat or a car or something.*

It was my kid brother Albert who snuck over to my bed and whispered, "It's the dead kid, isn't it?"

"Huh?"

"The dead kid. He talks to me in my dreams. He's told me all about himself. He's lost. His father's a magician, who is still trying to find him. There was a war between magicians, or something, and that's how he got lost."

"Huh? Is this something you read in a comic book?"

"*No!* It's the dead kid. You know what we have to do, David. We have to go save him."

I have to give my brother credit for bringing about my moral redemption as surely as if he'd handed me my sanity back on a silver platter and said, *Go on, don't be a pussy. Take it.*

Because he was right. We had to save the dead kid.

Maybe the dead kid talked to Albert in his dreams, but he didn't tell me anything. Why should he?

Still, I'd gotten the message.

So, that night, very late, Albert and I got dressed and slipped out the window of our room, dropping onto the lawn. *He wasn't afraid*, not a little bit. He led me, by the ritual route, under the arching bushes, through the tunnels of vines to all our secret places, as if we had to be *there* first to gain some special strength for the task at hand.

Under the bushes, in the darkness, we paused to scratch secret signs in the dirt.

Then we scurried across the golf course, across the highway, into Cabbage Creek Woods.

We came to the fort by the light of a full moon now flickering through swaying branches. It was a windy night. The woods were alive with sounds of wood creaking and snapping, of animals calling back and forth, and night-birds cawing. Somewhere, very close at hand, an owl cried out.

Albert got down on all fours in the doorway of the fort, poked his head in, and said, "Hey, dead kid! Are you in there?"

He backed out, and waited. There was a rustling sound, but

the dead kid didn't come out. So we both crawled in and saw why. There wasn't much left of him. He was just a bundle of black sticks, his head like a charred pumpkin balanced precariously on top. All he could do was sit up weakly and peer over the side of the box.

So we had to lift him out of the pit, box and all.

"Come on," Albert said to. "We want to show you some stuff."

We carried the dead kid between us. We took him back across the golf course, under the bushes, to our special places. We showed him the secret signs. Then we took him into town. We showed him the storefronts, Wayne Toy Town where I bought models, where there were always neat displays of miniature battlefields or of monsters in the windows. We showed him where the pet store was and the ice cream store, and where you got comic books.

Albert sat down on the merry-go-round in the playground, holding the dead kid's box securely beside him. I pushed them around slowly. Metal creaked.

We stood in front of our school for a while, and Albert and the dead kid were *holding hands*, but it seemed natural and right.

Then we went away in the bright moonlight, through the empty streets. No one said anything, because whatever the dead kid could say or hear wasn't in words anyway. I couldn't hear it. I think Albert could.

In the end the dead kid scrambled out of his box. Somehow he had regained enough strength to walk. Somehow, he was beginning to heal. In the end, he wanted to show *us* something.

He led us back across the golf course but away from Cabbage Creek Woods. We crossed the football field at Radnor High School, then went across the street, up in back of Wyeth Labs and across the high bridge over the P&W tracks. I was afraid the dead kid would slip on the metal stairs and fall, but he went more steadily than we did. (Albert and I were both a little afraid of heights.)

He led us across another field, into woods again, then through an opening where a stream flowed beneath the Pennsylvania Railroad embankment. We waded ankle-deep in the chilly water and came, at last, to the old Grant Estate, a huge ruin of a Victorian house which every kid knew was haunted, which our parents told us to stay away from because it was dangerous. (There were so many stories about kids murdered by tramps or falling through floors.) But now it wasn't a ruin at all, no broken windows, no holes in the roof. Every window blazed with light.

From a high window in a tower, a man in black gazed down at us.

The dead kid looked up at him, then began to run.

I hurried after him. Now it was Albert (who had better sense) who hung back. I caught hold of the dead kid's arm, as if to stop him, and I felt possessive for a moment, as if I *owned* him the way Luke Bradley had owned him.

"Hey dead kid," I said. "Where are you going?"

He turned to me, and by some trick of the moonlight he seemed to have a face, pale, round, with dark eyes; and he said to me in that bleating, croaking voice of his, actually forming words for once, "My name is Jonathan."

That was the only thing he ever said to me. He never talked to me in dreams.

He went to the front of the house. The door opened. The light within seemed to swallow him. He turned back, briefly, and looked at us. I don't think he was just a bundle of sticks anymore.

Then he was gone and all the lights blinked out, and it was dawn. My brother and I stood before a ruined mansion in the morning twilight. Birds were singing raucously.

"We'd better get home," Albert said, "or we'll get in trouble."

"Yeah," I said.

# V.

That autumn, I began junior high school. Because I hadn't been very successful as a bad boy, and my grades were still a lot higher, I wasn't in any of Luke Bradley's classes. But he caught up with me in the locker room after school, several weeks into the term. All he said was, "I know what you did," and beat me so badly that he broke several of my ribs and one arm, and smashed in the whole side of my face, and cracked the socket around my right eye. He stuffed me into a locker and left me there to die, and I spent the whole night in the darkness, in great pain, amid horrible smells, calling out for the dead kid to come and save me as I'd saved him. I made bleating, clicking sounds.

But he didn't come. The janitor found me in the morning. The smell was merely that I'd crapped in my pants.

I spent several weeks in the hospital, and afterwards Stepdad Steve and Mom decided to move out of the state. They put both me and Albert in a prep school.

It was only after I got out of college that I went back to Radnor Township in Pennsylvania, where I'd grown up. Everything was changed. There was a Sears headquarters where the golf course used to be. Our old house had vanished beneath an apartment parking lot. Most of Cabbage Creek Woods had been cut down to make room for an Altman's department store, and the Grant Estate was gone too, to make room for an office complex.

I didn't go into the remaining woods to see if the fort was still there.

I imagine it is. I imagine other kids own it now.

Later someone told me that Luke Bradley (who really was three years older than me) had been expelled from high school, committed several robberies in the company of his three goons, and then all of them were killed in a shootout with the police.

What Luke Bradley showed me was that I could have been with them, if Albert and the dead kid, whose name was Jonathan, hadn't saved me.

# FIGHTING THE
# ZEPPELIN GANG

Daddy, Pops, *Paterfamilias*, Father, you managed to convince me you were nuts at a very early age. I was, how old?—ten—when you dragged the whole family, me, Mom, and baby sister Way Up North one summer for a vacation in a state park in New England where the mosquitos were the size of small birds, and when the gutsy, he-man adventurer types (unshaven, in flannel shirts, just like on the covers of those magazines you used to read) saw you driving in with a suburban stationwagon complete with small kids and baby sister's teddybear in the window, *they* came to the same conclusion I did, probably with more reason.

You said it had to do with your work. You were never clear on exactly what you did for a living. I wasn't sure even Mom knew. This time you seemed to work for what a couple decades later we'd call an environmental agency, and it had something to do with capturing a rare insect—a butterfly I think it was—which could only be found at that particular place in that particular season.

"We'll all have fun," you said to me, and to Mom you added, "Might as well combine business with pleasure."

She, saint of infinite patience that she was, could only agree.

What I most remember about that trip were the industrial-strength mosquitos, not to mention the blood-sucking flies so massive they landed on you with a thump. We had to huddle within the smoke of our campfire to escape the bugs, and you had us all sing songs—and Mom, I could tell, was moving toward the consensus opinion about your sanity—and I remember watching with some fascination and a little dread as raccoons came into the smoke to stand up on their hind legs and beg like dogs.

But none of that was the point. The point was the ascent up the Mountain, where you supposed to discover the Alleged Insect, and you volunteered me to come along "for the ride," though there was no ride and we had to walk. Mom protested, but you got your way, and off we went, at dawn one morning while the mosquitos, having sucked us dry the previous night, now lay around like crab-apples with little wings and legs sticking out, too bloated to get off the ground and do any more damage.

Do I exaggerate, Daddy, just a little bit? Have you always told 100% of the truth?

I enjoyed much of the walk, in the cool morning air, and as the trail rose up out of the forest there were great vistas like nothing we'd ever seen in Jersey City, and, for all my ten-year-old self could never have articulated it and certainly would have been too stubborn to admit anything of the sort, yes, the landscape was breathtakingly beautiful, and images were to stay with me for the rest of my life. I felt as if a weight were dropping away from me—at my age, to think of such things!—and we were leaving civilization, our former lives, behind, like sinking into an ocean, deep, deep, the familiar sounds of traffic and TV fading behind us, *gone*.

But that wasn't the point, either. A ten-year-old has only so much attention span. As we started to seriously *climb*, it turned into *hard work*, and I became whiny and said, "Daddy, can't we *go back?*"

Very firmly, in a tone that almost frightened me, you said, "We cannot go back."

It was late afternoon by the time we reached the summit, then had to go over the summit onto a plateau. We were well above the timberline by then. The ground was covered with huge, round boulders, lichen, scrubby grass, and every once in a while a tiny tree, no more than a few inches high, a natural bonsai (as I would learn to call it much later) because the cold and the wind wouldn't let it grow any taller. I was beginning to sympathize. I was exhausted by then. I too could crouch down between who rocks and become shrunken, twisted, and just *stay there*.

I think you caught the butterfly. I don't even remember. Even that wasn't the point.

The point was that it was getting late and we were not going to be able to get down before dark.

"Mom will be worried," I said.

"She will *not* be worried."

In fact she was frantic, and she packed baby sister into the stationwagon and drove twenty miles to find a park ranger, by which point it was already dark and there wasn't much he could do because this was, after all, 1970, and if you think park rangers in those days had whole fleets of helicopters and infra-red sights to go looking for crazy campers and their kids in the middle of the night, you are sadly mistaken.

*That* was the point, Daddy, I understood even at the time. We might as well have been on Venus. We were *alone*.

So you made a campfire and we sat down behind a low ridge which would protect us from the worst of the wind, and we put on the extra wool sweaters you had been so careful to pack. We ate our supper and sat very close together, in the cold, while you told me to look out into the night sky—it was *dark* and moonless, and no one could ever believe there were that many stars—and you told me how, on certain nights, like this one, the "curtains in the sky" become very thin, or "open up" entirely and "powers" come through and walk the Earth. You told me that you, and a small number of others like you, some of whom were quite famous, though they all had secret identities, had learned to speak with these "powers" and gained from them powers of a different sort, meaning *abilities*, which is what made each of you special, and why each of you had to keep your identities secret. You told me that there were powers for good in the sky, but also powers of evil, which *also* came down on such nights as this and walked to and fro in the Earth and up and down in it—you used that odd phrase—and that our job, *ours*, which implied that I was supposed to be a part of this—to learn to distinguish the good from the evil, and ally ourselves with the former in opposition to the latter.

"Get it wrong, and the world will end. *Pffit!* Blooey!"

You pointed to how the stars were rippling in the sky now, like reflections in water when somebody throws a stone in. The "gates" were opening. Yes, the wind was very cold, and I think I had a dream that there *were* faces in the sky, and you were talking with them, and later something was all around us in the dark, after the campfire had burned low, something which *touched* me right at the left cheek-bone and made that mark on my face which is still there—it was so cold it burned—and I dreamed that a voice was saying, "Yes, his training must begin."

That *was* all a dream, Pappa, and you *were* nuts, and when we got back to the campsite the next afternoon, having somehow evaded the park rangers who were out looking for us, you merely pointed to my face and said, "He slipped and cut himself."

That Mamma, she of the halo and wings, did not sue for divorce on the spot was the most inexplicable thing of all. Maybe they didn't do that in 1970.

\* \* \* \* \* \* \*

*Ring, ring.*
*I pick up the phone.*
"Matthew, it is time."
"Dad, it is not time. I don't have time."
"Tonight."
"Dad, I am twenty-six years old. I am married. I have an infant son. I have a meeting I have to go to tomorrow. I have a life."
"None of that matters. What matters is that you meet me again, tonight, in the usual manner, in the usual place, in

uniform."

*  *  *  *  *  *  *

By the time I was twelve you started telling me about the
Zeppelin Gang, who spoke with the darkness the way we did,
but with a *different* darkness, *i.e.*, the bad guys, and how they
would destroy the world in a cataclysm of nightmarish horror
if given half the chance. You tended toward that sort of phrase-
ology, betraying a melodramatic streak, quite consistent with a
functional, though raving lunatic.

I still didn't know what you did for a living. I thought maybe
you were a writer, of books, or even comic books, but I never
saw anything you'd written, for all you were often locked in
your study typing "reports." It occurred to me, too, that maybe
you worked for the CIA, and when I blabbed that in school, said,
"*My* father is a *secret agent!*" Bobby Parker smacked me on the
side of the head with a ruler and said, "Then how come it isn't *a
secret?*" and I suppose he had a point.

The Zeppelin Gang was led by somebody called the Black
Scorpion, who wore a mask, whose face no one had ever seen.
*He* was a figure of purest evil, who gathered evil men around
him, all of whom travelled—or perhaps dwelt—in a fleet of pale
gray zeppelins with an emblem on them, a black scorpion in
circular field of white; which I thought would make them about
as formidable and scary as a fleet of Goodyear Blimps done
up for Halloween, but in that, you insisted, I was very much
mistaken. The fleet was never visible by day, but by night it
would emerge out of a fissure in the sky, from behind one of
those *curtains*, out of another reality or universe. Sometimes it
was possible to see them crossing the face of the moon. Most
people would just think they were clouds, but no, on nights
like that the Black Scorpion would drift over the cities of the
world, standing by an open window in the gondola of the lead
zeppelin, pouring out of his hands, like a farmer sowing seeds,
the very essence of evil, which brought plagues and wars and

death and madness—hands which few had ever seen ungloved, and which were reputed to be almost skeletal, but black and hard and spiked, like the claws of an insect.

I admit I was caught up in the story. "But how can anyone stop him?" I asked.

"There are ways. Secret weapons. We have our resources. Our greatest is courage, and the clarity of our purpose, but there is still something to be said for gizmos, atomic disintegration machines, that sort of thing. In time, my son, you will learn much."

\* \* \* \* \* \* \*

*Another cold night. Always on a cold, night, it seems, but there are no stars tonight. Overcast. Drizzle.* It is late October. I can almost feel ice beginning to form on the sidewalk.

But I must go, like the vampire's victim who steals away to ecstacy and certain death, like an addict addicted to a dream which will inevitably devour him.

My wife and child are asleep. I slip out of the house, roll the car out of the driveway without starting the engine or turning on the lights, only turning the key when I am halfway down the sloping street.

I must go, as I have always gone.

As I can't stop myself from going.

\* \* \* \* \* \* \*

When I was sixteen, you took me climbing again. Of course you were already dead by then, at least officially.

Father, that is why I have always hated you, in my heart of hearts, for what you did to me, to Mother, to Baby Sister—who wasn't a baby anymore—to all our lives. You spent more and more time away from home. I know Mother wept at night when she was in her bedroom alone and thought I couldn't hear her. She loved you, Dad. She would have stuck with you through anything, but you "sacrificed" her for the cause, or the greater good or something, and there were times when I wasn't sure who was more evil, you or the Black Scorpion.

Then you didn't come back at all. I was told that "something had happened," but no one, not even Mother, would tell me what. She had to raise us. I didn't know, then, that quite large checks came regularly in the mail, from a bank in Katmandu, and that helped, but it didn't help. Mother spent a lot of time staring out the window at the sky, I thought, as if she were waiting for something to drift across the face of the moon.

You and I had "issues," Father. Yes, indeed.

* * * * * * *

*I leave the car and switch to another, very different one, which is always left for me on these occasions. The towers of Manhattan gleam before me, across the river, though the gathering fog.*

I make a turn few people know about, down an alley, through what appears to be a solid wall, but is only a projection. I flip open the hidden control panel, and activate a field I can hardly explain, and then outside is only darkness, because the earth has swallowed me up.

I'll be there soon, Dad. I'm coming. But you knew that.

* * * * * * *

Then one day in junior biology class, I found a note, in my textbook, which I was certain had not been there the night before when I'd done my homework. It was from you, in your handwriting, containing a set of secret instructions, signs and symbols I knew from the Zeppelin Gang mythos, and directions, which involved Jersey Transit, a PATH train, the subway, Cleopatra's Needle, Grant's Tomb, a long walk in the Upper West Side and a secret door beneath a Civil War monument near the River, which led to places under Manhattan that weren't in any of the guidebooks.

It was all I could do not to make an excuse and run out of class. I went of course. I skipped my last class, and a date with my then girlfriend, and went, without bothering to phone home first. We are alike, you and I, equally inconsiderate. Would Mother worry? Did I care?

I hung around, waiting till dark, as you had instructed. I waited until the Moon rose behind the Manhattan skyline. (Did something drift across its face?) I slid my fingers, *just so*, as you had described, into a niche in the monument, and found the key you told me would be there.

I opened the secret door, descended the long, winding staircase, into the cavern, groping my way among stalactites into the very Bowels of the Earth, as the phrase would have it, though it felt more like a mouth. I was something very small crawling between the teeth of something very large. Sometimes, the very stone seemed to ripple and I felt a cold wind blowing through a very thin curtain that separated our universe from something else.

In the darkness, you spoke to me, Father. You brought me to a dimly-lit grotto, where I saw you for the first time in years, only I didn't really see you, because you were wearing a mask, and some kind of costume that had wings on it, which made you look like a huge, hunched-over bird.

There was a costume for me, too. You commanded me to put it on. It was featureless, all black, like a scuba-diver's wet suit, only it didn't feel like that against my skin. It became part of me. I felt amazing strength, and I had never been a big or muscular kid, but now I had become something else entirely. You told me to put on the mask and gloves and boots, and I put them on, and it had to have been a dream as we two climbed up through the earth, passing through solid stone as if through mist or through a curtain. Is that what we did? Up, we climbed, up, out into the glaring, but muted light of the night-time city in the fog. Up, and somehow the fibers of my fingertips and of my boots extended *into* stone and marble and steel, and I could feel the textures of these things as if they were my own flesh, and somehow the power flowing from them, into my body gave me my very great strength, so that I could climb as I did, and hang onto a ledge fifty storeys above the street with one hand and not be afraid.

"Dad, this is amazing," I said.

"Yes," you replied. "It is."

It was only when the moon broke through the clouds at last—I had the image of a spiderweb being torn away from the face of a lantern—that I realized where we were.

We were on a ledge, halfway up the Empire State Building, sitting next to an Art Deco gargoyle.

"Dad," I said. "This is so incredible. What does it mean?"

"You mean you haven't figured it out yet, son?"

"Not entirely."

You sighed, and I could sense the disappointment in your tone, as if to say to the gods, *I had hoped for a smarter kid, but never mind, I'll make do somehow.*

"I am the Night Hawk. The foe of the Black Scorpion. We two have been battling over the fate of the world and the future of mankind for a long, long time."

And you stood up on the ledge, and spread your wings.

I wanted to say to you, then and there, that this was all crazy, that you were a certified raving, gibbering, probably bug-eating lunatic, that you belonged not in a winged suit but in a strait-jacket, but there I was with you, in a similar, albeit wingless suit, on a ledge on the Empire State Building something like a quarter of a mile above Manhattan, and so I couldn't quite bring myself to raise those objections.

You folded your wings and sat down beside me. You put your hand gently on my arm. I felt a tingling through the suit, as if power somehow passed from you to me, just then.

"There are others like us," you said, "who are better known. They keep their daily identities secret, of course, but their *personae* are known, even famous, even the subject of treatments in various media. But they are mere distractions, a kind of smokescreen. We, who remain much less known, do all the serious work."

And I saw my whole life falling away as surely as if I'd suddenly taken a flying, albeit wingless leap.

"Let me guess," I said. "You want me to be your sidekick."

"More of a boy wonder, if you will excuse the phrase," you whispered into my ear, laughing.

When I got home the next morning, Mother looked pale, ill. She had been up all night. "You're not into drugs, are you?"

I assured her I was not.

She wept softly. I think she knew what was going on. I think she had always known. I think she began to die that night.

* * * * * * *

*Onward and upward, into the cave, into the secret laboratory, some of which I understand, some of which I have been denied access to, despite my many "training missions" over the years. I suit up.* All this has been my secret, my thrill, my delusion. I cannot remember all that we have done, even in my dreams. Most of it is just tales, things you have done on your own, and reported back to me, because I am not ready yet for the "real thing."

Up, climbing through the earth as if through smoke. Up the side of smooth stone and glass, like an insect. Into the street, moving swiftly in the shadows. Up again.

The Empire State Building. The ledge, where we have met so many times before, next to the gargoyle we have nicknamed "Bruce."

There. You are waiting.

For once we climb even further, to the very top, onto the highest observation platform at the base of the radio antenna.

The city spreads before us, the world in light and fog, the faint sounds of traffic and ship horns from the river like a whispering of a tide.

"This is the last time, Matthew," you say. "From now on you

must go it alone. No more sidekick."

"What are you saying, Father?"

Again I can sense that faint exasperation in your voice. You explain what you'd hoped would be obvious.

"It is time for you to take over. You must become the Night Hawk."

"No," I say softly. "I can't."

"I didn't raise you to be a coward, son. I raised you to be a hero. Maybe you're not the most heroic hero to ever come down the pike, but dammit, you're going to have to do. You're all I got."

"There was Baby Sister," I say bitterly, "and Mom."

"Your mother is dead. I regret that very much. As for your sister, Gwendolyn—"

"I'll tell you what happened to my sister, Gwendolyn. I don't think you know about this, because it just happened, just two days ago, and besides, you were away all the time and never gave a bug's ass about her, did you—?"

"Son, you know I have other preoccupations—"

"Well Gwen grew up—is growing up, she is only nineteen—rather confused, and, lacking any guidance, even from me because I too was preoccupied, she fell in with some very bad company indeed, Father, and I must confess to you that with some of the tricks you've taught me I found out all about it, every last sordid detail, like the party where she got herself so shot up with junk that she didn't know what was going on even when she got gangbanged by an entire fraternity. You know what I did? After hours, when the party had thinned out a bit, I went in and cleaned things up, not wearing any magic suit, not using any super-powers, with my face covered with a knit ski-mask and armed with a baseball bat. I smashed a couple guys up pretty badly, Father. I could have *killed* them. Easily. And, you know, I *wanted* to. I felt entirely justified in doing so. I might even have *enjoyed* it.

But somehow I didn't, not quite. I carried Gwen back to her dorm and told her it was all a bad dream, and I felt so *dirty* telling such lies, having done such things and thought such thoughts, that I *know*, Father, I am not the stuff that Night Hawks are made of."

For the last time, you put your hand on my shoulder gently, and I feel a tingling, of some mystical energy passing from father to son, and you say, "On the contrary, you've finished your training. You are ready. You have learned to act decisively, to draw on the darkness within yourself, to harness even that for the greater cause—"

"No, Father. I came here tonight to tell you that I quit. I've concluded you *are* a fucking lunatic after all, that none of this is real, that both of us are fucking lunatics, that we should both turn ourselves in to the police and hope they put us away in a rubber room where we won't hurt anybody—"

You shake your head sadly. "I'd hoped it wouldn't come to this, but it has. I had wanted to grow old as your curmudgeonly mentor, maybe playing the outward role as a faithful butler or something, all part of the secret identity stuff, but the reason I called you here tonight, son, on this night, for the last time, is to tell you that there are shortcomings to this line of work, and sometimes bad things happen, and it so happens that I am dying, son, of an incurable disease, which I must have acquired dodging too many death rays, or from the Black Scorpion's poisons. It couldn't have come at a worse time. I know the Enemy is planning a new assault, and must be stopped at all costs. Therefore you must take over the family concern, *now*, tonight."

"Why you crazy—"

But before I can say anymore, you press something into my hand, and climb back over the metal fence that is supposed to prevent the observer, so high up, from yielding to perverse and terrible impulses. But you scale it with ease, as might an insect—no, that's not right—as might a huge, black bird.

You stand up and spread your wings.

"Matthew, become the Night Hawk now. Fulfill your destiny."

"Father, no!"

It was only then, in a moment of sheer, helpless terror, that I truly understand that those wings, whatever enhanced powers your suit might have given you, are for decoration, or psychological effect only, as in *not functional*.

You fall away into the darkness.

* * * * * * *

*It is only much later, as I cling to the iron fence, sobbing, and I hear sirens in the street below, that I realize that what you pressed into my hand is an envelope. Final instructions, of course.* And a key, which will not only give me access to every part of the laboratory, but also open a certain locker in which hangs another suit, like yours, with wings.

I am ready to put that suit on now. I am not ready to try to fly with it. Not yet.

The Moon comes out. Something, not clouds, drifts across its face.

I hear engines thundering in the night.

# SWEEP ME TO MY REVENGE!

The thousand injuries of Professor Cranchberger I had borne as best I could, but when he ventured upon insult, I vowed revenge; and if I were a Poe scholar I would doubtless carry on in such a vein of increasingly purple prose for a while before contriving to brick up my rival in one of the dim alcoves in the musty cellars below the Liberal Arts Building. But I am a Shakespearean, and so I should be thinking more in terms of bloody daggers not necessarily of the mind, *multitudinous seas incarnadine, gashed stabs like a breach in nature* and *horror! horror! horror!* such that *tongue nor heart cannot conceive or name*, or, more satisfying still, a *pound of flesh*, which is what I would have from the arrogant bastard.

It is true that my vanity had been pricked; I will admit that much, and even concede the young twit's claim that as I approached retirement I had become a tenured, potted plant without coming up with a new idea in twenty years. But in my calling, what would otherwise seem intellectual stagnation is merely the recognition of eternal verities, for, century in and century out, Homer is as great as he ever was, and the same can be said for Dante, Cervantes, Milton, and most especially Shakespeare; and if there is nothing new under the sun it is because the winter of our discontent is made glorious summer by the Bard, illuminating all the dark nooks and crannies of the human condition.

But try to tell that to Cranchberger, *the* one and only Lee

Allen Cranchberger, the cock-of-the-walk, twenty-nine or thirty-something, just out of graduate school but already a professor on account of his undeniable brilliance as a flatterer and flimflam artist and fake and razzle-dazzler, who had made himself the darling not only of the Department Head but of the President of the University himself, and now proposed to overturn the life's work of all of us old *potted plants* and show us how proper literary scholarship is done.

So much for the thousand injuries—I once thought of specializing in Poe, and admit he has a few good lines—but the insult came when Crancho, as we all called him behind his back, brought out another of his interminable tomes from the most prestigious publisher imaginable and was allowed, nay, ordered by the Powers That Be to invade *my* Shakespeare class as a guest lecturer to promote *The Shakespeare Fraud Unmasked: Final Proof That Edward De Vere Wrote the Plays.*

My students found this all very amusing. One of the brighter ones did pipe up with, "Excuse me, Sir, but didn't De Vere die in 1604, eight years before Shakespeare stopped writing?"

Crancho was ready for that one, of course, and even for the two class wiseasses—I always thought of them as Heckle and Jeckle, but for once I was glad to have them and mentally cheered them on.

"How about Marlowe, then?" said Heckle. "He died early too. He could have stashed away a whole trunkful of stuff he was working on, like *Hamlet*—"

And Jeckle said, "Well what if Christopher Marlowe didn't actually die? I mean, maybe he was a vampire or something. He'd need a front-man to pretend to be the author of his later work, and it's obvious that he was *great* writer—"

Everybody started tittering, but Crancho, I must admit, had the teacher's essential skill of calling things back to order with a glare, or a gesture, or just a change in his stance, and you *knew* that, all kidding aside, we were going to get serious now.

"I can well imagine," he said, "that, had he lived, the author of *Tamburlaine the Great* and *The Tragickal History of Doctor*

*Faustus* would have become a formidable rival to Edward De Vere, but Christopher Marlowe actually was killed by a dagger thrust through the eye in a brawl in at Dame Eleanor Bull's tavern on Deptford Strand, May 30, 1593, more or less as reported, and such details as are uncertain are of no relevance to the present argument—"

That was when I, I admit, lost it, and broke in to my guest lecturer's lecture in the rudest possible way, and said, "Damn it, we've been over and over this before, and you know goddamn well it's all crap, and I ask you this, *yet again*, why doesn't anybody try to prove that Edward DeVere or Francis Bacon, or Marlowe, or the Fifth Earl of Rutland or Charles Blount or Sir Walter Raleigh or the Queen herself or Attila the Hun actually wrote the works of *Thomas Dekker* or some other suitably obscure, second-rate playwright of the period—no! No! Don't answer that! I already know what your mealy-mouthed, stinking, oily, two-faced answer is going to be—"

"I think you're mixing metaphors—" he broke in.

But my fire was up, my words swept over him like a roaring tide, and never mind the goddamned mixed metaphors. I hadn't been this passionate since the time I delivered Henry V's "Once more into the breach, dear friends!" speech in undergraduate drama. "The reason you pick on Shakespeare, why you have to knock down the grandest and most visible edifice rather than just vandalize a dirty window in a back alley, is that if you did less, *no one would care*. It's why the science crackpots go after Einstein, instead of someone nobody has ever heard of. Only the biggest targets, so *your* ego can be sufficiently inflated. To give an *honest answer* to the young man's question—" I nodded toward Jeckle, whose deer-in-the-headlights expression made it clear he wasn't sure *what* he had started he was beginning to wish he hadn't—"*If Christopher Marlowe had lived*, and become the greatest of all Elizabethan playwrights, vermin like you would be trying to prove that De Vere and Bacon wrote *his* work and you'd leave Shakespeare alone!"

After that maybe my shortness of breath caught up with me,

because I was left gasping and stuttering, and one or two students tittered, but most of them just gaped, as Jeckle did, not sure *what* was going on, and that was when Professor Cranchberger, shaking his head sadly as if he felt sorry for me, put his hand on my shoulder and said softly—but loud enough for everyone to hear—"I'm afraid your Shakespeare is a limp spear. You've got to move with the times, Chuck, or you'll lose it entirely."

*That was it!* He called me "Chuck" in front of my students, undermining my authority forever! Such impudence! Such uncalled-for familiarity!

I vowed revenge. A pound of flesh.

\* \* \* \* \* \* \*

But we live in quieter times than the Elizabethans, and I am, in any case, hardly in good enough shape to best a man thirty years my junior in a back-alley duel with swords; but still I fulminated *revenge* and I would have blood or something fully as satisfying. Poison at the departmental Christmas party? No, it might get the wrong person. A pistol-shot through the head from behind? Messy. Besides, he was six inches taller than me and had reflexes like a cat.

It's at times like this when I have to either sell my soul to the Devil or go see my brother Francis. I chose the latter because he was closer. He worked at the same university, just across campus, in the Physics Department. I walked into his office and said without any formalities, "I want to borrow your time machine."

Francis took this in stride. Since we were boys, he had been used to my eccentric moments. He invited me to sit down, fetched some coffee, and suggested we talk about it.

Actually he did most of the talking. He'd been like that since we were boys, too, when he used to prattle on in a monotone, non-stop, about equations and angles and dimensions at the dinner table, while my sisters and I stared at the ceiling or at our plates and our parents beamed with pride at their *little genius* even though they only understood one word in twenty if they were lucky.

I got some of it.

"You can't *borrow* it because it's not portable. It's the size of a building. This building. It occupies all the cellars underneath us, and some new corridors and chambers which had to be dug to accommodate it. And it's not really a *time-machine*—not like Mr. Peabody's Wayback Machine—but a *place* where the angles of the time-flow are twisted and redirected through a pseudo-gravitational matrix—"

I have to admit he was starting to lose me again.

But when he said, "Perhaps it is best explicable to the layman as a series of *doors* which lead backward or forward into time—"

I broke in, "Fine, have you got a door to 1593?"

Of course my brother objected that sending a *person* back in time was as yet untried, and much too dangerous, and worse yet, suitable mechanisms had not been set up to recover all the data from such an experiment, and so on and so on and so on in such a vein until I redirected the word-flow of the conversation and with such a burst of eloquence and persuasion as I hadn't displayed since my undergraduate days—when, I must admit, my temporary sojourn as a drama major had in fact taught me something—and I argued that we were, after all, brothers, and maybe he owed me something for sitting through all those dinner-table lectures of his which might have so stunted my childhood that I grew up to be a serial killer or worse; but somehow, through saintly forbearance, I had not, and so on and so on in *that* vein until *his* eyes started to glaze over—

Now I will spare my reader a recitation of the tedious details, much less any scientific explanation. Suffice it to say I still had friends in the drama department, and was able to borrow, without too far-fetched an explanation, suitable Elizabethan garb, though at my age and girth, I had to accept Falstaff's costume, which was usually worn by a twenty-year-old with a fake beard and a pillow stuffed into the front of his doublet. From an Army-Navy Store I acquired a not very convincing, but serviceable dagger, just in case, and I practically had to empty out my retirement account to pay certain coin dealers for a handful of genuine Elizabethan gold, sovereigns and what were called "angels," and I had to hurry them along because I wasn't at all concerned about condition, much less rare mint-marks.

Then the time-flow was reversed, or twisted, or whatever happened to it in a pseudo-gravitational matrix underneath the physics building, in the middle of the night with my brother Francis at the controls and not even a graduate assistant on hand to do the real work, and I stepped through a metaphorical door (though it was more like a cross between a smoke-filled room and a funhouse mirror) and found myself on Deptford Strand, the last coaching stop before London, across the Thames and downstream a bit, on the morning of May 30th, 1593.

It was fortunate that I had done my research thoroughly, and more fortunate yet that the sixteenth-century street maps I had been able to examine were more or less accurate, so I didn't have to stop and ask directions, because, despite a lifetime of Bardolotry I found spoken Elizabethan English almost incomprehensible, at least at first, not like the speech of the low characters in the plays, none of this "hey-nonny-nonny" stuff, but somehow gutteral and sputtering and lilting all at the time time, like a drunken Irishman trying to speak frog-German while strangling a Scot. I was able to find Dame Eleanor's Tavern all by myself, which was just as well. People were staring. I couldn't figure out precisely why. Maybe it was the spectacle of an unaccompanied gentleman of my age wandering alone in such a place—hence the emergency dagger, because Elizabethan back alleys were *not* safe—or maybe it was just because I was *clean.* The stench of the place and the people took more getting used to than I had time for.

I found the tavern and I found the private room that the poet Marlowe and his lowlife companions, Ingram Frizer, Robert Poley, and Nicholas Skeres had taken on that fateful day, which would be, unless circumstances were altered, Marlowe's last.

The poet himself confronted me at the door, hissing, *"Who did bid thee join with us here?"* with foul breath.

It was all I could do to prevent myself from breaking out laughing, then explaining at length in my best professorial tone that those were the very words first spoken to the Third Murderer in *Macbeth*, a play which hadn't been written yet. Shakespeare, in 1593, was an upstart crow, a nobody.

But I controlled myself. I eased my way into the room.

"I am a friend," I said, and before I could say anything more the others had twisted my right arm behind my back and an even more malodorous, rat-faced little man whom I later learned to be Frizer snatched my dagger out of my belt and poked it under my chin and whispered, "I think thou liest, and I'll have thy guts for garters."

It took my entire repertoire of eloquence and tricks to get out of that one, a shift in stance, in tone, a gesture, to re-establish control, as a teacher does with a restless class. That, and with my free hand I reached into my pocket—one of the things that may have been an anachronism, there was a pocket in my doublet; I'm not sure pockets had been invented in 1593—and produced a gold coin.

"This, for friendship."

In time, I sat with them, and even got my dagger back, which indicated some degree of trust, though the wariness never left them, for these men were, after all, spies, petty criminals, and very likely, already, murderers. Probably Marlowe himself was more like them than his admirers centuries later would be comfortable to admit.

They were unarmed. They'd left their swords and daggers with their cloaks in the hall outside, *except*—it was very important to note that my research had been correct on this point—Frizer, who wore his dagger over his behind, so it dangled over the edge of the bench while he sat.

They took me for a foreigner. I drew on what acting skills I had and what research I'd done, to drop hints, and names, and let slip just a *little* knowledge I shouldn't otherwise have—just enough to first alarm them, but not too much, then intrigue them, then appeal to their greed as I spun a fragmentary (and probably incoherent and contradictory) web of lies and half-truths and things scholars had figured out four hundred years later, enough to suggest that I was a representative of either the criminal underworld or of world of Elizabethan espionage. (On which side? Protestant? Catholic? Both?) I had their attention. What they concluded ultimately didn't matter. That wasn't the point.

I spent money freely, calling for a meal, then for more wine, and more wine, until all of us grew considerably tipsy, and once Marlowe said to me, "Thou art not a spy, but the very Devil, come to tempt me," and I said "No, to save thee," and he, "Indeed?" raising his right eyebrow. Some while later we walked in the garden, speaking softly. Some while after that, awash in wine, in the hot, stuffy room that swayed like a ship at sea, arms on one another's shoulders, almost tumbling off the bench, roaring out enough verses of "The Pope is an Ass" to exonerate Marlowe of any hint of the subversive sympathies with which his enemies were at this very moment charging him, I achieved my carefully planned goal.

I got behind Frizer and pulled out his dagger, then broke the point on the stone floor.

He looked back, blearily.

"You dropped this, my friend," I said, and slid it back into his scabbard before he could see what I had done.

Mission accomplished. After that, all I had to do was somehow extricate myself from this cheery, albeit sinister company and make my way back to my own time.

\* \* \* \* \* \* \*

I was still drunk when I arrived. This should have fascinated Francis, because it was theoretically impossible, he had previously explained at considerable length, for me to actually leave anything physically in the past, or to bring anything forward, which was a kind of temporal failsafe to prevent serious messing with history. But the 16th century alcohol, in my system, had definitely done a bit of time-traveling, and what was I doing but seriously messing with history?

My mind cleared only very slowly. I realized that I was in the basement of the Physics Building all right, and dressed as Falstaff, and drunk as a skunk, but there was no time-corridor. It was just a storeroom, full of boxes. And there was no sign of Francis.

*What* had I done?

The only answer, at a time like this, is research. I hurried across campus, sticking to the shadows, hoping I would not be spotted. The library was closed, but I had the key to the English Department. I let myself in, sat down in my desk.

The room was still swaying, a little, though the cold night air and the adrenaline rush of getting here had cleared my mind considerably. I paused, gasping for breath, then fingered through my Rolodex for Francis's number.

He lived in Arizona now, not Pennsylvania anymore.

I called him up. With the time-difference, it wasn't too late. He sounded puzzled, even a little alarmed, as I rambled on, trying to pump him for information without admitting I was doing so. "Chuck, Are you *all right?*"

"Yeah, yeah, I'm fine." He at least was allowed to call me Chuck.

I hung up.

I glanced around at the shelf behind my desk, and saw my familiar Penguin Shakespeare, but, beside it eight fat volumes of *The Collected Dramas and Poetry of Christopher Marlowe*, and next to those a biography: *Marlowe: the One-Eyed Poet* by a respected colleague; below that, a whole shelf of issues of *Marlowe Studies*, and several copies of a book with my own name on it: *William Shakespeare, Friend of Marlowe* by Charles Henry Tillinghast, Ph.D.

*Oh my God*...I could only sit and tear my hair, and then frantically search the internet. First, the little things. My brother.

Arizona, yes. Lived in Tempe. Taught in the university there. *English.* I had changed history, all right, and in this new history my brother had given up physics in college and switched his major to English because he was so carried away by...a performance he'd seen by the Royal Marlowe Company of *Jenghiz Khan, Lord of the Earth.*

I web-searched frantically. Yes. Marlowe had survived. Circumstances were mysterious. It was uncertain how many people had been with him at Dame Eleanor's Tavern on Deptford Strand that day in 1593 when he and his fellows got into a quarrel over the bill—but *why, why?* I'd left them with a lot of gold, hadn't I, more than enough to pay for meat and drink...unless, unless, my brother in the *other reality*, the one who became the physicist, had been correct, and you can't leave something in the past, so the gold I'd brought there vanished when I did— *where?* I don't know, scattered along the timestream somewhere. Maybe it materialized on a contemporary London street. The net result, the money disappeared, Marlowe and his pals were suddenly embarrassed for cash, the much-studied brawl ensued. Marlowe, in a drunken rage, snatched Frizer's dagger from behind and beat him over the head with the pommel, whereupon Frizer twisted around, grabbed Marlowe's wrist, and shoved the dagger point-first into the poet's face.

But the point was broken off, almost square, and the dagger took out Marlowe's right eye, but did not kill him. He lived. He became the legendary One-Eyed Poet of Elizabethan and Jacobean theatre, who had wrapped the whole of English dramatic poetry of that period around himself, so that Shakespeare, Ben Jonson, Beaumont and Fletcher, Thomas Dekker, Thomas Heywood, John Webster, and the rest of them were remembered as *contemporaries of Marlowe.*

I was still tearing through websites when I heard keys jangle, the front door open, and someone come in. It was all I could do to rush into the back of the office, change out of the Falstaff costume, and make it back to my desk before—who should poke his unwelcome head into my little world, but my nemesis,

Professor Lee Allan Cranchburger?

"Hey, Chuck," he said. "Working early—or late?

"Just working."

That I wore an old jogging suit didn't faze him. That was all there'd been in the closet in back.

"How, how did you like my guest lecture the other day?"

"Great, just great."

"Why thank you, Chuck. You know, I think you ought to be thanking your lucky stars that you specialized in the second banana, Shakespeare, because I've got the Marlovians shaking in their boots."

"Yeah, I'm sure you have." I kept clicking through web-pages.

"My book *is* a smash, you have to admit, Chuck. I'd meant to drop off a copy for you." He thunked a thick tome down on my desk. "I see you're busy, so I'll be on my way. Oh...would you like me to autograph it before I go?"

\* \* \* \* \* \* \*

*Ay, here's the rub.* As I paged through *The Marlowe Fraud Unmasked: Final Proof That Edward De Vere Wrote the Plays*, I realized that I had been short-changed my pound of flesh. I had proven myself right, but as the only survivor of the old reality, which my meddling had otherwise wiped out, *only I knew that*, and I could convince no one. Some revenge, huh? The following weeks revealed that there were occasional improve-ments in this new version of things, notably that my brother the English major had married a nice girl in Arizona and was now a proud grandfather, as opposed to my brother the physicist in Pennsylvania who was messily divorced, bitter, and obsessed with his work—but in *my* situation, there was no improvement as all. Cranchberger was as insufferable and dismissive as ever. I did not have my revenge, and without my brother being a phys-icist, there was no time machine. I could not meddle my way out of this one.

At times like this I think of murder, or call my brother (which would not do much good) or consider selling my soul to the Devil.

I clicked to the university directory. Did we have a Department of Demonology?

# A LOST CITY
# OF THE JUNGLE

"It was upon the Congo River," the Oldest Member said suddenly, "where I discovered the way to the City of Dreams."

The conversation had been ranging over many topics, while the Oldest Member seemed submerged in a reverie. When he suddenly spoke, in little more than a whisper, it had the effect of a thunderbolt. We all knew that he had been many places and seen strange things in his youth, and, to some of us at least, his stories were more than just idle yarns. He was, in odd way, our prophet. Here was a man who had been to the proverbial mountain, and had come back to report on countless wonders.

Or so it was still possible to believe, though age had wearied him, and his mind was, admittedly, not as focused as it had once been.

The waiter quietly refilled the Oldest Member's glass.

"What—? Huh—? What was I saying?"

Gently, with a slightly pained look on his face, another member said, "You spoke of the City of Dreams. On the Congo."

"It might have been the Zambezi—"

"You mean you don't *remember?*" sneered the Skeptical Member.

There were mutterings, glares. Instinctively, I edged away. I never had liked that fellow. He could be a boorish drunk when cold sober, and I wasn't sure—nor did I care—about his state now.

I should explain that all of this happened long ago, in one

of those London clubs that used to be much commoner than they are today, the sort of place where gentlemen could come after hours to leave the world behind in the midst of a very select company. This particular establishment had existed for some centuries, and it was jokingly explained to me once (when I inquired about a certain coat of arms on the wall, above an ancient suit of armor) that one of our founders had been knighted by Richard the Lionhearted during the Third Crusade. Certainly there were trophies here from exploits of more recent vintage, medals, elephant tusks, mounted animal heads, framed photographs and even a curious jade skull, about which many stories were told. I was awed and honored to be in such a place, particularly at my age, for I was barely twenty, and only allowed there because of who my father had been.

Perhaps it was because I was just young enough to have missed the Great War—though I remember seeing zeppelins overhead, and I told my mother they looked like mythological monsters which Perseus or St. George would soon slay—that I was still able to believe in Romance. I had grown up reading of the olden days and far away, of the great explorers and travelers; and also pure romance, from Mandeville to Haggard, not to mention Tennyson and William Morris. I had little sympathy for the new age that was upon us now with its noise and speed and ugly music—the age of which the Skeptical Member, for all he was a few years my senior, was so obviously a denizen. (He too in the club because he was the son of somebody rich and famous, but he had, alas, no appreciation of the privilege.)

Therefore, while everyone else was too flustered to know what to say, I turned to the Oldest Member and said, "Please, Sir, tell us the story."

* * * * * *

It was upon a broad and muddy river (the Oldest Member began), of the sort celebrated in that vulgar old song, where "black fever makes the white man shiver" and what you have for supper, unless you bring your own fare, is more likely to turn a European's stomach than nourish it.

Slowly our expedition pushed onward, amid swamps and bellowing hippopotami, until the water was too shallow and too clogged with fallen trees and hanging vines thick as curtains. We had to abandon our small steamer and proceed further upriver in dugout canoes, guided by natives, whose loyalty could be bought with trinkets or gleaming coins—one made a point of polishing one's pennies before handing them out, for the black folk thought them less valuable if tarnished. Still one could hardly share one's thoughts with such people, and not merely because of the language barrier. Even Zango, a multiply mixed-breed who spoke tolerable English and a plethora of local dialects and functioned as our interpreter, was as inscrutable as the Sphinx, as mysterious as the dark, dank depths of the jungle itself. You could see it in his eyes. There was, I say, a vast gulf between us, which contained secrets he would not, or could not, ever put into words.

Therefore my two white companions—the half-Spanish Garcia-Smith, and the military man, Colonel Balderston—and I might as well have been the first humans to reach another planet, a hellish place of searing heat and pestiferous insects, where, in the night, strange birds screeched and monsters of the river coughed.

Our guides paddled on stoically against the sluggish current, and muttered among themselves or sang songs that sounded like dirges when we drew up onto the shore to camp. I assure you that, as our elected leader, I was not so foolish as to regard them as little more than pack animals, to mistreat them or otherwise deal arrogantly with them, if only because our very survival depended on their guidance, but also because it was clear enough that they were men, brave fellows all, just not our sort of men. We could not truly understand what they knew or felt or dreamed.

"The river is full of ghosts," Zango said to me one night. "It flows out of the mouth of the King Crocodile, who is God, who gives both life and death. Look, up above," he said, pointing, "those are not stars, but the teeth of the crocodile."

Now someone of a more...skeptical turn of mind would have dismissed all this as superstitious native rubbish—

\* \* \* \* \* \* \*

*"Damned rightly too!"* said the Skeptical Member of our club. He waved his glass for the waiter to refill it.

"Will you *be quiet*, Sir?" another member whispered through gritted teeth.

The waiter brought the Skeptical Member more whiskey, and he gulped it down, which silenced him for a time.

To the Oldest Member, I said again, "Will you continue your story?"

"Oh, yes, my story. It was long ago, on some river or other, in the darkness which never seemed to end, even when the sun rose, and after a time the jungle canopy was so thick overhead that one forgot that it ever *did* rise...the twilight, then night seemed to go on forever...."

Several minutes of silence followed. The Oldest Member seemed slipping into one of his reveries, from which, it was distinctly possible, he would not return this evening at all. I was acutely aware of the clock ticking, then chiming—eleven PM; it was getting late—and of the Skeptical Member fidgeting impatiently, and of one of the older members breathing in such a steady, rhythmical manner that I feared he might be going to sleep, which might affront the Oldest Member and preclude the continuation of the story.

I myself wanted more than anything else to hear the rest of that story, and for it to be true.

Therefore I did something which might have been a breach of good manners, though in the presence of the Skeptical Member it was hard for anyone to notice such smaller infractions.

I reached over and touched the Oldest Member on the arm. I nudged him.

"What—? I say...."

"You were speaking of Zango, Sir, and of the river that was filled with ghosts."

And the Oldest Member continued his narrative.

* * * * * * *

Zango said that the river was filled with ghosts, that the dead swam there, that the other men knew this and saw their ancestors just below the surface of the water some nights, and even conversed with them—and that this was not necessarily a bad thing.

Zango was undeniably brave, but also one who had ventured into realms few men of any race ever had, I am sure. He was, to me, like an ancient and mysterious book, which I had only begun to decipher.

"It is a thing of great fear," he said, "but not always bad. Great danger for white men, for Zango too, for black fellows, for body and soul both—but not evil. Not good. Not evil. Both. Neither."

I couldn't get him to explain, but the words thrilled me. Here, perhaps, was something unknown to both Western science and Western occultism—

But I am ahead of myself. I should have stated earlier that the ostensible purpose of our journey, the reason for which rich men and institutions financed us, was indeed to find what was unknown to Western science, certainly unknown to biology and medicine—for Garcia-Smith was a botanist and he took and preserved thousands of plant specimens along our way—but the main interest was geographical. In those days much of the interior of the Dark Continent was still unexplored. For all it seemed to consist of endless stretches of pestilential swamp and the country of wild and potentially hostile savages, we actually hoped to locate an ancient city so thoroughly lost that it had a thousand names and none at all, a place which formed the basis for the legends of Kor and King Solomon's Mines and Atlantis, a realm already hoary with fantastic age when Great Zimbabwe arose amid blood and thunderous drumming, a figment of a nursery-tale or a terror tale (depending on which of the many contradictory sources you followed) when Prester John ruled the land—yes, *that* sort of lost city, which, I thought, and Zango would doubtless have agreed, actually *belonged* thousands of miles beyond the edge of any map, in the darkest jungle imaginable, on the banks of a midnight-black river which flowed out of the gaping maw of a god.

I wish I could have questioned Zango more about this, but the opportunity did not arise.

That very night, he wandered but a short distance from the firelight.Suddenly there was a loud, horrible scream, the likes of which you'd never believe could issue from a human throat. We heard a great thrashing about in the underbrush and at the edge of the river, then...nothing.

It was all over in a second. We were all too stunned to react at first, either my companions or the blacks, until Colonel Balderston drew his pistol, took up a lantern, and said, "What the Hell—?"

We scurried to investigate. What little we found we wished we hadn't. Zango wore European-style boots. I know they had cost him a lot and he was very proud of them. Now we found Zango's shield, shattered, about half of his spear, the iron head snapped away, and those boots...with his feet still in them. But we didn't find Zango.

Now it would seem obvious that he had been taken by a crocodile, but it was impossible to believe that so experienced an adventurer as he could have been so careless. On that dark night, the few stars we could see where the canopy broke above the river really did gleam like the teeth of some enormous demon-god, and it was certainly possible to entertain the notion that Zango had incurred unholy wrath for revealing, or merely hinting at...*too much.*

I could see that Garcia-Smith was thinking along similar lines, and the black fellows jabbered among themselves, wide-eyed and very much afraid.

Colonel Balderston didn't share the notion, you can be certain. He was a no-nonsense, capable sort, they very man you wanted at your side when you faced orthodox dangers, no matter how severe; but he lacked, to put it mildly, imagination. In his view, we were here to show the British flag, perhaps to claim territory for the Queen and discover resources worth exploiting, but to him a lost city was only a pile of old stones.

"Well, damn it all! Aren't we in a bloody fine fix?" he said, and, while Garcia-Smith and I were still too stunned to do anything, he took charge. When the blacks looked like they might bolt, he fired his pistol into the air and shouted angrily, and they stayed where they were.

We were in a fine fix, quite literally in the middle of nowhere, hundreds of miles from the coast or the nearest European outpost, now unable to converse with our guides, with the expedition in command of a tyrant whose manner, Garcia-Smith darkly whispered, was over-compensation for a military career which had not been...ah, entirely meritorious.

A brave man, I am sure, a capable man in many respects, and a stronger personality than either Garcia-Smith or myself— I will admit that we were nearly as afraid of him as the blacks were—but not the sort of person who could make our tiny band hold together under such circumstances.

He behaved like a fool with the natives, as so many white men do, assuming the role of master, shouting what few words of Swahili he knew (though these natives didn't speak Swahili), waving his pistol about, even thrashing one of the fellows "to restore discipline," as he put it.

When a native bowed down before him and spoke the word *"Bwana,"* everyone but Balderston could certainly detect the malicious irony in the man's voice, though we understood none of his other words.

But at least Balderston managed to get the expedition moving forward, though in a very different spirit now. Every second seemed fraught with danger. We three white men sat with rifles in our laps while the natives paddled, and slept with rifles at our sides. The blacks, who had been more or less friendly before, now were sullen, but more afraid of Colonel Balderston than anything that might haunt the river or the jungle.

Or so it seemed. I could be wrong. I think I *was* entirely wrong. I think they were just *waiting*, and had some idea of what to expect, when again, in the night, when we still pressed on in the darkness because we had found no suitable place to land, *something*, a *thing*—I cannot say what, a tentacle, a enormous serpent, an animate vine—but *something* which seemed to have a face and certainly had a hideous laugh reached down out of the overhanging vegetation and *snatched* Balderston away even as a capricious puppeteer might yank a puppet off the stage with a sudden, sharp flick of his wrist.

The Colonel didn't even have time to scream. Garcia-Smith and I both cried out, and we both fired our rifles, wildly, but it did no good.

Then we were drifting in silence on the river, and the black men exchanged glances without a word, looked at us, and up into the darkness.

Garcia-Smith went to raise his rifle again, but I steadied his hand.

The two blacks who had been paddling our canoe handed us the paddles. We could do nothing but take them. Then they stepped into the other canoe among their fellows.

One man rummaged among the supplies. He said something to his companions, and all of them sorted out a certain amount of medicine and supplies, which they handed over to us. They even handed over the wooden boxes containing Garcia-Smith's journals and plant specimens.

In their own way, I don't think they meant us any harm. At least they intended to give us a fighting chance. One of them pressed into my hand a kind of fetish, carven out of a tooth. He pointed to the fetish, to me, then to the sky. He held up two fingers. He pointed up river.

I wasn't sure what he meant. Two miles up the river, or in two days, the fetish would have some purpose?

It was clear enough was that if we were to persist in what must have seemed to them to be a completely lunatic expedition, the natives were having no part of it. Without further ado, they paddled away down the river, back the way we had come.

Now Garcia-Smith and I were indeed, as Balderston had so aptly phrased it, in a fine fix.

* * * * * * *

*"As are we all!"* bawled the Skeptical Member, disgracefully drunk. "It's all bloody fine rubbish and lies, fetishes, native hoodoo...not fit for a white man to listen to. *Gad!* Wake me when it's over."

The Skeptical Member stretched in his chair, threw back his head, and began snoring loudly. There were further angry mutterings. When I reached over and placed my handkerchief over the fellow's mouth to stifle the noise, several of the older members smiled approvingly.

The waiter came in and served a final round of drinks. He glanced at the Skeptical Member with a raised eyebrow, but made no move to interfere. Then, because it was late, he was given permission to retire.

Outside in the hall, the clock struck one.

The rest of us gathered closer around the Oldest Member, who resumed his tale with some vigor now. There was no danger of his slipping off into a reverie. The memories had fully awakened him. His fire was up.

* * * * * * *

We were indeed in a fine fix (the Oldest Member said). It got worse almost immediately when Garcia-Smith succumbed to jungle fever, and within a few hours lay delirious in the bottom of the canoe while I paddled desperately on.

It seemed useless to go back down river, knowing that I could never overtake the natives—though I did not think they would actually harm us if I did find them—and well aware of how far we had come and what little chance I had of making my way all that distance back to the coast alone.

No, whatever slender hope remained must lie ahead, two miles or two days or two bends in the river ahead, whatever the black man had meant.

I'd have to find out. When I could, in the dim light, I got out the carven fetish and examined it: made from the tooth of some large carnivore, exquisite workmanship, depicting a crocodile devouring—or perhaps disgorging—an entire city of beehive-shaped towers.

It too was part of the mystery, to which we were now inextricably linked, into the very heart of which I now pressed on.

Perhaps it was just an impression, but it seemed to me now that the night was endless. Enough time passed that the sun should have risen. What few stars I glimpsed through the now almost solid jungle canopy seemed unnaturally pale and faint, forming no constellations I knew. If I could keep track by my fitful sleeps, two full days should have passed, after which, precisely as the man who had given me the fetish had prophesied, I beheld in the midst of the river a large, squat hut made of grass and logs and vines, crouching on pilings like a huge spider.

I pulled alongside, caught hold of a railing, and secured the canoe. Garcia-Smith, who lay in the prow, was almost lucid now, but too weak to rise.

"Wait here, old chap," I said, "while I go have a look."

He muttered something in the Spanish of his childhood, about El Dorado and the Seven Cities of Gold.

I climbed up onto a rude porch or landing, and rapped on the arching doorway of the hut, the opening itself being covered by a bead curtain.

There was no response. There was nothing else to do but enter, so I did.

Inside, crouching in the light of a tiny lantern, was an old, wrinkle-faced native, who showed no surprise or alarm at my presence. He rose. The garment he wore, which seemed mostly made of beads and bones, rattled.

He said something in a language I did not know, and when I tried to indicate that I didn't understand, he reached over and touched my forehead. Then he smiled and said *in perfect English,* "You have come far on your journey. Your friend, in the boat, has gone on ahead of you. He is very close to his destination. You have a greater distance to go before you reach yours."

I protested that Garcia-Smith and I were going wherever we were going together, that under no circumstances would I abandon him, but the old man, the wizard or shaman or whatever he was, merely smiled, shook his head, and sat down beside a wide, round dish he'd placed on the floor, into which he poured some dark, oily liquid out of a gourd.

He held out his hand expectantly, as if fully aware of what was in my pocket.

I gave him the fetish.

"Do you know what this is?"

I replied that I did not.

He touched it to the oily stuff, which suddenly burst with light and smoke, as if set aflame, though there was no heat from it. The old man blew away the smoke, and then I saw clearly, in the bowl, a vision of a huge crocodile resting in black water. As I watched, the monster opened its eyes, which were bright, like moons. Its enormous jaw gaped, and I saw that its teeth gleamed, like stars, and seemed to fill up the whole sky, the whole of creation. I turned away quickly, lest it devour me.

But the old man said, "Be not afraid. Now that he knows you are coming, he will spare you." The old man gave me back the fetish. "This is a key," he said, "also a sign of safe passage. With it, you may go on your way to the end."

I made some remark about how tired I was, how my companion was sick, and we both needed to rest.

The old man shook his finger. "No. For you there is no rest."

He bade me look again, and this time, in the vision, I saw

the city we had so long sought. It indeed had beehive-shaped towers, but of gleaming marble, and walls, battlements, roofs, and great stairs which rose tier upon tier into a black sky. All the windows were aglow with lights, their reflections gleaming on the black water of the river; and silhouetted against that light, on the river, I saw myself and Garcia-Smith in our dugout, drifting toward the shore.

Some of the details of my journey become...uncertain...after this point. I have no clear memory of leaving the black wizard's hut, or even of turning away from the vision for a second time... but I know that the old man gave me a parting gift, a bag or mesh made of some animal gut, tied on a thong, so I could wear the carven "key" around my neck and be guided by its light at all times. Indeed, the thing glowed now with a light of its own, which was the light of that Lost City we now approached.

I remember being on the water again, with Garcia-Smith, and telling him that we had to press on, that there was no turning back, not now, not ever. He nodded, and said something more in Spanish about the Seven Cities.

How, exactly, we came to that city, I cannot fully say. Perhaps I merely paddled against the slow current for several more days, which my companion sank into delirium and I feared for his life. Certainly our medicines did him little good. Whiskey did no more. He sat with his eyes open, staring up into space, as if he could already see something which held him completely enraptured.

I can only say that we came to the Lost City at last, and as I tied up our canoe at the quay, I saw poor Zango there, standing in the shallow water. "I can't go in," he said. "Got no feet. But I happy to come this far."

"Nevertheless," I said, "I'll see if I can get the rules changed." I left him smiling hopefully.

With Garcia-Smith leaning on my shoulder, more than half carrying him, I made my way up from the river, into the light, while trumpeters in plumed helmets blew a blast from the battlements to welcome us, and the great, golden gates swung wide.

It is harder still to describe what I saw within. There can only be impressions, of crowds of men from many ages and lands who had reached this place before me—Egyptians, Babylonians, Greeks in crested helmets. I think there were maidens there too, more beautiful that imagination could have ever made them. I think there was a throne-room of sculpted fire, and that a queen dwelt there, amid fires that did not burn, while living, golden elephants knelt down one by one as I passed. I think there were angels among the multitudes that acclaimed me, and dragons curled in the rafters. I think, too, that Garcia-Smith beside me did not see or experience the same things I did, for he exclaimed something about El Dorado and the Queen of Heaven, then he seemed to recover his strength, break away from me, and run forward with his arms wide to embrace someone or something I could not see.

Alone then, I approached the fiery throne of that queen who was not, I think, of Heaven, but of Myth, neither holy nor unholy, neither good nor evil, as Zango had perhaps been trying to explain to me so long before.... I approached, and sat on that throne, and for the first time I was aware of a deep, solemn, measured drumming—I more felt it than heard it—like the slow beating of an enormous heart.

Amid such splendor, to the sound of that drumming, I allowed a golden crown to me placed upon my head, and a scepter in my right hand, I took the Queen's hand in my own, and together we gazed out into the Worlds of space and among the stars, and saw the dreams of mankind forming there amid waves of luminous foam, and where it pleased us to darken them, or make them brighter, to bring despair or hope, we did so, but mostly we just let them flow past our throne like a vast, black river, on which our palace and the whole Lost City floated like a fantastic barge into infinity....

\* \* \* \* \* \* \*

And the Oldest Member grew silent, concluding his tale,

while the rest of us gaped at him, slack-jawed and amazed. I cringed to think of what choice words the Skeptical Member would have for all this. Fortunately he was still asleep, and although he'd told us to wake him when it was over, no one did so; for I was not certain that it was over, nor have I ever been even unto this day.

The clock in the hall struck three. It was indeed very late.

Now the Oldest Member rose to his feet, a little unsteadily. I rose to help him.

"I really must be going," he said. "I have overstayed my time."

"Would you like me to help you upstairs?" I said, knowing there were rooms provided for members in special circumstances.

"No, I must be *going.*"

"But, *Sir,*" I said, almost stammering, struggling to express myself. There were so many things I needed to ask. How could he leave off such a tale, hanging in mid-air, as it were? I could, indeed, imagine what the Skeptical Member would say, though I desperately wished to believe that such accusations were unjustified.

The other members glanced at one another, but sat still, as if paralyzed by the black wizard's magic. I alone was able to move, as I helped the Oldest Member on with his coat, and followed him toward the door.

"Sir," I pleaded with him, "tell me, at least, *how you got back—*"

He smiled at me gently. "What makes you so certain that I did?"

"But—you're here, with us—"

He took my hand in both of his and pressed something into it. He held me, like a father imparting some last precious bit of wisdom to a son he never expects to see again. "They are dreams, my boy, all of them, Shamballah, the Earthly Paradise, El Dorado, the Seven Cities, Kor, Opar, Atlantis, the Plateau of Leng, whatever wonderful or terrible place we are so certain must exist beyond the map or over the horizon or around the bend in the river. They're all in the Dreamlands, which border on the lands of the dead, which is why Zango got there first. I can only tell you that whoever finds such a place never truly returns from it. He may walk among men in the everyday world, but more and more it is that everyday world which seems the dream to him, and the other increasingly real, and, in the end, he must *awaken*.... There is little more I can say. You must *believe*, my boy. You simply must believe."

"I do, Sir."

And he let go of my hand and turned toward the door, pulling the door open just a bit.

It was then that I heard the drumming.

What followed is difficult to describe. I can only say that when I followed him to the doorway, he was already gone, and that I looked out on a vast, sluggish river, where stars sparkled in the black water. I glimpsed a barge, ablaze with lights, propelled by black oarsmen in plumed headdresses. Distant trumpets blared. Then the stars themselves rippled and flowed and took the shape of a vast crocodile, his mouth wide, swallowing up the whole world, but also disgorging it. I cannot explain. There was a blinding light. I looked away, and stood for a long time in the doorway, until the cold, winter rain had thoroughly soaked me, and the sound of a steamer's horn on the nearby Thames broke my reverie.

Only much later did I examine what the Oldest Member had pressed into my hand: the ivory fetish of the crocodile and the towers.

# OUR FATHER
# DOWN BELOW

Exactly why Brian, who hated me, woke me at all, much less shared the adventure with me, I never expected to know. I was twelve then. He was fifteen. The difference was just enough to make me a tag-along nuisance and worse.

But he came to my bedside in the night. He didn't swat me with a paperclip on a rubber band or poke me with a pin, but instead he shook me gently and whispered, "Get dressed. Come on. Be quiet."

Why he was up and already dressed, and how he knew where we were going and what we would find, were likewise mysteries. They gave the experience a certain archetypal continuity, staving off the incoherence of a dream: two brothers, perhaps rediscovering some faint affection for one another for the last time, afraid but lacking the words to say so, slipping out together into the dark.

He took me by the hand.

"This way."

We crawled out the window of the bedroom, rather than try to sneak through the center of the house to the door. That might alert Mom.

"Where...?"

"Don't say *anything*...."

And we stood for an instant on the lawn, beneath the brilliant stars of a moonless summer night. There was *silence*, like a tangible thing, draped over all, the night birds and insects inexplicably hushed, as if the doorway to another world had swung open in that darkness and something was about to come through.

For an instant, we waited. I could feel, almost hear my heart beating, but there was, as I say, no sound.

We walked, in the darkness, in the silence, our footsteps noiseless in the dew-sodden grass, and we leaned to pass under the forsythia bushes that arched like too-low cathedral vaults. We were getting too big for this. For smaller boys, those bushes held vast fascination, the vaulted ways underneath like tunnels into some inner, hidden mystery. Now we had to crawl.

And we came to that spot which was still special, enchanted with memories of games and whispered secrets, where adults could not follow, the place we called our "fort" and had built up against the fence at the edge of the yard with sticks and vines woven through the bushes. There we had cleared the ground and carved our cryptic sigils into the dirt. There we had buried our treasures.

There my brother got out his penlight and pointed the beam at the earth and I saw the thing he had brought me here to see:

Our father's face, perfectly formed in the mud; our father who had "gone away" five years ago, and whom I could still remember vividly, a fearsome, shouting man, who dispensed blessings and beatings as arbitrarily as the Old Testament God I had learned about in Sunday school. Daddy, who could smite as well with a folded belt as with a thunderbolt, whom I loved as well as hated, for whom, sometimes, I would have done anything just to avoid his blows and win his smile. Now he was in the earth, not walking to and fro and up and down, but seemingly asleep.

Then he opened his eyes.

I screamed.

"*Hiya* kids!" He grinned impossibly wide, like a movie monster morphing into all-teeth, and he babbled so fast I couldn't make out what he was saying. But I heard his thoughts in my mind. I saw his ideas forming, like shapes out of smoke.

I was afraid, and I wanted to defy him, and, more in a spasm than by an act of will, I *reached out and touched* that awful face, to make it shut up, perhaps, and my hand passed right through it—it was all gooey, like overcooked spinach – and then the face was gone and all I had was a handful of muck.

Brian smacked me on the back of the head and said, tearfully, "Way to go, asshole."

I wept too, and held the muck up to him, and said, "What do we do now?"

But before either of us could say anything more, the earth seized me by the ankle, a hand forming out of the mud, but hard and cold as iron. I screamed as it dragged me down through the ground as if through the surface of a scummy pond. I thrashed about. I reached for Brian. I think I caught him by the knee, for just a second, but he peeled my hand off; and then I was tumbling in the darkness with my cold, wet father, and he whispered in my ear, "Now Joey, what you tried to do wasn't very nice, but I will forgive you because I am your father and I've missed you since that worthless bitch your mother made me go away, and I want you to see where I live now and meet a few of my friends—"

The dead were all around us, drifting like logs in a sluggish stream, big-eyed and staring, their eyes lit like those of luminous fish, stupid and terrible.

I saw Grandma, as waxy as she had been at her funeral.

There was Mr. Brand, the crossing guard who got run over by a truck in front of the whole school, his head a red smear.

And my father spoke to me, walking up and down in the earth, telling me that I was his favorite, not Brian, but when he called out in the night, somehow it had been Brian who had heard him, not me.

I wondered what he had said to Brian.

"I'm sorry, Dad. I was asleep."

"Like a log. I know." He reached out and ruffled my hair, as he did sometimes when he was happy and his anger was far away, like a thundercloud below the horizon. He took me by the hand, and we walked together, among the dead, and he told me who he truly was and who I was and was to become, and he said we'd be joined together, here, in the new neighborhood he'd moved to. He said we'd all become one, and grow very powerful, and live on, in dreams, which are better than actual life. Many things he said I did not understand at all. "But first," he said, "there is a thing you must do."

He whispered it into my ear, and I did not doubt that I would have to obey him. His voice had that quality, that inevitability, and I was terribly afraid of him, even though I knew that I loved him.

He let me go. I drifted from him like a balloon. I saw him for just an instant, his arms wide, his hands drifting from side to side as if he were a conductor directing an orchestra; and he was smiling that impossibly wide smile yet again.

I rose up. I swam, then crawled, then clawed my way through the dirt, spewing out muck, grasping desperately for breath. I caught hold of my brother's wrist and pulled myself up. He yelped and tried to shake free. He kicked, but missed, and I got hold of his belt, and crawled up out of the ground, onto him, holding him in a ridiculous embrace.

He rolled and heaved me off. As I opened my eyes and wiped the mud away, the look on his face told me everything. I knew. He knew I knew. I knew he knew I knew, so very knowing were we two brothers, which, as I have said, gives the whole experience a certain peculiar quality which raises it above the incoherence of common dream or nightmare.

Not a dream at all. No. Real. I had no doubts.

I did what I had to do, and very quickly, before he could react, because he would have done the same to me, because he wanted to usurp my place in Daddy's favor; and our rivalry ended forever; and my father was Saturn, devouring his children, or at least one of them.

Very solidly, stinking of earth, I entered my mother's bedroom and touched her gently. She mumbled something, turned on her side, flicked on the light that was on the nightstand, then drew breath in astonishment and said, "Where in God's name have you been? You're absolutely filthy."

"I've been with Dad," I said.

She slapped me in the face. "No, you have not!" Disgusted, she tried to wipe some of the slime off her hand with a tissue.

"I'm sorry," I said, but without tears, feeling only a hollow resignation. "You have to come. It's Brian. He's hurt."

No, he wasn't exactly hurt, but the mind has to invent excuses sometimes, to fill in the void until the impossible can shape itself out of smoke into something which can be described, so we tell a little lie now, and we stutter, *um, um, um*....

Mother got up, pulled on a jacket over her nightgown, slipped her feet into loafers and followed me, somewhat less archetypally out the door rather than by the window, while muttering about the beating I was going to get if this wasn't "damn good," whatever that meant. We entered the silent darkness.

She halted at the edge of the bushes and wouldn't proceed.

"Brian?" she called out, scarcely above a whisper, her voice faltering with disbelief. "Brian, are you there?"

But it was an entirely different voice which called her by her own name, "Inez...come to me, sweetie pie...."

She let out a little cry and whimpered, and turned toward me as if I could do something, or explain, but I couldn't do anything, of course, or say anything.

"I...*nezzz!*"

Then she couldn't disobey that voice any more than I could, and she got down on her hands and knees and let me lead her under the forsythia bushes, through the vaulted tunnels to the childish holy of holies, which, just this once, was to be violated by an adult.

Brian's penlight was there, and one of his shoes, but Brian was not.

I pointed the tiny beam, and I whispered, "Daddy came back."

Had she not been in such a cramped position, she would have hit me again. Instead she refused to look. She did not see. "Your father is dead."

"He told me that you murdered him. You tricked him out here on the Fourth of July when the fireworks were going off, so nobody would hear the gun."

Down below, Father had explained all this to me, and he'd showed me a trick with the bullet, sticking his finger into the hole in the back of his head and squishing it around. Then he opened his mouth to reveal the bullet on his tongue.

"Your father was an evil man."

"No, Mother, he was a god. I am the son of Thunder."

(For Father had told me that I would be great, and I would reign with him in Death, whatever that meant.)

"He sold his soul to the Devil." Right there, under the bushes, she knelt and crossed herself and began to tell herself those little lies we throw up as a smokescreen against the impossible: *This isn't happening; I didn't kill him; he had it coming; I loved the boys; I only did what I had to—*

The eyes of the mud-face opened, all aglow, as sudden as bursting fireworks.

*"Hiya, Honey!"*

She screamed only once as he caught hold of her. She didn't call my name, much less hurl me aside like the proverbial baby out of the burning building, and she certainly said nothing like, "Run! Save yourself!" which a mother should have.

I was angry. She should have done all that.

My father had called her a worthless bitch after all.

Worthlessly, she grabbed onto the bushes, then tried to beat daddy with Brian's shoe, and after a few seconds she was gone. The ground rippled once, like a scummy pond, and settled down.

Silence.

But only for a moment, because Father reared up out of the ground like a shark leaping from the water, and he was grinning that impossible, toothy grin and his arms were stretched wide and he said, "Joey! Joey! My favorite Joey! You're next!"

I could only snivel and say, stupidly, "I don't want to go."

"We'll be one big, happy family," he said, smiling, and then, not smiling, he said, "Don't make me angry."

*Why?* I wanted to ask him but could not. With Daddy, always, *what* was totally clear, why something he did not deign to reveal.

The darkness trembled, in anticipation of thunder.

"Come," he said.

I could not resist his voice. I reached out my hand to his cold, wet touch.

But that was when the miracle happened, when my mother came back and was wrestling with him. I was in the darkness with them, in the cold, wet nothingness with the dead people all around, and there was Mother screeching and trying to claw out his eyes; and the power of his voice faltered.

For an instant it was Mother who had me in her arms. She heaved me up, onto the solid ground, and she did indeed cry, "Run Joey! Get away!" like she was supposed to.

Then Father caught her by the hair from behind and yanked her down, and I thought he'd broken her in two. I didn't see her again, ever; and Father and I faced off in the darkness under the bushes. Before he could speak again, I scrambled away backward and kicked him squarely between the eyes and his face *splashed* the way Mr. Brand's had when the truck hit him in front of the whole school.

But, unlike Mr. Brand's, his face came back together again, and he was almost pleading. "Come to Papa, Joey, and we'll be happy together."

I screamed and crawled and ran. I went into the house and crawled back into bed, filthy as I was, and lay for what must have been hours, clinging hard to the bedpost so no one could drag me away, while in the darkness, outside the window, my father shouted, "Joey, don't make me angry," and the thunder rumbled and the rain fell, rattling down on the window's glass like an endless avalanche of stones; and I called out, helplessly, uselessly, to no one in particular, to make it all go away, to make it stop, while my father raged outside in the soft earth but could not get into the solid house.

I was so sorry, so sorry for it all.

I was sorry even for Brian, but mostly for my mother, because she had *wasted* her effort. If she had known what she had saved, she might not have. That was the worst of it all, the thought that the miracle of my mother's return had been a waste, too late to redeem me.

Because the darkness was already within me, and the mud, and the cold, in my heart. I had hit my brother expectedly on the side of the head with a stick and tumbled him into the Pit.

I bore the mark of Cain, in my heart.

I was my father's son, truly, in my heart, thought apart from him for a little while, yet one in being with him, of his kind.

I think that Father understood that after a while. The storm ceased. There was silence beyond the window. We spoke in dreams, and were reconciled.

In the morning I found an old bullet outside, on the window-sill.

# THE MESSENGER

He had come a long way and he was very tired, both in body and mind, and covered with the ash of burning cities. Behind him, all along the horizon, black columns of smoke smudged the sunset like malignant growths; but when he crossed a ridge-line and directed his horse down into a valley, he seemed to have entered another world entirely. Here was an eternal and timeless place of cultivated fields, white towns, and rivers stretching like silver bands revealed gleaming in the moonlight.

Somewhere, far away, bells rang softly.

He came upon his goal suddenly, for, as he had read in the classics—and in the long years without war he'd had the time for such things as reading—one discovers the capital thus, however one approaches it.

Indeed, appeared as more an apparition than a solid thing. The landscape rippled into little hills, then dropped into a lower valley, and he turned a corner around an outcropping, where the path twisted sharply to his right, and suddenly there spread out before him the city and palace and fortress of the Great King of Glory, the Emperor of All Eternity, who had more titles than even one who took the time to read about such things could remember.

The capital seemed more than a building or a series of buildings, with its thousand spires and its lighted windows as countless as the stars. It was more as if a great sea, golden and white, had raced frothing over the world, then frozen there in place beneath the moon. Or it might have been an enormous, divine spider-thing of infinite complexity, a creature of a million gleaming legs now standing perfectly still; or perhaps a kind of forest; or a cloud, taken solid shape.

His mind could not grasp all this. It sufficed that he felt a kind of ecstasy at the apprehension that mankind, or even the gods, could have achieved such greatness, that from here radiated the serene power which held all the world in its place, and that he, in some small way served that power.

This was more than the stuff of legends; it was the stuff of dreams.

Yet he could only think of his mission. He was suffering from hunger and thirst and many wounds. His mount was nearly dead beneath him. Still he could not rest, for he bore a message from the Captain of the Farthest Frontier to the Emperor, beseeching the Lord Above All Lords to take up once again the Sword of Empire which he had received from the hand of Heaven long ago and come forth as his ancestors had done; for now, as had been darkly and obscurely prophesied, the walls of the frontiers were broken, and barbarians of inhuman ferocity were pouring in.

Now the distant cities burned.

When his horse dropped to its knees and could go no further, he paused a moment, tossing aside bridle and saddle to let the beast fare as it would, and continued his journey on foot.

It took the whole of another night and a day. Once, dreaming as he walked, he thought fires burned all around him. He could remember such things. Past and present were as one for him now. A weeping, screaming woman ran alongside him, holding out her child to him, begging him to bear it to safer place. But he saw at once that the child was blue-faced and dead, and, in the dream, the woman too was dead, and yet she spoke his name in a kind of prophecy that filled him with great fear.

And he awoke from that dream or fell unto a further one. Still he staggered on toward the gate before him, which rose high as any bank of clouds on the horizon. The sun had set again, and in the darkness, the countless windows filled with light, like all the stars in the heavens come out at once; and it was in the darkness that he finally reached the gate. He pounded his fist against it, crying out that he bore an urgent message for the Emperor.

But he heard only the wind blowing among the battlements, and the cries of night birds, and, very far away, another sound, which might have been the beating of a drum, or a bell.

The gates felt smooth to his touch, cold and hard like marble, and, as he ran his hands over them from left to right and right to left, he understood that carven here were countless figures, tens of thousands; and the walls, too, were covered with images of men and demons and gods, of burning cities and monsters, of ships crossing great oceans. Here, at the center of the world and the Hub of Eternity (for so he had read, but when he'd had leisure) were recorded all lives that ever were, or are, or are to come. Thus was it declared that the Holy Empire over which the Emperor ruled was for all time and could not end.

Yet the messenger, who stank of sweat and ash, knew it to be a tapestry already on fire around the edges, burning toward the center. He could not comprehend, but he knew.

He shouted. If anyone patrolled the top of the walls, they did not answer.

He could sit there before the gate. He could lie down and rest, sleep, dream, perhaps die; but he was sworn to uphold his duty, and therefore he marched, for at least when he was moving it felt like he was doing something.

He followed the circumference of the wall, running his right hand over the carven figures; and again he dreamed while yet on his feet, in his exhaustion, and it seemed that he saw amid the carvings a figure very much like himself; and this figure moved with him, wriggling between the other figures like a fish swimming in a rippling stream. And it seemed, further, that by some transition too subtle to follow *he* moved amid the carvings. He saw before himself towers and forests of stone, and he walked among people and beasts of living stone like himself. He reached out to touch, with his left hand, the fingertips of a flesh-man in the outer darkness who faded away from him and was gone.

Then he awoke into blinding light. He sat up, to his astonishment, in a green meadow beneath a blue sky.

He crawled to the edge of a stream and drank, and saw his own haggard face reflected in the water. He washed his face, and saw, around him, reflected likewise, men and women clad in white, regarding him with some concern but no fear.

He turned and demanded of them where he was and how he had come there.

They could only reply that he was within the wall.

He explained that he had a message for the Emperor.

An old man smiled and shook his head. "We worship the Emperor as a god, and our philosophers debate whether there ever was such a physical being, or if he represents an abstract concept; but no one, I assure you, has ever actually *seen* him, much less ventured into his presence—"

The messenger raged that they must all be insane, because *he* must venture into the Emperor's presence most urgently, for the cities were burning, hordes pounding over the landscape, the sky filled with dragons, the dead rising from their graves at the behest of barbarian sorcerers to devour the living—

He fell down faint again. He was vaguely aware that the people bore him up in a cloak as if in a litter. There were gaps in his memory after that. He lay by a stream, being bathed, his wounds cleansed. He lay in a cottage, in a soft bed. A maiden played upon a harp and sang a song so exquisite that it seemed time had stopped and eternity was *now*, like a firefly encased in amber, its light too captured for all eternity.

Yet he was arguing. He was trying to spread the alarm. But no one understood. Perhaps they thought him delirious. Perhaps he *was* delirious.

He was given wine to drink and good food. Again his wounds were tended to and anointed with sweet-smelling oil. He lay in a soft bed for a time he could not measure. His clothing was taken from him, cleaned and returned. His benefactors handled his mail-shirt and his steel cap and his sword and his bow with wonder, as if they had never before seen the accoutrements of war.

He got up and spoke of urgency.

The maiden said that she did not understand such things, that he should dwell with her and they would be wed.

He put on his clothing and his mail-shirt and his cap and took up his weapons. He slung over his shoulder the pouch in which he carried the message for the Emperor, and set forth.

An old man, the wisest among the people, followed him for most of a day, trying to explain to him that the Emperor had dreamed all things and all possibilities into existence, or perhaps he had caused them all to be illuminated into an infinite book (there were competing schools of thought; most present philosophers favored the dreaming theory); but in any case it was universally agreed that there *was* *nothing else*, that the world the messenger described could only be a delusion, and therefore any attempt to depart to another place was also *ipso facto, q.e.d.*, also a delusion and futile in its very essence.

The philosopher was still debating (more or less with himself) when they came to a golden ladder that stretched down from a circular point in the sky.

The messenger put his hand on a rung.

"Oh yes, *that*," said the philosopher, "we haven't quite worked out an explanation for *that*. The prevailing speculation is that Our Lord the Emperor put it here to humble our pride."

The messenger began to climb. The philosopher shouted after him. After a while the messenger couldn't hear the shouting.

\* \* \* \* \* \* \*

*For a thousand thousand thousand years had the Holy Empire of the Ancient Word spread across all the Earth and subdued it, and a thousand thousand thousand emperors whispered from father to son that single word which was given to the first of them by the gods on the day of creation; and from the reiteration of that Word a thousand thousand thousand times arose all things that were and are and shall be, made as one in the dreams of Our Lord the Emperor of the Ancient Word....*

So the messenger had read in a book once. So he recited to himself now, in his mind, as he climbed, so high that the ground below him seemed as cloud, and the circular spot above him which was his goal appeared no closer.

But he took more comfort in memory of the passage which told how *the Emperor of the Word and Lord of Eternity took up his Sword and drove back all the darkness, all the fears which besieged mankind, making the world pleasant and obedient to his will....*

Weariness came over him again, and he was tempted, as if a voice whispered in his ear, to let go of the ladder and lie back upon the air, and rest upon it, assured that it was such a great distance to the ground that he would die of old age before he ever fell that far.

But, resolute in his duty, the messenger continued, until he hit his head against a hard ceiling, and reached up to push open a circular hatchway. With a heave, he emerged into darkness, a darkness that became absolute when the hatchway fell shut with a heavy thud and the light from below was blocked out.

He found that he had crawled onto a damp, cold stone floor, gritty to the touch, as if covered with wet sand.

He stood up, his shoes scraping.

Very slowly, his eyes adjusted, and what he thought were specks of light drifting before his eyes resolved into other sets of eyes that he did not like at all, cold and harsh like the eyes of predatory birds, and he discerned, very faintly, hunched, dark shapes towering over him, and long white, folded claws before each figure.

*"What is this that has trespassed among us?"* came a whisper like the wind through a stone ruin.

He drew his own sword, which was not magical or handed down from Heaven, but just a piece of wrought metal. Yet it was all he had, and it gave him courage, and clutching the sword and the satchel in which he bore the message, he made his way forward, and the dark things before him parted, as insubstantial as shadows.

He passed through a tall, pointed archway and then into twilight, into what he first took to be a forest, but then saw to be a forest of stone pillars beneath a vaulted ceiling. High above, windows of colored glass shone as if from a sunset. Between the pillars, stone kings, tall as mountains, knelt in homage, their bowed heads and crowns pointing the way he should go.

Yet beyond this place was a garden under the full light of day, with neatly planted trees and enormous rows of blood-red flowers as tall as men; and moving to and fro among these, tending the garden were persons clad in gowns the same color as the flowers, most of them thin and soft-faced, all of them beardless. He might have taken them for boys but that some of them were gray, stooped and lined. When they spoke, among themselves, startled at his coming, they murmured softly, like pigeons. He understood that these creatures were not men but eunuchs, and he knew that it was the custom for such to serve the Emperor, made by their strangeness utterly dependent upon him, since they could have no concerns in the world.

But at least, he thought, they served him.

At least, he hoped, they might know where he was.

Yet when he questioned them, they only fluttered in confusion, as if the words he spoke were not words at all, just unfamiliar noises.

Finally the chief of them said, "Sir, what you ask is most improper. Your presence here is most improper. If Our Lord The Emperor in all His Majesty should glorify this place with his presence—for He would shine like the rising sun and fill our humble garden with light—if that happened, I say unto you, it would not be *proper* for there to be even a blade of grass out of order, or anything disturbed, much less the likes of you, untidy—"

The messenger grabbed the fellow by the arm and shook him hard.

"Do you say that the Emperor comes here? That if I wait I

might *meet* him here?"

The eunuch squawked, then wriggled free of the messenger's grasp, and stood apart, straightening out every crease and fold in his robe, as if *his* dignity had been affronted, and said, "The Emperor has *not* taken His pleasure here in all the time I have served Him, but He *could*, and for this reason all must be perpetually in readiness."

Then the messenger grabbed the eunuch again, by both shoulders, whirled him around and shoved him in the direction of a parapet. All the others shrieked and cried in a weird chorus of something other than words, but they did not stop him.

The two of them stood by a railing, gazing out over the Holy Empire from an astonishing height, but the messenger had no concern for the magnificence of the view, though he could see half the Earth from where he stood. He pointed to the columns of smoke from the burning cities on the horizon, which seemed more numerous now, and closer.

*"That,"* he said, "is improper and *that* is most irregular, and the Emperor must see and know of it."

But the eunuch could not seem to grasp such a concept in his mind, and could only say, "The Emperor's majesty admits nothing which is unpleasant."

The messenger could have hurled him over the parapet in exasperation, but he saw it was useless.

He let go. The chief eunuch clapped his hands and shrilled commands, and before long the others had fetched beautifully embroidered silk tapestries stretched between tall poles, and placed them along the parapet and around the edges of the garden to block the view.

Later, having left the eunuchs, the messenger came to a vast library of many levels, filling many galleries and vaulted rooms, and he walked for hours in twilight amid row after row of dust-covered volumes, until at last, far ahead he saw a flickering light.

He ran toward it, kicking up dust. Then he shouted to a hunched figure in a dark robe that he saw seated at a lectern poring through a huge volume.

As he drew closer, the man in the dark robe—it was an ancient man, with a furrowed face, and long, white beard and hair—held up a finger to his lips in an angry gesture to be silent.

The messenger looked around. He didn't see anyone else who could be disturbed. Besides, he didn't care who he disturbed at this point. He hurriedly explained. He got out the very letter and showed it to the old man, pointing to the raised golden lettering and the raised seal which identified as a message from the Captain of the Farthest Frontier to the Holy Lord Emperor himself.

The old man did not look up from his reading. Straining his eyes, leaning closer, he ran a withered finger down a column of text. "I am of the opinion," he said, "that there isn't even a palace, much less any world beyond it; that the universe consists of nothing but this library, which is infinite—"

The messenger drew his sword again. He could have lopped the man's head off in sheer fury, as easily as he might have cut through a dry stick, but instead he merely touched the man under the chin with the tip of the blade and raised him up from his reading.

"If that is so, then were did I come from?"

"That is a proposition like 'what is the sum of infinity plus one?' On one level it's nonsense, but I am sure that I can find a reference for it somewhere—"

\* \* \* \* \* \* \*

*Great and wise are the holy emperors, infinite their power and their justice, for they are served by all that are worthy and they reward all who are true and brave and loyal in their duties—*

So the messenger recited (from some book or other) as he climbed a cobwebbed staircase littered with bones, threw open a pair of black doors and plunged ahead into darkness, where huge and impossibly loud bells rang overhead somewhere far above, proclaiming the glory of the Emperor. The sound struck him like a physical thing; it deafened him until he could only *feel* it as pain, and yet he made his way onward, until he came into light again and his ears were bleeding.

*Yet the emperors command and are served not because they lack any thing possible to desire, but because by such service are the souls of men forged and made right—*

He faced a dragon in a long corridor, and suffered wounds and burns, but slew it.

He crossed a gallery filled with statues that ground to life, turning after him, but he held up the message and proclaimed the name of the Holy Emperor, and they paused, and let him pass.

Once something like an enormous worm, but with a pasty, soft human face disturbingly like that of the chief eunuch blocked his way as he tried to ascend a stair through a passage, and the only thing he could do was split the creature's face in half with his sword, then cut his way all the way *through* the thick, foul-smelling body which blocked the passageway, until he had emerged at the upper end, covered with steaming gore.

He made his way through long galleries and along hallways, where servitors stood in endless lines to present the Emperor with rich gifts, or banquets on golden plates; yet all were made of stone, and the plates held only dust.

He faced many more dangers. One he ran along a beach where the very stars in the heavens splashed as foam around his ankles while he battled sea-monsters; but at the very last, exhausted, more than a little bit mad, he reached the very pinnacle of the palace (which, he understood, is also the axis on which the Earth turns) and he stood outside a door of black ivory, which he knew, because there could be no other possibility, must open into the throne room of the Holy Emperor himself in all his incomprehensible glory; and if the door was locked and no servitors or guards stood outside, that made no sense, but it was just more of the eternal mystery which reflected the Emperor's eternal majesty even more clearly—so clearly that his mind was overwhelmed until, indeed, nothing made sense anymore and all those inspirational passages he had memorized from books were the murmurings of pigeons.

He pounded his fist against the door, and fell down, weeping and at the end of his endurance. His mind was not right. He knew that. What if he...what if he...? Just went away and assumed the Emperor wasn't interested in messages? What if he just slipped the message under the door? What if he lay down and died there and waited for it to be discovered?

But no, he had been trained as a hero, to do brave deeds, to serve and never to desert his duty even as the Holy Emperor in his benevolence had forged his soul and the souls of all men by such ordeals.

*For the Emperor is the hope of mankind,* he recited. *This is our faith.*

And it came to him that the only recourse now was to run his sword through his own heart, so that his ghost, which *could not rest* with such a mission left unaccomplished, would eventually find a way to deliver the message.

This made as much sense as anything. Finding a little more strength somehow, he tossed away his steel cap and pulled off his mail shirt, and made to stab himself; but his hand was as unsteady as his mind was dazed, and he missed, and gave himself no more than a bloody but superficial cut across the breast, and he fell down in despair against the door, sobbing, staining the message with his own blood.

Then, to his amazement, as he rolled against the door, touching it with his head, the door swung open as easily as silken curtains might part.

He crawled on hands and knees before the Holy Emperor, the Lord of All the World.

The room was dark. Starlight shone through distant windows, but still he recognized the crown of the one seated upon the throne at the far end of the room—a gleaming disk set upon it like the rising sun shrouded in thick clouds, but burning through nonetheless. He knew the majesty of the figure seated there.

He actually staggered to his feet, and spoke, explaining his mission, explaining the peril, shocked and amazed that he was doing this, doubtless violating protocol; ashamed and afraid and *not* ashamed at the same time. Boldly then, at the very last, he did his duty, and when the Emperor made no response he thrust the message into the Emperor's right hand, which remained motionless on an armrest at the side of the throne.

And as the messenger watched, the Emperor's crown fell down into a rising cloud of dust, and a *stream* of bones and dust and scraps of rotten cloth *poured* down out of the throne to settle around his feet.

There was nothing more he could do. He had left his sword on the floor by the door. He couldn't even fall and die in the honorable fashion.

There was nothing. Nothing.

He picked up the message and, though that part of his mind which was still sane reeled at the blasphemy, he broke the seal.

Then someone took the message gently out of his hands.

He turned and beheld one like a skeleton shrouded in black, holding an hourglass. This one read the message with hungry, empty eyes, turning its head slowly from side to side.

Then this one looked up at the messenger, and were it possible for such a being to express pity—it was not—this one might have.

"Don't you know who actually rules the world?"

But at this point the messenger was entirely mad. Whether he actually *heard* that voice, as the bells ringing in his ears receded a little bit, he knew not. He cared not. He leapt. He twirled about. He sang. He snatched the hourglass out of the apparition's grasp and flipped it over. He ran up to the throne and sat on it, brushing away bones and dust. He placed the gleaming crown on his own head. He reached up and took down the Sword of Empire from off the wall, and held it aloft in his right hand, even as it crumbled into rusty flakes in his hand and the blade broke off and fell to the floor.

He sat there on the throne and said softly, "Yes, of course I understand who rules the world. *I* do, for *I am the Emperor* of Hosts, the Lord of the Ancient Word which was given by the gods to the first of *my* line and whispered from father to son a thousand thousand thousand times. I believe you have a message for me."

The shrouded one handed him the message.

It was blank. Perhaps the hungry eyes of the other had devoured the words right off the paper. Perhaps there never were any words in the first place. It is, in the end, a mystery.

\* \* \* \* \* \* \*

The palace dissolved, like a dissipating mist. The messenger awoke in the bright morning on a hillside. He had lost his steel cap and his weapons and his shirt of mail. He was bleeding from a wound across his breast. His right hand was stained red with rust.

He sat poring over a blank sheet of paper, turning it over and over, struggling to discover its meaning.

So the barbarians found him. At first, when he did not resist, they surrounded him, mocked him, and abused him, but when he held up the message so the Captain of the Farthest Frontier might read it—for the Captain's head was there, stuck on a spear—they saw that the messenger was mad and honored him; for among the barbarians it is held that madmen are touched by the gods and sacred. Indeed, he became a prophet among them. He took their chieftains to hilltops at dawn and bade them behold, there within the sunrise, the infinitely glorious palace of the Emperor of All the Earth, who commands the Ancient Word. At first none of them could see, but after a time a few could, then many, until he had converted the entire nation, and it was they who bore him up in a litter (for he was very old by then) and insisted that he lead them on to the palace of the Emperor so that the message might be delivered and his duty fulfilled.

# THE LAST OF THE
# GIANTS OF ALBION

*I have crushed the cities in my hands; I have tram-
pled the nations beneath my feet.—*

*Nemesis* XI, 11-14

The giant dreamed in the earth for he was of the earth. He
dreamed in stone for he was of the stones; a stone had been the
mother of his race, the father a fallen star; begotten was he in
fire upon cold stone; smoldering in slow rage, he dreamed away
the centuries, beneath the earth.

He heard the Romans come into Britain, and he walked amid
their dreams, that they might never know ease or rest. He knew
their speech. He heard them leave. He heard the coming of
robbers into the land thereafter, felt them like insects crawling
upon his skin, awakening him from his thousand-year dream.

He knew that fire and the sword were the law now, that blood
flowed in rivers through all the forests and hidden valleys of
Britain, as on the plains.

All this he found good, for he hated mankind.

Therefore he rose through the earth, toward the light, like
a great leviathan swimming up majestically out of the darkness and deep. His journey through the years slowed. A decade
passed. A single year. Rain fell and wind blew. Gradually the
stone itself was shaped, soil fell away, and if you stood just so,
in moonlight, his broad face was clearly visible on the side of
a hill.

He stirred in his sleep and an avalanche buried a town.

He opened enormous eyes with startling suddenness; they gleamed like two additional moons, risen at once.

\* \* \* \* \* \* \*

King Arthur saw these things in a dream and awoke with a shout. Courtiers came running, but Arthur sent them away and summoned Merlin. The two of them conversed privately in the king's chamber. Arthur was a young man then, newly crowned, resting in Camelot for a single night between the wars.

"But I have not rested," he said, and he told Merlin what he had dreamed.

"This is no mere vapor of the mind," said Merlin, "but a true thing."

"Explain it to me."

Then Merlin laughed a little and held up his hand. "Such haste, my Lord? You command, but sometimes not even I can fulfill all your desires." Merlin grew grave again. "There is much here to be uncovered. I can tell you only that you have dreamed a true thing, and surely it is the beginning of an adventure."

Arthur rose from his bed. "Then let me be armed, and call together my knights—"

"My Lord, again, be not so impatient. This adventure, which you and none other has dreamed, is therefore for yourself alone. You must go without your knights, to uncover the mystery by yourself."

Arthur nodded toward the door to the chamber. "How can I do anything alone? My servants are without. I am sure they are leaning against the door, trying to listen, as if I did not know. But they only seek to know my mind and serve me better. And my knights lie beyond them, asleep in the great hall. They too will rise up to assist me." Now it was Arthur's turn to laugh a little, as he said, "A king is never alone, so I have found out, having become one. He can scarcely scratch himself without a bevy of chamberlains to oversee and assist and flatter him."

So Merlin whispered to Arthur a secret word, which was known only between the two of him, to reassure him, as sometimes a master must reassure his student. Merlin had spoken this word to Uther the night Arthur was begotten. Now he spoke it again, and by magic he made a *seeming* of Arthur lying in the bed and a *seeming* of himself standing there.

Then he bade Arthur dress and arm himself, and commanded him to cover himself with his cloak; and Merlin covered himself with his own cloak; and the two of them went through Camelot invisible, while the *seeming* Arthur slept and the *seeming* Merlin stood watch over him. He knew that with the dawn the false Arthur would arise and speak with his warriors, and feast, and jest, and even fight in the joust, and none would be the wiser, though a *seeming* is but vapor and dust shaped together.

Meanwhile he and King Arthur took horses from the stable and journeyed through the night. Dawn found them in the marches of Cornwall. There they paused to break their fast, still invisible. They passed by the town of Totnes, on the River Dart, near the coast, and did not reveal themselves to the people of that place, but continued on, across mountains, into a very remote region, where a forest stretched before them, dark as night even though it was day.

Arthur and Merlin dismounted and entered the forest, groping their way through the thick barrier of underbrush. Once Arthur heard Merlin whisper to him, "The vision and the adventure have come to you alone. Even I am blind here."

Arthur made to reply, but then he realized that Merlin was no longer with him.

He groped on alone through the darkness of the wood, and the wind rattled the branches over his head. Cold rain fell, and the tree trunks gleamed with ice, though it was early spring already and should have been too late in the year for ice. Arthur trembled. His breath burned in his chest. Once he thought he saw two moons before him, rising suddenly, light flickering like burning rain between the black boughs, but then the light was gone as if two vast furnace doors had shut.

There were ghosts around him, groping, clinging to him like mist, whispering in his ears, imploring him to right ancient wrongs, to put away their pain; and he knew that these were all the men who had died in this place attempting to fulfill whatever quest he must now fulfill.

Arthur put his hand on Excalibur. He did not pray to God just then, but merely trusted his own courage. That was, perhaps, a folly.

* * * * * *

Now there was a more steady light ahead, flickering, yes, but growing ever brighter as Arthur drew nearer.

He saw that it was a fire, and in a clearing, before the fire, sat a giant roasting a whole ox spitted on a tree-trunk.

The monster put down its supper as Arthur emerged into the firelight.

"Do you know who I am?" said the giant, and the very earth and air trembled as it spoke. "Arthur, king of the Britons, answer me."

"How do you know my name?" demanded Arthur.

"Because I have dreamed of you. Because I felt you draw Excalibur out of a stone, which is my flesh. Now I ask of you again, do you know me?"

"I know that you are my foe," said Arthur, "for there is enmity between your race and mine." And he unsheathed Excalibur in challenge.

The monster stood up, towering over him, covered from head to foot in scale-armor, which was of stone, and therefore not a garment at all, but the giant's own flesh. The creature hefted a stone-headed mace and took up a stone shield and stepped across the fire to contend with Arthur.

The two of them fought. Sparks flew like lightning flashes were Excalibur struck, and the giant drew back, amazed and in pain. He stumbled over his fire. He stumbled once more at the edge of a pit where the earth had been heaved up, as if some great leviathan had breached there from out of the world's core.

Yet the giant was not truly hurt, though his blood flowed over his stone armor. He could not kill Arthur, for the king was too fast, and Arthur could not kill him, because his shield and his armor were too strong. Wherever the giant's mace struck the ground it left a crater. Where he swung to one side or the other, trees crashed down.

After a long time, by mutual consent, though neither of them called for quarter, the two of them rested, and there was a truce between them.

Arthur sat on a fallen tree-trunk. The giant leaned on his shield.

"Once more I ask, Arthur, King of the Britons, do you know who I am?"

Arthur was too exhausted to think of a clever answer, or of any stratagem, so he merely shook his head.

"Ah," said the other, "at least I get an honest reply, and in the same spirit I tell you that I am Gagonerok, son of Gogmagog of great fame, and I am the last of the giants of Albion. I say to you further that this is *my* country into which you and your people have come trespassing, and I will be revenged."

"Ha," said Arthur in contempt. "There are many giants and monsters in Britain. I have slain any number of them. My knights have slain more. What makes you so special?"

The giant glared at him, and once more the earth shook. Stones fell echoing into the nearby pit. For a moment it seemed that the giant would break the truce, and raise up its mace to strike. Arthur held on tightly to Excalibur. But the moment of anger passed.

Arthur considered what Merlin might advise him to do in this situation, and was certain that the wizard would tell him to learn something. It was sound strategy, to spy out his enemy's strengths and weaknesses.

"So, speak more of yourself and your illustrious parent," said Arthur.

Now the giant sat down, setting his shield aside, toying with his mace before the fire, at ease, as if actually flattered that someone would want to know. Idly, he picked up the roasted ox and took a bite, then offered some of the meat to Arthur, who ate of it.

"There are many giants," said Gagonerok, "and other monsters, it is true, but they are of fleshly nature. Most emerge from the bellies of women who consort with demons. Some are merely malformed men. But Gogmagog my father was made of stone and fire, and he coupled with a mountain, and so the earth split apart and I was born, as were all the other true giants of Albion, who occupied this land before men came."

Arthur glanced around at the broken earth. He remembered the mountains he had passed through on his way to this place. "Where are they now?"

"When Brutus the Trojan and his band came into Britain, they overthrew Gogmagog's progeny, all of whom were my brothers. A Trojan called Corineus cast our father into the sea, where he fell upon a sharp stone far away from the shore and was dashed into a thousand pieces. The waters ran red with his blood, and the pieces of his body formed a deadly reef, which mariners, to this day, still fear. I am glad for that."

"I have read of this Corineus," said Arthur. "He was a great hero."

"He was a pirate, thief, and murderer."

"He won a homeland for his people, whose own had been destroyed."

"On the way he killed thousands in Africa, pillaging to take what he wanted."

"What he needed," said Arthur.

"He and Brutus and the rest would have killed the entire population of Gaul had they not instead come hither. Not that I would have seen any wrong in that, but the Gauls might have, don't you think?"

"Why didn't he kill you?" said Arthur.

"Only because he did not find me. I was the last-born of my

father's children, still asleep in my cradle of earth. So I was orphaned. Yet I saw everything in my dreams. Corineus, Brutus, and the other Trojans killed many children, in Africa and Gaul. They did not even bother to eat them, which seems a waste."

Arthur let this last comment pass.

"I ask you," said the giant, "are these the deeds of heroes?"

Arthur thought again of what Merlin would advise him. He was uneasy now, without Merlin at his side, but if a part of his mind, remembering the teacher's lessons, could become a *seeming* Merlin, then all yet might be well.

Merlin might tell him that a king must be more than merely brave; he must be clever; and he must be more than merely clever. He must be just.

"I will grant that you have been wronged," said Arthur, "that I too would hate someone who had killed my brothers and cast my father into the sea."

But he was not sincere. He was being more guileful than truly weighing the rightness or wrongness of the thing.

Yet Gagonerok smiled broadly. He extended his empty hand.

"Then let us indeed have a truce between us. Let us even be, for a time, allies, and adventure about the world for a time. No one has ever shown me sympathy before, or tried to."

Arthur did not take his hand, fearing he would be crushed in it. The giant shrugged.

"I will go about the world for a time," he said, "swimming."

He allowed Arthur to climb onto his back, behind his neck, and crossed the countryside in great, broad strides, shaking the earth until he came to a cliff overlooking the sea, which Arthur knew was where the giant's father had died, and is thus called Gogmagog's Leap.

And the son leapt also, with Arthur on his back, into the foaming sea, and with great, broad strokes swam, and dove deep to converse with leviathans, while Arthur gasped for air and struggled merely to hold on, lest he be swept away in the currents and depths.

At last they came up on the shore of Ireland. The giant showed him where a sea monster, one of the very leviathans with whom he had held converse, now ravaged a town, turned over a castle, and devoured men even as a beast might devour ants kicked out of an anthill.

"They are but pagans," said Arthur, "and therefore my enemies. I should delight to see them destroyed."

"Really? Even as Brutus and Corineus delighted in seeing thousands of innocents slain, the women and children of Africa or Gaul who could have taken no part in their quarrel with the men there?"

Arthur felt unease. He knew that the *seeming* Merlin would counsel him to do the unexpected, to think before he spoke or acted, to weigh everything carefully.

"If they are pagans now, perhaps they may yet be redeemed from Hell, or their children might be, but if they are all dead they're just—"

"Dead meat?" said the giant, idly picking his teeth with a broken house-beam.

"We must save them," said Arthur.

"I'll do it for sport," said the giant.

"And I for mercy."

So they fought with the monster and slew it. Gagonerok broke its back over his knee while Arthur struck off its head with Excalibur. But the men of Ireland fled in all directions in fear. Their salvation would have to be brought to them later.

Smiling broadly yet again, his enormous teeth glistening like white stones in the rain, the giant said, "We work well as a team, Arthur of Britain, but perhaps I tire of this now and will merely leave you here while I swim back to Britain and devour all your countrymen."

The giant laughed. He bent over laughing, until all of Ireland shook and the seas leapt up, and mountains fell and the land and the islands thereabout were reshaped and reformed. And the men of Ireland were very much afraid, of both the giant and of Arthur. They stayed far away.

Acting swiftly, Excalibur in hand, Arthur hollowed out the

severed head of the sea monster, stretching skin over its eye-sockets until he had made a boat. From its guts he made a strong rope, from its claws a hook, and when the giant leapt once more into the ocean, Arthur hooked it behind the neck and was towed back to Cornwall, up the River Dart past Totnes (where the people looked on in wonder and dread), then dragged over the mountains, through the forest, while the giant tried to shake or scrape him off, but could not.

In the clearing, by the fire, amid the dark wood, Arthur once more drew Excalibur and said to the giant grimly, "We had a truce and were allies, yet you would devour my countrymen. My duty as a king is clear."

Said Gagonerok, "Are you sure?"

Again they fought, and sparks flew like lightning, and the earth and sky shook with the combat, yet neither prevailed, because of the sharpness of Excalibur, the swiftness of Arthur, the strength of the giant's mace, and the sheer impenetrability of the giant's stone flesh-armor.

At last the giant threw his shield down on top of Arthur. It fell on him like the collapsing roof of a great hall, and pressed him to the ground. The giant reached underneath and caught him in his hand, holding him up before his gleaming teeth.

"I could devour you now, Arthur King of the Britons, but as a morsel you taste no different from any other, and I desire more sport."

So he hurled the king as a player hurls a ball, and Arthur sailed deep into the wood, clinging to Excalibur. The blade, flailing wildly, hewed down trees, but at last Arthur was caught in branches, and thus fell to the ground, sore and bruised and bleeding from many wounds, but still alive.

He lay in the soft loam, beneath the dark trees, while the wind blew around him and the cold rain fell down. It came to him, as if in a dream, that he was lying deep underneath the earth, as in a grave, but conscious as years, as centuries passed overhead. He could hear the earth groaning as the roots of the trees grew, as the water from the rain worked its way into the stones and the winter froze the water into ice and the stones slowly cracked. He heard the mountains breathing very slowly as the land of Britain rose and fell on a scale imperceptible to human senses; but clear enough to him, as if it were he himself breathing in his sleep, in his dream, in his grave.

It was at this time that shapes rose around him out of the darkness like great leviathans breaching. But their faces were man-like, yet he knew from their speech that they were not men. They whispered and made the earth tremble; indeed these were the ancient gods who dwelt in the earth, walking to and fro and up and down in it, now trapped there, no longer worshipped by men since Christ had banished them hither.

Yet these gods, these ancient powers, who were in and of every tree, every stone, every mountain in Britain, whose voices were the wind of the air, whose blood was the rivers of Albion, these gods called out to Arthur and said, *Let us have a truce between us and be made allies, and we will overthrow Gagonerok even as you could flick an insect off yourself.*

Arthur wanted to call out to Merlin, to ask what he should do now, but he could find no voice, for when he opened his mouth it was filled with mud.

So the gods entered into him and filled him with their strength and their guile and their ancient hatreds, and Arthur rose up out of the earth like a leviathan breaching. He felt the winter's rains cracking stones, washing away the earth above him, until he opened his eyes and beheld the dark forest—yet he could see in it, by some gleaming light flickering between the boughs like fiery rain.

He emerged once more into the clearing. His mind was filled with a thousand voices now. He could not find any *seeming* Merlin to advise him. Indeed, he could not even find Arthur. He had forgotten who he was.

He saw the giant Gagonerok, son of Gogmagog, crouching before a fire, beside which he had laid out the corpses of thousands of men that he had slain. As Arthur watched, the giant scooped up a handful of the dead and sprinkled them into a boiling pot, which he stirred with a broken tree trunk.

He looked up, grinning, his teeth gleaming.

"Ah, will you join me in my supper?"

And the gods whispered to Arthur, within his own mind, that a king or a hero must be greater than all other men and above common morality. Therefore to do mighty deeds, he must also be terrible, and partake of terrible things.

So he sat down beside Gagonerok and ate of that supper, dipping his helmet into the broth.

But as soon as he tasted it, his mind cleared, and he knew what he had done. He called out to Merlin, but Merlin did not answer. He called out to Christ, for the salvation of his soul, and the voices of the ancient gods were silent; they tempted him no more. He wept, knowing himself to be a wretched sinner, who could never be the true and perfect hero he had aspired to be, merely a flawed, weak, and mortal man, who now sat all but helpless beside a grinning giant who regarded him with bemusement, apparently unaware of what had happened.

The giant gulped the broth. He belched loudly and lay back, saying, "Yes, my friend, our life together will be good together, now that we understand one another."

Arthur, left alone now with merely his wits to save him (for he was certain that Merlin would tell him, *think before you do*, or something like that), swore eternal friendship to Gagonerok the son of Gogmagog. He forced himself to taste even more of the stinking broth and eat of the hideous meat.

He knew that he had perjured himself merely to survive, but that if a king himself is recreant and false to his oaths, then there is no order in the universe, and a giant might as well eat everybody, for all anything mattered further.

Yet when the giant asked him to repeat the oath, he repeated it.

Gagonerok hummed softly to himself, interrupted by belches. He stirred the soup and sprinkled the last of his gathered ingredients in.

He lay back and patted his stomach.

"Tell me a story," he said. "I think I'd like a story now, before I rest."

Once, when he was a child, Arthur had done some wrong and tried to conceal it from Merlin, which was of course useless. *"You'll always be a bad liar,"* Merlin had said. *"You have no talent for it."*

So it was now. Arthur wept. He feared for his soul. He couldn't lie anymore, but could only tell the truth, of how in his pride he had thought to become the greatest of all heroes, how he yearned to be as great as, indeed, Brutus the Trojan and Corineus (Gagonerok growled at the mention of the name), or like Aeneas and Alexander, or like Joshua, David, and Judas Maccabeus who were favored of the Lord. He told of their heroic deeds, of the victories they won, the enemies slain. He told of other heroes of the Britons, of Dunvallo Molmutius who was famous for his laws, of Belinus and Brennius, rival brothers but great men both, of the peerless Ambrosius Aurelianus and of the famous victories of Uther Pendragon, his own father. He wept as he told these tales, certain that he would never measure up to any such persons, that he himself was a mere *seeming*, a shadow-hero, just pretending.

Gagonerok must have thought Arthur's weeping was just so much noise, like the wind in the trees. He eased toward sleep.

"Those are good stories," he said. "I liked them. I am glad that you have sworn to be my friend. Haven't you?"

"Yes," said Arthur, "I have." And he wept again, knowing that he had perjured himself before God.

"I think I'll eat the rest of the British in the morning," said the giant, belching, then snoring.

And Arthur, who had sworn now three times, waited only until he was certain that the giant was asleep, then drew Excalibur from its scabbard and climbed up onto the giant's face.

The giant snorted and his nose twitched, as a man's might, if an insect were crawling on his face as he slept. Arthur clung to the giant's moustache so that he would not be swept away.

Then, stealthily, praying to God that this act might somehow redeem all he did, he drove Excalibur into the monster's eye and pushed the blade down all the way to the hilt, into the monster's brain, and so slew Gagonerok, son of Gogmagog, last of the true giants of Albion.

\* \* \* \* \* \*

But Gagonerok the giant awoke briefly with a shout, knowing that he was slain, and he cried out, calling Arthur recreant and traitor. Yet, then, as he was dying, he seemed to lose his anger, and he whispered, "Arthur, you have murdered me, but you were also the only friend I have ever known. I enjoyed having you by my side in adventures, and at supper. Therefore, I make you a gift."

He yanked the smallest and sharpest of his teeth out of his mouth, and affixed it on a wooden shaft, fashioning a spear, using his blood to bind it together.

He gave the spear to Arthur saying, "Take this. It will make a mighty man out of you."

"It will do me good? It is not a trick?"

"I *swear*," said Gagonerok. "You will conquer with it. You will even kill your own death with it."

Arthur took it. The death-rattle was upon Gagonerok. Grinning, teeth gleaming, he died; and as he died, the sky grew brighter. For the first time since Arthur had been upon that adventure, he saw the sun rise. He saw that the dark wood was merely an ordinary forest. He saw that the dead giant was merely a pile of broken stones.

But hundreds of corpses still simmered in the pot. Weeping, burning his hands as he did so, Arthur tipped over the pot and sent it rolling down a slope into the forest.

Then, weeping still, leaning on the spear, Arthur prayed to God for the souls of the dead, and for the salvation of his own soul, which he knew had been compromised.

When he looked up, in the bright sunlight, he saw Merlin.

"You have done well, My Lord," said the wizard.

"I don't think so."

"The monster is slain. The countryside is relieved of the danger. You yourself have grown in wisdom—"

*I have learned*, thought Arthur to himself, *that the king, to be a king, must sometimes do the hard thing, the terrible thing, the filthy thing, though others may praise him for it later and make songs and stories of his heroic deeds.*

"And, look, too. You've gained a powerful weapon, which will make you all the stronger."

*The king can't afford to worry about his soul. That is in the hands of God.*

"Yes, a powerful weapon," said Arthur, standing up, hefting the spear. "He said I would kill my own death with it."

At this Merlin grew silent, for he saw the future clearly, and he knew that Arthur would indeed carry that spear in all of his wars, and long after he himself was beguiled and trapped in the crystal cave, unable to be of any more help, the king would carry that spear into the last battle at Camlann, and impale Mordred with it even as Mordred slew him.

Tearfully, Arthur turned to Merlin even as a child turns to his teacher, and said, "But I have compromised my soul—"

Merlin forced a little laugh. "No one but you and I and God need ever know. God probably won't tell anyone. So be of good cheer. More good will come of it than ill, in the long run." But his words seemed hollow just then, as they never had before.

# HOW IT ENDED

Jehan, a knight of Auvergne, who had been called the Brave in his youth after he had taken up the cross and served in the holy wars, and now was called Jehan the Good to his face and Jehan the Placid or even Jehan the Fat behind his back, stirred awake on a winter's morning.

He sat up in bed, shivering. His breath came in white puffs. He reached over to the nightstand, broke the ice in the finger-bowl, then wiped his face.

The sharpness of the cold air on his wet face was good. It reassured him.

Yet he sat with his knees raised up under the covers, his arms locked over his knees, and he was not reassured.

"The dream again?" The lady Asenath stirred beside him. Her grey hair had come undone and streamed all over the pillow, yet her face was still marble-white and beautiful. It made her look, he thought, like something cast away among leaves and vines.

"It was the dream."

"Vapors of the mind. Forget it."

But he could not forget how he had dreamed of *a slain knight lying in an empty field, beneath the sun and stars. All his short life this young knight had served God and the cause of righteousness, and yet now God and righteousness seemed to have tossed him aside like so much rubbish. Seasons pressed gently yet relentlessly upon him, first the dry leaves, then frost gleaming off his shattered hauberk (for he had been struck with a spear through the breast); and then snow covered all.*

*In spring, flowers grew between his bones, birds took the last strands of his yellow hair to make their nests, and his great helm was made the habitation of worms.*

Jehan dreamed these things in the night, and in the morning the dream was not quite over, lingering even as he regarded his wife sleeping beside him, as he thought of his three sons, as brave as ever he had been, all of them now gone to the Holy Land to fight for God with great distinction. The youngest, knowing he would inherit no lands, had even carved out a dukedom for himself by the Sea of Galilee, in the very homeland of Our Lord.

Should he, Jehan, not then be content?

Yet he was afraid as he regarded the age spots on his hands, as he thought how the top of his head was bald and his whole body grew gross and decrepit. These were the first touches of the grave, he knew. He thought it even as the dream did not end, but continued while he sat awake, in his memory like an echo *and the soul of the slain knight lingered, and could not rise up to Paradise nor slide into the pit, but struggled to get free like an animal caught in a trap. It cried out in a voice that was no more than a faint breeze rustling last autumn's leaves, but a voice nonetheless, filled with sorrow and longing and bewilderment that all his courage and chivalry had brought him to this.*

Jehan looked at his spotted hands and wept softly, for something he could not put into words, a truly nameless dread.

His wife got up, wrapped herself in a robe, and came around to his side of the bed. She kissed him gently on the forehead, then tugged him by the arm.

"Come here."

He let her lead him to the window, where he stood in the bracing cold and beheld his own lands, untroubled by war and witches all these years, stretching as far as the eye could see. True, he held them in trust for a duke, who held them for the King, but for all practical purposes they were his, and he had grown fat on the profit of them.

The fields lay brown and still beneath a steel-grey sky. He could smell snow in the air. Crows soared above the stubble of last year's crop.

He saw the mill by the river, near the castle gate, and beyond, a new cathedral rising up, one tower complete, the other half-built; and houses clustered around like piglets around a great sow. His wife said, "Look. This is *not* a dream."

It must have been in a dream then, still dreamed while he stood there awake, *that the slain knight heard a voice calling his name, out of the darkness on the first evening of summer. Dared he hope to awaken from the nightmare of death? Dimly, his mind came to itself. His limbs stirred. With a great heave, he stood up. Worms tumbled onto his shoulders.*

*And a voice sang to him, beautiful beyond words, it seemed, and he dared further to hope that it was a voice of an angel, summoning him to paradise. Yet he did not rise above the earth.....*

"Be thankful for what you've got," Jehan's wife said. "God has been very good to us."

"How can I be certain?"

Playfully, half-angry, she buffeted him on the temple. "Ah, you've got worms in your head. They've eaten your common sense."

*Clumsily, groping, like a player impersonating his way through a play when he has completely forgotten his part, the dead youth walked, his armor rattling, mud pouring out of the joints, scraps of rusting metal trailing behind. Yet he found some semblance of strength, as bone came together unto his bone, and the mud and rotted leaves and few scraps of flesh remaining fused together in imitation of life.*

*He opened his eyes.*

*And the voice sang in his mind, as if in a dream that lingered even when he stood there awake; and the voice was not that of an angel, for there was an edge of sorrow in it, but it called him nonetheless; and he could almost make out the words.*

But Jehan's wife only laughed and said, "Do me the favor of remaining alive for a while. We have work to do." She put her arms around him from behind, placed her chin on his shoulder, and nuzzled her cheek against his. "Besides, I still love you. What would I do without you?"

What indeed? Therefore he rose and dressed, called for his servants and his breakfast, and went about the business of the day, some dull matter involving rents and tenants and an inconsistency in accounts.

All the while, as he endured these things, listening to stewards complain about one another and about the burghers, and to the burghers complaining about the stewards, Jehan the Good, the Gracious, Generous, Caring, or Reasonable (called thus to his face) otherwise known as Jehan the Old, the Inert, Stingy, Bald-Head, or Sluggard realized with the force of quiet revelation that he could not be absolutely certain that he had ever awakened from his dream at all. He could just as readily be a dead man dreaming himself alive.

It was like the first piece of plaster falling from a ceiling, a tiny speck, but the beginning of the end nevertheless.

*Adventures came to him. As a knight, he turned toward adventure like a plant toward the sun. A demon swooped down out of the sky, its black, swirling wings blotting out the sky like ink spilled on an illuminated page. Stars shone faintly through it; and a face like a leprous, pale moon rose and spoke to him, bidding him to lie back in his grave, to rest and be still.*

*"I cannot rest," said the dream-knight, for the music within his mind would not let him rest, nor had he any grave.*

*The blackness darkened, the stars gone. Only the moon-face remained, rising slowly above the horizon, saying, "Tarry then, and despair until my master Satan fetches thee."*

*Yet again a maiden's voice, sorrowing and beautiful beyond words, called the knight by his name. Therefore he did not despair, but with greater urgency drew his rusted sword and struck. The demon's blood poured down through the sky like an aurora; and the leprous face vanished.*

*He walked more surely now, beneath a summer sky filled with brilliant stars.*

The afternoon was better. Jehan's groom brought a new stallion for him to ride. He could still do it. He still felt young in the saddle. He trotted the horse around the yard, faster and faster; and within his mind he heard that infinitely haunting song all the while; and his doubts increased, like plaster falling; and he saw *the dead knight in the worm-filled helmet, walking amid wolves, which closed around him, then drew away, disturbed, but able to dismiss him as carrion too far gone to be worth devouring.*

*The earth trembled. A dragon reared up, filling the sky, its flaming breath roaring over him. Yet he divided the fires with his sword as a ship's prow divides the ocean, and the dragon fell away, and the sword was made new and strong by the heat of the flames, and the fire was the slow and gentle sunrise, and still he heard that voice within his mind.*

He startled the groom by spurring the horse suddenly and riding out of the castle yard, through the gate, down the curving path past the mill, over the bridge until he drew up at the rectory behind the new cathedral and pounded on the door, while the townspeople gaped and remarked that old Jehan (whatever they called him) had not moved like that in twenty years.

In his mind, more plaster fell from the ceiling. In his mind, the earth shook. In his mind, he heard, still, that bewitching, yet not at all comforting song he could just about make out as, in his continuing dream of memory, *he came to a town, where all fled before him in terror, but for one dirty-faced child, who spoke with the voice of prophecy, saying, "Your lady awaits." But a mounted knight waited for him in the middle of the road, beyond a ruined bridge at the edge of the town. There was no challenge. The knight lowered his spear and charged; and the dead youth in the worm-filled helm caught hold of the spear with more than human strength. He yanked the horseman out of the saddle and swung him shrieking down onto the ground, like a thresher threshing wheat; and the rider died in the roadway, his neck broken, his ghost stirring in confusion like a little whirlwind amid the dust, before it found its way either to Paradise or the Pit.*

*Yet the young knight who had arisen from the dead had no such relief. He seized the terrified horse, holding it to his will. He mounted and galloped, as memories rose in his mind like bubbles from the depths of a dark pool, summoned by that song he constantly heard, beautiful, terrible, almost resolving itself into words of infinite mystery and power.*

Jehan pounded on the door, which opened. He sent novices scurrying to fetch Father Giles, a learned and holy man. He spoke to the holy man in a torrent of words, a great tempest of sputtering fears which ended over and over again in the question, "What if—? What if—"

And Father Giles took him aside, into a great hall, where massive books were kept chained to desks. He opened a volume of chronicles, pointing to the pictures and running his fingers slowly over the words as he read how Jehan the Brave, in the eighteenth year of his life, had put on the cross and journeyed to the Orient, where he won great worship as a servant of Christ, riding at the side of the hero Godfrey of Bouillon into Jerusalem when the city was taken and the streets ran with blood of slaughtered pagans up to the knees of the horses, all for the glory of God. This was all written down. It was certain: the deeds of Jehan, his return, his marriage, the births and exploits of his sons.

But Jehan told how he had dreamed of a young man who took up the cross, yes, but also carried his lady's glove beneath his surcoat, thinking on her when he should have been thinking on God; how he was killed over some trivial point of chivalry before he even got to the Holy Land and left like a heap of rubbish in a field, rotting and rusting while his soul was caught like an animal in a trap.

"These doubts are like scabs," said Father Giles. "Don't pick at them."

Yet Jehan felt the cold earth upon his face. He felt the wind and the leaves and the frost upon his bones. Nervously, irritatedly, he brushed his shoulders.

He fled from Father Giles and leapt onto his horse, riding

back up the long, curving road to the castle in the evening twilight—for the day had somehow fled all too fast—and he felt the stones become an avalanche in his mind, the plaster gone now, the edifice of his life and sanity collapsing. He saw a dragon rearing up behind the castle. He saw the leprous moon above the towers, calling out his name; and the stars were blotted out as if ink had been spilled over them. He reared up his horse and called out a challenge, yet no one answered him, save for that singing voice he still heard within his mind, beautiful, shrill, bewitching, horrible, telling him in words he almost entirely understood now, that at long last he had *awakened*, that what he had thought to be real life was a dream and his dream was reality.

He trembled. He wept. Like a player who has forgotten all his lines and has to pretend, fooling no one, he dismounted and entered the great hall of the castle.

There a dirty-faced servant child stood before him, and spoke with the voice of prophecy.

"The Lady Asenath awaits you."

Now he heard the music of his dream clearly, and he understood the words without any doubt. When he confronted his wife, her eyes widened, and she *knew* that he knew and with a long, despairing wail, she fled from him.

*And the dead knight, returning home from the wars, greeted the Lady Asenath whom he still loved, and he removed his great helm, scattering worms. She screamed and screamed. And her scream became a kind of music, the echo of it a song just at the edge of understanding; and she did not sing alone, but joined her voice with another, one who cried out in anger and pain and the despair of utterly lost hopes.*

There was, in this castle, a certain room Jehan was not allowed to enter, far below in the vaults, a room kept barred with heavy bars, chained and locked, blocked with stones, forgotten in the darkness and damp. It has been Asenath's castle before it was his. Her father had died without male heir, and he gained the place through marriage, having proven his worth in the wars of the Cross. But he married and gained the castle on the single condition that he never go down into that vault, unbar that door, or discover the secret of that room.

At the time he had laughed about it. "I don't have to know everything," he'd said. "Just let it stay where it is and I will stay where I am, and all will be well."

And his bride Asenath, who loved him, laughed and agreed.

But now she turned from her flight and followed after him. She shrieked and clung to him, and fell to her knees, begging that he remember his promise, that he just leave things alone and let all go on as before.

"If you love me—" she cried. "If you love me—"

He did love her, still, but he could not. It was too late. He had awakened. The singing voice inside his mind revealed all. Outside that barred door, he heard that voice, not in his mind but with his ears, like any other sound.

His wife shrieked and no servant dared stop him as he hurled away the stones. He had but to touch the door and the heavy bar, the locks, and chains all fell away like dust. The door swung open, and there within, revealed by some unnatural light of vision, was a harp set upon a stone coffin. The harp was made of human bones and strung with golden hair. It played itself and sang with the voice he had heard all these years in his dreams. And as he looked there rose up from out of the stone coffin the ghost of a maiden, who sang and played upon the harp now, where before it had played alone.

Jehan turned to Asenath and demanded in astonishment, though he already knew the answer from his dreams, "What is this?"

She fell to her knees, sobbing, and said only, "I did it all because I loved you."

He listened as she told how she had drowned her own sister, Eleanor, down by the mill.

"But you didn't have a sister."

"You could not remember her, for she was not part of the new thing I made by—"

"By what?"

"By witchcraft." And Asenath told him how her younger sister foolishly loved Jehan the Brave also, though he was betrothed to the elder. When word came back that Jehan was killed in a duel, and the younger dared mock the elder, all else followed: the murder; the frenzy of younger sister's absurd, twisted love, her anger, and pain bound into the harp by Asenath's great magic; the harp commanded by Asenath to call Jehan back, to alter the very course of time and turn their lives in another direction.

"This was surely a great sin," said Jehan. He drew his sword and struck a blow, smashing the singing harp. In profound silence, the spirit of the murdered Eleanor drifted up. It gazed upon Asenath in terrible reproach, but only for an instant. Then that gaze turned to things beyond the living world, and the spirit passed through the stone ceiling and was gone.

In silence, Jehan beheld his wife, on her knees before him, her face wet with tears.

"It was for nothing," she said softly.

*In the final instant of the dream, Asenath recovered her composure. She stopped screaming and spoke calmly, saying, "Welcome husband. I have waited long for your return." And trembling, she accepted his embrace.*

Old Jehan knelt down and raised her up. He realized that he should be angry. He should condemn. Yet he could not.

He got out her glove from beneath his clothing, where he'd always kept it as a love-token, and pressed it to his face as if it were the sweetest-smelling of roses.

A worm fell onto his shoulder, and another.

She looked at him, wide-eyed, brimming with tears, but silent.

"I cannot judge," he said at last. "I can only say that these things are for God and that from God you should seek forgiveness, not from me. A true knight must defend and succor his lady always, or else he is not a knight." He took her by the hand and said in a low voice, "Hurry, I don't think we have much time."

He led her upstairs into the great hall. He commanded that a feast be set and that all make merry. But he and his wife took their supper in their own chamber while the household celebrated, uncertain what was being celebrated.

He ate little, gazing into her face all the evening. Once a worm fell into his wine cup. Discreetly, he spilled it out.

While he still had the strength (which was failing fast), he led her to their bed and lifted her onto it. He lay beside her. They did not touch, but merely lay there, on their last night together, speaking of the love of two young people who lived long ago. Was it not expected, he put to her, something you read in the chronicles anyway, that a knight's love for his lady should transcend all things, even morality? Did it not follow, she rejoined, that hers should do likewise?

He supposed that it should. "Let God sort it out."

Later, he held her hand in his, though his hand was no more than bone and a few scraps of flesh and old leaves. He was afraid. He asked her to comfort him, to tell him that yes, somehow, they really did have three brave sons, that such sons would be possible, born out of illusion, begotten by a corpse, and still be living sons.

"Let God sort it out," she said. "I think so."

"Truly ours is the greatest romance in all the annals of chivalry," he said.

"I think so."

"I love you," he said, but he did not say, *more than God*, nor did she say it.

And so it ended.

\* \* \* \* \* \* \*

In the morning, then, the servants found her kneeling by her bed, weeping before some old bones which had somehow come to be there. This was a great prodigy, they knew. Father Giles was sent for. Asenath confessed to him, and gave over all her riches and lands to her sons. She put on the veil, spending the rest of her brief life as a penitent, beseeching the forgiveness of God, and of Jehan, and of her sister Eleanor.

But that same morning, just before dawn, Jehan saw the leprous, devil-faced moon crumble into sparks and shooting stars. He saw the sun rise. His soul broke free, like an animal out of a trap, knowing that the quest of his life was complete, that his knightly task had been nothing less than to draw Lady Asenath back from the brink of the Pit.

He had done it, by the grace of God, and he gave thanks.

His soul leapt up. The angels caught hold of him.

# THOUSAND
# YEAR WARRIOR

## I.

Shall I tell you the story then? Surely you already know it. Everyone does.

The Thousand Year Warrior.

Here, in this place, where the ghosts come howling out of the rocks, sweeping down toward the sea on such nights as this.

*They call it Cape Howling, you say.*

Yes, they do, and that's why.

Thousand Year Warrior. Thousand Year Bay. That is what they have also called this place. It all happened here. It is happening here. It will happen here.

You try to make yourself, comfortable, boy. Yes, the fire will warm you more than it will me. Get close to it. Fine. Stretch out your stiff leg, which no doubt pains you. On such a night as this, winter, by the sea, the bitter sleet in the air, you need all the comfort you can get. More than I do. Humor an old graybeard, will you?

You sit still, and are attentive. That's all I ask.

I was telling you a story, wasn't I? About how there was a battle here, on these waters and these beaches, a thousand years ago, between the two great houses of Vasilios and Venn, and in the end the Venndite warriors were victorious, which is just as well—

*Our king is of House Venn, you say.*

It's just as well, because House Vasilios served Razates the Demon King, who wanted to devour the world, like some enormous crocodile. Like a what? A big lizard with teeth, as many teeth as are stars in the sky. The Lord of House Vasilios gave over his soul to Razates, and, were it not for the bravery and sacrifice of House Venn, the world would have been swallowed up. Only death would remain. The sun would not rise.

If not for the Thousand Year Warrior, who was their champion.

In the end House Vasilios was entirely destroyed, its fighters perishing to the last man, the remnant hurling themselves into the sea, the heir to the house, a boy about your age, taking hold of his most loyal retainers in either hand, and leaping likewise to his death.

You're right. They were all very brave too. Evil, but almost incomprehensibly brave.

An old story, yes? Something to explain the gloomy name of this gloomy place. But I tell you that the story is not over yet, because the Thousand Year Warrior, the champion, can never rest. Razates the Demon King is a shadow cast out of the nightmares of the gods, equal and opposite to them, and still the darkness pushes in upon the world like a tide, and still the Thousand Year Warrior must push it back.

I? You have not seen armor like mine before. This breastplate, which looks like the bare torso of a giant, or a god, it's made of leather and bronze. Nobody wears helmets with horsehair crests like this anymore. This sword is probably obsolete too. The ways men have of killing one another progress constantly, I do not doubt.

I? The archetypal warrior from out of the heroic past, crouched down by a fire on a winter's beach in the dark, amid the howling winds, as clouds cover up the moon; telling his story to a mop-headed, bug-eyed, and somewhat lame, scarecrow of a boy for no particularly good reason?

It's not as simple as that.

# II.

There was such a boy. In fact, there were two of them, Ulric, the elder, and Bauto, the younger. Their father, Duke Vahendobad, was a great man of the Empire, or at least he was supposed to be; a huge, bear of a man, always towering over his sons (even over Ulric, who was the tall one) in his heavy furs and his helmet which had spikes and teeth on it. When he lowered the visor, that helmet made him look like a metal beast. Their mother being dead, Duke Vahendobad took his sons everywhere he went, on his endless peregrinations as inspected the various farms and castles and holds and towers the Emperor had given him in trust.

His fur and armor, his beast-mask of a helmet, his rattling swords and daggers, his troop of knights who accompanied him were all for show; for there had been no war in many years, and he was halfway between a semi-impoverished country gentleman and a clerk, pretending to be a war-duke.

Everything was for show, even his sons, that he might show off the strength of his line and his loins.

Or it may have been that the Emperor kept him so occupied, and away from court, because he did not love him.

Even as the two sons feared their father and feared that he did not love them.

Even as Ulric, the older, desperate for his father's affection and jealous of his younger sibling's very existence, definitely did not love *him*.

False love, treachery, a theme we will develop.

It so happened, then, that on a wintry night filled with ghosts, in the darkest time of the year, Duke Vahendobad, his sons, and his threadbare retinue of knights (with one wobbly wagon to carry the supplies) came calling, as they always did, at the tower of the Howling Cape, and while the father sat with the warder inside the tower, discussing ships and storms and fish and taxes, with some mention of the ghost situation, it was not too difficult for the two boys to sneak away.

Bauto thought it was a game.

His brother reached over and flicked his finger behind his ear. He was always doing that, as if to emphasize that his reach was so much longer. Ulric was fourteen that year, Bauto eleven.

"Hey runt, get up."

"Huh?" Flick! Snap.

"Be quiet and get up!"

So they pulled on their heavy boots and their coats, and it was a simple matter to lower themselves out of the window of the barn in which they slept, hang for a minute, then let go and fall into a pile of old hay. A dog barked. One of the tower-warder's men shut it up. It was easy to get away.

They both found stout sticks, pretending to be brave heroes on a quest. They paused to duel with their sticks, all this so Bauto would think this was a game. Around them, the wind blew as it does on such nights, speaking with the thousand mouths of the caves and pits and crevices in the sea-cliffs. Something passed across the moon, and in that moment of darkness, Ulric proposed to finish the game, which was called murder. He grabbed his brother by the scruff of the neck, forced him to his knees, took a stone in hand, and raised it up, to bash in his brother's brains. (The rest of the game involved heaving Bauto off a cliff, where the tide would carry him away and the crabs would eat him.)

But in that instant, the miracle happened.

From among the ghost-voices there came the clear blast of a war-trumpet and the thunder of drums.

The moon uncloaked itself, low, down toward the southwest, spreading a golden band across the dark water. Something slipped across that golden band, like a bug scurrying across the light when a door has been left open a crack.

Then there was another, and another, and it was clear these were not scurrying bugs, but *ships*, galleys of a most ancient type, like nothing either boy had ever seen before, massing toward the shore like a great wave, the water foaming beneath their oars.

The trumpet blew again, and there were voices on the wind.

"Get down, you idiot!" Ulric hissed. He yanked his brother into a nearby stand of tall grass, and the two of them watched, until the both of them could see, clearly, the fierce eyes painted on either side of the bows on the oncoming galleys, and the emblem on their black sails: a rearing dragon circled in flame.

These were the ships of House Vasilios, come out of the darkness one more time, from out of the mouth of the Demon King Razates, whose teeth are the stars, who sought to devour the world.

But horns sounded along the stony beach below, from out of the caves and hollows and crevices, like the wind over a bottle's mouth, only louder, fiercer; and there came racing down to the shore a great host of men, all clad in ancient molded-leather armor that made them look like muscled giants, in brazen greaves and trimmings that gleamed in the moonlight and helmets crested with feathers and horsehair that gave them the aspect of predatory birds. They swarmed out of the cliffs, out of the earth itself, swords drawn, spears gleaming, banging their weapons on their shields to make a thunder like the tide at storm-time.

On *their* shields was the familiar Venndite symbol, the sun and the eagle's face.

Their ships lay at anchor. They waded out, clambered aboard, and set forth, oars churning, drums keeping time like the beating of a single, enormous, muted heart.

So it had been for a thousand years, the ghosts of the slain risen upon again to defend the world against the Demon King, even as the Thousand Year Warrior must lead them, and never rest; and the sounds of the sea and the wind became those of clashing swords, the crash of tearing wood as rams pierced the sides of ships, the screams of dying men, dying all over, again and again and again. They were fighting on the beach now, too. Some of the enemy had reached the shore and more warriors raced down to meet them.

A spear whooshed through the grass and landed with a thud, so close Bauto could have reached out and grabbed it. Then, for whatever reason, he *did* reach for it. He got up. His brother grabbed him from behind and yanked him down, but it was too late. Armor clattered all around them. Tall, crested figures loomed. Someone shouted, "Here he is! A fine warrior!" and they laid hands on Ulric, the elder, and dragged him off kicking and screaming into the thick of the battle.

For Bauto, the rest was delirium. He tumbled onto the beach, actually trying to rescue his brother. The air was thick with shouts, with the smoke of burning ships. Arrows buzzed around him like angry bees. Once he actually saw his brother, somewhere in the press ahead of him, clad in black armor, with a tall helmet on his head, wielding a sword. There was a sign on his shield. Bauto couldn't tell which side he was on. He called his brother's name.

Then something kicked his feet out from under him, and he could only lie there, huddled and sobbing in pain, and that was how his father's men found him in the morning, with a wrought-iron dart of an antique type through his leg, the point protruding several inches out from the knee.

## III.

Quite some story, eh?

*I knew most of that story already, because it had already happened, years before, and I was almost a man now, and had managed to grow up, more or less, but as a cripple, because my leg never healed and I could not run or ride a horse and would never be a warrior. How my father the Duke raged, that the gods had taken his good son and left him the lame runt. "Just be glad you still have your stones, boy, that they didn't make a girl out of you; you're not entirely useless," by which he meant that at least I might gave him a decent grandson to be duke after him. But his anger never left him, and filled with rage, he made his rounds, from castle to castle, demanding, threatening in the Emperor's name—but not in the Emperor's name really, for the Emperor did not love him and it was only a matter of time until enemies at court whispered certain accusations, and when we finally came, in the dark of a winter's night, to the tower at Howling Cape, there was a band of imperial soldiers waiting for us. Father fought, of course, howling like a beast, striking to left and right like the champion my brother and I had always known he was; but it was to no avail. In the end the soldiers bound him in chains and killed everyone else, even the warder of the tower and the servants and all the knights, because they didn't want any witnesses, I guess, and they heaved them all off the cliff for the tide to carry away; and they found me and took me there too, and laughed as they forced me to my knees and made to strike off my head.*

*But then the further miracle happened, and I began to prophesy, to speak with the voices of all those dead soldiers who rise up to follow the Thousand Year Warrior and fight forever against the Demon King. This was not the wind howling over cupped stones, or the waves on the beach, but the true voice of the Thousand Year Warrior speaking in an ancient tongue no one could understand, but which filled them all with dread.*

*So they left me there, alone, amid the ruins of the tower, to dwell among the ghosts, concluding I was mad, or touched by the gods, or possessed by ghosts, all of which are pretty much the same thing.*

*And I dwelt among them for many years, and learned deeply the secrets only the dead may know.*

## IV.

A fine story, yes. Let me tell you the part about how Bauto lived for years and years in the ruined tower and spoke with the ghosts as if he were dead, learning their secret language, which is universal among the dead of all nations; but he was not dead, though his hunger and misery were great. Somehow he found enough to eat by the shore. Perhaps a god sent him fish and bread every day, carried by a raven. Perhaps the country people cared for him, for he was a kind of oracle now, who could be called upon to prophesy; and as long as he kept things sufficiently incomprehensible, his words sufficed, for they could be interpreted by the priests. Thus the gods were praised, the spirits appeased, and little sacrifices made.

The best part is how Bauto grew to be a man, old enough, in fact, that his beard went gray. He hobbled along the beach, leaning on a stick as always, his wild hair streaming in the wind, while the voices of the ghosts spoke to him from out of the cliff-mouths on a moonlit night. On such a night, in such a place as this, he met his brother again, the one who had tried to murder him, Ulric, who was *still a boy* because time does not move among the dead as it does among the living. Once the ghosts had carried him off into battle, he might have fought for a thousand years and suffered ten thousand wounds, but he was still fourteen years old, tall and thin as a reed, in armor that did not fit him and chafed.

They met, and they sat down together by a fire, and each told his story to the other, and they wept and embraced and tried to forgive one another. It was Ulric who said that they must rescue their father. No, Bauto argued, that was a long time ago, but Ulric said that among ghosts it is always *now*, and so the two of them set off on their quest, in the company of ghosts, and they walked on the water and on the wind and on the beams of moonlight; and the distance was as nothing to them, nor was the passage of so many years other than an instant for them, but when they arrived in the capital they found their father dying, not yet dead, for the Emperor had crucified him in the public square, and his death was very prolonged.

To Duke Vahendobad this seemed, no doubt, but one more episode of his delirium, and he and his son the oracle prophesied together, incomprehensibly, speaking the language of the dead and of the gods, and they told the tale of the Thousand

Year Warrior; and when his two sons took him down from his cross, he was already dead, and only his ghost came with them upon the wind, upon the moonbeams, walking on water in the company of other ghosts.

On the rocky shore by the Howling Cape they armed him, dressing him once more in his furs and his spiked armor and his bestial, toothy helmet. Then both his sons asked him for his blessing, and received it, but their reunion lasted no more than the flickering of an eye.

The trumpets sounded. The ships appeared out of the darkness, and Duke Vahendobad led the host, out across the water, to do battle with the forces of Razates, the Demon King.

## V.

Here's the rest of the story.

*When I was still a boy, fifteen or sixteen or thereabouts, I had been alone for a few years already, always in pain because my leg never healed, and perhaps I was a little mad. Perhaps it was only a vision that I had, but it seemed that I met an old man with a streaming gray beard and wild hair, and he sat me down by a fire on the beach and told me the story, very much as I would have told it to him.*

*When he had done telling it, we two sat there in the darkness, as the fire went out, and the wind whistled and moaned around us, and the tide came in, splashing cold spray over the stony shore.*

*The ghosts among the cliffs and in the crevices and on the wind were not silent, nor had they found rest, nor had there yet been any victory.*

*The old man told me what I had to do, and I did it.*

*I stood up and waded out into the frigid water. I didn't have boots, only rags wrapped tight around my feet, and so in an instant I was burning with cold, then numb, and for the first time there was no pain. I waited there, until the trumpets blew from* out of the cliffs, and the clouds parted, and by the light of the fading moon I saw black ships scurrying like bugs across the floor when you've left the door open a crack.

I waited until the galleys clashed once more, all around me, until the oars churned up the sea and arrows swarmed like angry bees; and I waited for the warriors to take me. I was seized by either arm and hauled aboard a ship. I did not resist or scream. I let them dress me in armor. I took sword in hand, and raised up my shield, and I led them into the battle, I, who called out to my father and my brother to follow me.

Our ship crashed into the foe. We stove in their sides. We sheared off their oars. We boarded and slew and pressed on, forever, it seemed, not for a single night, but in a battle that went on for a year, for a thousand years, until I was no longer young, but an old man, with wild hair and a streaming beard gone gray, almost white.

Somewhere, beyond the edge of the world, with the moon adrift off our bow and the stars foaming beneath our oars, we came upon a black galley, vaster and taller than any other we had seen, its countless oars streaming through the darkness like rays of light, the eyes painted on either side of its prow burning with the flames of red suns, and alive. We threw our grappling hooks over the side and boarded. We slew the demons that confronted us, and at last I, sword in hand, shield upraised, led my father and my brother and countless other warriors into the gaping jaws of Razates the Demon King, into the cavern of his belly where his heart was like a great drum, beating in the darkness. We marched for a year, for a thousand years, for no interval of time measurable at all, and we cut out the Demon King's heart, so that its beating stopped, and we were all awash in his blood.

Then we beheld the Demon King seated on a throne. He was dead. His heart had been cut out and the front of his gown was soaked in blood, but he opened his fiery eyes and spoke through his crocodile jaws, and he told is that he too was weary, and desired nothing more than rest, but the shadows from which

*he sprang are eternal, cast by the gods out of their own night-*
*mares, so that neither shadow or light will cease until there are*
*no more gods to have evil dreams or cast shadows, until both*
*the Thousand Year Warrior and the Demon King are no longer*
*to be found within the hearts and minds of men; until men stop*
*dreaming of them.*

*In the end, the tide of blood carried me away, and deposited*
*me on a stony beach, where I met a boy with a crippled leg and*
*told him this story. In the end of the story, as I told it, the old*
*man, infinitely weary, lay down beside him on the stones, and*
*both of them slept, each comforted by the warmth of the other,*
*and the old man died, and that was the end.*

## VI.

I awoke with a start. I staggered to my feet. My bad knee
was so stiff I could not stand on that leg at all, but leaned on
my stick.

It was dawn. Seagulls cried out overhead. The sun was just
rising, somewhere behind distant hills.

I was alone on the beach.

I looked out over the sea and beheld ships of no kind I had ever
seen before, with fire in their bellies, belching smoke. Later I
encountered some people who spoke strangely, so I could barely
understand them, and they did not honor the gods. I began to
prophesy, and they called me a lunatic. Most just laughed and
went away. A few looked on me with puzzlement, even dread.

The wind blows over the mouths of stone. The ghosts still
speak. They do not rest. It isn't over. Perhaps I shall, at intervals,
even snatch happiness from the clutches of jealous time, which
is all any of us can do; but I know that when I am old, I shall
tell this story to a boy I meet on the beach, who is the Thousand
Year Warrior.

I hope that this will end, when the gods die at last.

# INTO THE
# GATHERING DARK

*This much is known. It is written down. It has many witnesses:*

That when his mortal life was done—for it was given to him to know the exact number of his days—True Thomas of Ercildoune, called the Rhymer, the poet who was a prophet, whose tongue could not lie, received word that there waited for him in the street outside his house a white hart and a white hind, miraculous beasts, which feared not mankind, and which no hunter's weapon might touch, though some hunters had tried, thinking to take such splendid prizes for themselves.

"No, they're mine," whispered Thomas, dismissing the amazed, almost speechless messenger.

Then he rose from the dinner table and offered a toast to all his guests, both friends and kinsmen, bidding them health and long life, giving his farewell, for he knew he would never see them again.

True Thomas, who had learned many secrets that are not in the world during his famous sojourn in Elfland, was accustomed to miracles, and took this one calmly enough, or at least he maintained an outward appearance of calm.

"Play your harp for us one last time!" someone called out, and the others echoed this, and it seemed fitting, Thomas thought, that he should be remembered this way. So he did play, remembering as he did all the beauty of Elfland, which he had seen, and all of its songs, which he had heard, and which are not of the world; and he played until all before him wept. He himself felt tears streaming down his face. Then, in the impenetrable silence that followed, he bowed low, as a servant might before his master or a courtier before a king, and he took his leave of them.

Only one followed him outside, into the cold and gathering dark where the beasts waited, a priest who was also his kinsman.

"Thomas, Thomas, wait—"

"I cannot wait. You know that."

"I will pray for you then, for the forgiveness of your sins."

"The foremost of which is pride. Yes, Father, I know that."

And Thomas paused for just an instant, as if he were going to say something more, but he did not, merely turning to follow the white hart and the white hind into the gloaming. He was never again seen on Earth.

* * * * * *

*This much is avowed, and averred and repeated in story and song:*

That the Queen of Elfland, who had carried him off once before, came to him again in the darkness. It was she who had sent the hart and the hind, of course. This he knew. He had been expecting her. He bowed low, as he had before, though this time he neither made the mistake nor indulged in the flattery of addressing her as the Queen of Heaven, for he knew who she was and why she had come. She and her train bore down upon him, the fairy knights in armor that gleamed like shards of moonlight, the ladies in their splendid gowns and their mantles streaming like spider silk on the night's wind. Then came her pages, musicians, and even those servants less readily described, whose heads were those of beasts, whose forms rippled like shadowy water, and who rode upon steeds or were a part of those steeds, like centaurs or something far stranger. Overhead, more of them flew upon great, dark wings.

All of these bore down upon Thomas, with silver bells

dangling from the bridles, with horns blowing and harps and fiddles playing, with hooves pounding, *and yet there was no sound.* They turned suddenly, swirling around him like the cloud of a whirlwind, while the Queen of Elfland drew up her horse and bade Thomas, as he had once before, climb up into the saddle behind her.

Willingly he mounted and rode. He disturbed the dreams of sleepers as he passed, knowing the thoughts of a great lord in his castle as he sat up in his bed with a shout. That lord had been dreaming of wars and the pomps of rank, until he heard Thomas's voice in his dream, *All is vanity, all folly, gone in an instant like the dew.*

Thomas would have given him wise advice if they'd had more time to converse.

The company passed two lovers who had come together in secret, thinking to run away together as if the whole world would welcome them.

*Ah, sweet, false hope*, whispered Thomas.

"It's just the wind," said the young man to the maiden, throwing his cloak around her. "Let's go." But the maiden looked behind her into the darkness and was troubled.

On rode Thomas and the Queen and the magical troop. They crossed a field, where a thief was digging a hole to hide both the treasure he had stolen and the corpse of the man he had murdered to get it. Thomas, by his prophetic sight, knew how all this would end up—he had a vision of a gallows—and said nothing at all, for all the wickedness of the world was clear to him that night, and all its follies as numberless as the stars in the heavens.

But the ghost of the murdered man, hovering over the corpse, cried out, and the robber fell down in terror.

When the company came to a wasteland, almost beyond the world, but not quite. They came to a lonely cottage, and Thomas whispered into the ear of Elfland's queen, "Grant me but one thing. Pause here. I have had a further vision, informing me of small matter I must tend to."

"One thing?"

"Then I am yours forever."

"I know your tongue cannot lie, Thomas. I made it so."

"I am bound by my honor."

She drew rein, and Thomas dismounted, while the Queen and all her company rode around and around the cottage in utter silence, the wind of their passage gently buffeting the shutters and the thatch.

Thomas knocked on the door and there was no answer. He found it unlocked and went in.

Inside, over a fire, an old woman stirred a cauldron. Thomas knew this is be a cauldron of prophecy, which gave the woman a magical sight like his own, but of a less wholesome kind. The woman was a witch.

"Thomas," she said, without turning to face or greet him.

"Aye."

"Do you remember poor Annie, Thomas, that loved you until her heart burned?"

Now on this night of nights, being as he was at the end of his mortal days and halfway out of the world, he could read her thoughts and her memory like an open book, and so he knew that there had once been a girl called Annie, who was poor and ragged and not very beautiful, whose mother was shunned for witchcraft even as she later came to be. Young Annie, on occasion, ventured into Ercildoune, and gazed upon Thomas the Rhymer from afar, dazzled by the splendid figure he seemed in her eyes, listening to the tales of his deeds and, when she could, to his music. On one night in particular, when he had played at a wedding, and she, ragged and poor that she was, could only creep in secret beneath a window and lie there, and listen to his beautiful harping until her tears ran and her heart burned—and all this was *before* he had gone into Elfland and returned to his greatest fame, but it was already enough to dazzle Annie and turn her wits.

Thomas had to admit that, at the time, he had not even known she existed.

"But such things happen," he said softly. "I can't help it."

"I hardly could have presented myself to you," she said, "or spoken out. You only would have mocked me. Already you could have had any lady in the world, and you no more would have taken my hand into yours than you would have picked up dung off the street."

There was a moment of silence. Thomas could not deny anything she said. He knew that as the witch stirred the cauldron and breathed the vapors that rose from it, she could see as clearly into his heart as he could into hers.

"What am I to do" he asked at last, "to right this wrong I have committed against you?"

She did not answer. He, seeing into her heart, already knew the answer.

He got out his harp and began to play, thinking first to give her the pleasant gift of his music for her to remember him by, to dream over, and perhaps be comforted by; but as he played, as the music itself grew in wildness and intensity as if of its own accord, he understood that there was more at stake, much more, for the days of the witch's life were also accounted and done, and the Devil was coming for her this very night. He saw how young Annie, in her pain, her heart already afire, thought the fires of Hell could be no worse. She had despaired when he vanished into Elfland for seven years, then came back famous, admired, and not aged a day, while time and nature had not been at all kind to her. Therefore, on a lonely night in winter, she had gotten out her mother's old book and summoned the Devil over her threshold and into her bed, and didn't think she was any the worse for it at the time, having lost the impossible love of the Rhymer.

Now the theme of Thomas's music darkened, and he who could split the hills and draw tears from a stone with his harping summoned all his power and his passion, and as he played the ground shook and the cottage trembled and the air filled with a foulness which came not from the cauldron.

Thomas knew, too, that it was too late for her to repent, to call upon God, for she had signed her name in blood upon the Devil's contract, and such were the terms that she would be torn limb from limb before she could utter a word of prayer.

So he played, and he *prayed* for her, not with his lips but with his fingers.

Then the air itself split apart in a burst of blinding light. Still he played on, and when he could see again he beheld standing over him a massive figure like a thing of living, molten stone, black, veined with fire, with eyes like furnace pits. A clawed hand reached for Annie, who now had stopped stirring her cauldron, and cowered by the hearth.

The face was too hideous to look upon, too filled with mad malevolence. The thing wore a crown of glowing iron spikes. This truly was the King of Hell.

It spoke in a voice so terrible as to stop the heart of any who heard it, save for one whose days were already over, who was already doomed.

"You are come for. This night our bargain is complete."

But Thomas's hand and voice faltered only for an instant, and regained their poise, and he sang and played the most beautiful songs he had learned in Elfland, and so great was their power that the Devil himself was distracted by them, and the Devil danced and clapped his hands, and tried to sing along, however badly, and his attention wandered for just an instant.

And it was in that instant that Thomas worked a miracle, or at least a miracle was done. Thomas, with his prophetic sight, recognized it, and Annie, with hers, saw it too. A certain way opened up, a tunnel into the shadows, between the angles of the air, back into time—for time was much disturbed and its normal flow suspended that night. Annie could run, into that tunnel—back, back before the time of her despair, before her sin, until she could take a different path where she had once misstepped, and so relive her life and make it come out better again, to a new ending.

She ran. She diminished into the air, growing younger as she did, throwing off her vile, black years, until she was a ragged girl again, and perhaps not as unbeautiful as she thought.

"I shall love you always Thomas!" she shouted, and then she was gone.

The tunnel vanished, like an eye winking shut.

Thomas stopped playing.

Now only Satan, cloaked in flames and smoke, stood before Thomas. The cottage burned away in an instant and he saw that the night had passed, and he was in the midst of a lonely moorland. The east was aglow, just before sunrise.

*"Thomas, what have you done?"* said the Devil.

"What honor and chivalry required."

"Then you must come with me instead, and play your harp in the court of Hell, until the end of time, and see if you can please me *still*."

Thomas bowed low before the Devil and said, "If this is the bargain I have made, then I must honor it, for my lady's sake."

Now the wind blew all around them in a fierce whirlwind, and it was the Queen of Elfland who cried out in fiercely, *"And what lady is that, Thomas? You are* mine, *Thomas, and may go with no other!"*

She and her knights bore down upon him. Because Elfland is neither of Heaven nor Hell, the Devil had no power over her. He snatched at her, as an angry cat would, but he might as well have been trying to catch smoke in his claws.

Meanwhile the Queen hauled Thomas up onto her horse again and the company galloped off, westward, into the fading night.

"You're slippery as an eel, Thomas, but I have you now."

"I knew you were coming," he said. "I was counting on it."

"You must feel very pleased with yourself, Thomas. You must think yourself very clever."

"I do. I admit it."

"Your pride, Thomas."

"I put it to good use."

"But it will be your undoing?"

"Am I undone?"

"You must love me, Thomas, not the world of men, not Annie, not even yourself. For you, I think, that will be very hard."

"My tongue cannot lie."

"It's not your tongue that I want, Thomas. It is your heart."

\* \* \* \* \* \* \*

*This much is revealed. It is a vision:*

That as the dawning light overtook them, Thomas saw that Elfland's Queen had become a loathly hag, that all her knights and ladies were hideous corpses, and her other followers monsters astride monsters, impossible to describe.

Still he clung to her, and they rode on, under a stone and under a hill, for forty days and forty nights, wading in red blood to the knee, through the ocean made by all the world's slain, until they reached the further shore, where, though she was still a thing of charnel tatters, Thomas kissed the Queen of Elfland full on the lips, and in an instant her beauty was multiplied ten thousand fold. In that instant, Thomas gave himself over to her utterly, beholding as he once had before, all the splendid colors of Elfland, which are not of the world or in it.

In that same instant he heard the exquisite music of Elfland, as the bells on the bridles rang, as the horns blew and the fiddlers and harpers played, and he made to join them with his own singing and his own harping, but to his dismay he was like an ape chattering before the heavenly choir of angels, utterly unable to replicate in the smallest degree the glory of that sound, as no mortal man might ever do.

Then, as quickly, the music and the colors faded, even as the gold of Elfland is actually brittle leaves, as its fruits do not nourish, as the wine of that country tastes of cold, wintry air. He was a dead man now, unable to understand how or with whom a bargain had been struck, that he should go neither to Heaven nor Hell, but remain here; and it was fitting that he should.

"It is enough," said the Queen, as she sat on her throne in the midst of her realm, and Thomas's reply was a faint wind, whispering in her ear and stirring the grey dust at her feet.

"Enough."

# SECRET MURDERS

*...but why* will *you say that I am mad? Hearken! and observe how healthily—how calmly I tell you the whole story.*

—Poe, "The Tell-Tale Heart."

I remember it this way. My brother Edward, with whom I had very little in common, begat three children, which was three more than I ever did and something of a sore point between us. He had no appreciation of the arts. In his view, the only difference between a real man and a bum was money and kids. Here I was, allegedly celebrated painter and sometime author, frittering my life away on trifles.

Thus it may be tactless to mention that, dear kid brother Eddie, successful sales representative for the Engulf and Devour Corporation, American consumerist to the core, once made a deliberate wife-shopping tour of Third World countries in search of a "traditional" mate of the barefoot-and-pregnant variety available in this country only in Christian fundamentalist communes—we won't talk about it because Eddie was someone steered through life entirely by himself, and in an odd way I admired his ability to take charge and make things happen, whereas I am more of the passive and reactive sort.

So forget that.

Forget also that he *almost* bagged himself a Burmese wife, but that didn't work out for reasons which remain perpetually obscure and have something to do with his showing up on my doorstep one night with a big pile of Burmese cash and minus most of his possessions.

We didn't have much to talk about.

I remained dubious about his efforts at matrimony.

Then he proved me wrong and actually located a curiously porcine creature with the unlikely name of Tiffany somewhere in the wilds of New Jersey, and they were fruitful and multiplied. I was glad for them. This was what my brother really *wanted* out of life, and Tiffany didn't have a lot of other prospects, so maybe they *were* right for each other.

I enjoyed being an uncle. He had two *beautiful* daughters, Shariann and Rowena. I couldn't get enough of those two. I joked that I'd steal them home with me, and while Ed and Tiffany never got the joke and looked uneasy, the girls loved it, and it was our private little tease. We used to pretend we'd run away together and plot our journeys to exotic places. When the girls were old enough to write, we exchanged secret letters, filled with maps and drawings and childish attempts at code.

But I am getting ahead of myself.

I am forced to acknowledge that Shariann and Rowena had a brother, actually older then them, called Mark.

The first time I saw Mark, the proud parents held him up to examine, and when I went to tickle him under the chin, he threw up down my sleeve.

*That*, his father thought was funny.

I think that if the girls hadn't come along two and four years later, I never would have contacted my brother again. Meanwhile, Mark grew into the proverbial Horror spoiled by indulgent parents, downright feral, crapping in the back yard in full view of the neighbors at the age of five. Whenever he came to visit, his unerring sense of what to deface or destroy suggested that somewhere within his dim and fetid brain was a guidance system worthy of a cruise missile. Like that Christmas when I foolishly allowed the lot of them into my apartment. There, in the living room, was proudly displayed my award-winning *Cubist Landscape with Windmills* which was actually going to be displayed in the Metropolitan Museum of Art in New York in a few weeks. Tiffany squinted at it, wrinkled her snout, and said, "Not very realistic." My brother just said, "I guess it's good for what it is—whatever that is," and snickered, appreciating his not otherwise appreciable wit. But before the evening was out, and as soon as my back was turned, *guess* where little baby Markie deposited the steak knife?

He also tore pages out of several of my best books.

But I shall not dwell on this.

I attempted, more than once, to actually befriend him. I told him we were going to be pals. But he just spat back, "Pals," as if that were a dirty word.

Most of the time, I only saw my brother's family at his own palatial but somehow shabby sty (for Tiffany was *not* a good housekeeper, alas), and I *did* continue to enjoy the girls, despite Markie's efforts to make things, ah, tense.

He was successful more often than not. That guidance system of his would have been the envy of the U.S. military if they'd known about it.

Like the time he piped up in the middle of a Christmas dinner, amid the assembled aunts, uncles, business associates, in whose company I was sort of a freak anyway: "Is Uncle Henry a *homosexual?*"

There was a moment of shocked silence. Tiffany nudged her spawn as if to say, *Shut up and I will tell you later.* Edward sort of choked and said nothing, so the Apple of His Eye went on.

"...but he's older than Daddy and he's not even *married*—" Tiffany had the surprising good sense to try to gag him, but he bit her hand and blurted out, "There's gotta be *something* wrong with him—"

And again, I must move ahead in my narrative.

It *is* true, I will admit, that, using the excuse of my devotion to the Finer Things In Life, I managed to get by without quite supporting myself, living in my old room, prolonging adolescence into my forties. But I wasn't sponging off Mom. I *did* produce worthwhile material. I *had* acquired some reputation. She alone in the family understood that. Neither of us thought my life wasted. But I had never quite gotten around to marriage. Then I finally *did,* meeting at last my beloved Anne, who was twice divorced and a little older than me but *perfect,* a patient, lovely person with a day job who would continue to indulge me in the manner to which I had become accustomed. We moved into a rowhouse together and were perfectly happy. It had nothing to do with any sexual insecurity produced by Markie's question. It was just a coincidence that I married less than a year later, and *another* coincidence that the following year, on Thanksgiving, our whole family gathered for the last time at our aged and widowed Mother's converted farmhouse in rural Bucks County, north of Philadelphia.

Now Edward and I actually had something in a common just then, a desire to let Mother enjoy as many more of her traditional gatherings as she could manage, for all our respective wives did most of the actual cooking and preparation.

So, coincidentally, I say, on an unseasonably warm November afternoon, I happened to be taking a break from the festivities and sitting in the doorway of the Log Cabin in the back yard—one of those prefabricated things everybody got for their kids when Davy Crockett was all the rage, since converted into a shed. I sat there, sketchbook in hand, gazing out over the sloping brown landscape, noting how, as the sun set behind distant trees the colors all faded into a slightly bluish, battleship gray. A flock of geese went honking overhead. It took all my aesthetic integrity not to start knocking off Andrew Wyeth imitations for the shopping-mall market. In the midst of this spiritual struggle, along comes Markie, now eleven, about to shoot up into bean-pole adolescence, my brother's long face, blue eyes, and shock of red hair repeated in himself, but somehow, if I may use such a melodramatic term, *perverted.*

This apparition firmly planted itself, feet spread apart, in my light, and would not move when requested to. He snatched the sketchbook out of my hand, took one look, said, "The usual shit," and threw it into the bushes.

He jutted his chin out, as if daring me to smack him, and said, "Why don't you have kids? My Daddy says *normal* men get married to have kids."

Very coldly, I said, "I don't have to explain anything to you—"

"I already know!" he said, and before I could react he produced an *enormous* hatpin from somewhere, lunged forward, and jammed it as hard as he could into my crotch. I let out a yell and caught hold of his sweatshirt as he tried to wriggle away, and *he* made only the briefest squawk of surprise as I *heaved* him around into the Log Cabin like a hundred pound sack of potatoes and started *slamming* his face into the floor again and again and again; and contrary to what you read about such things, I didn't blank out or go into an animalistic rage which subsumed all reason. It wasn't like that at all. Whap! Whap! *Thunk!* More like an out-of-body experience in which I floated up above somewhere and watched, and thought to myself, hey, I'm really doing it, I'm really getting into forbidden territory here; hey, he's stopped struggling; thunk, thunk, thunk; his head bobbed up and down like potatoes tumbling out of the sack, losing a bit of definition; and I only stopped shaking when I was hoarse and gasping for breath and the pain reminded me that there was still a five-inch hatpin transfixing my scrotum. I rolled over onto my back, but couldn't stretch my legs out, then fell onto my side into an almost fetal position as I drew the pin out with agonizing, desperate care.

Then I lay there, almost weeping, and it slowly came to me that I had murdered my brother's only son, violating a taboo so basic to all human societies that nobody, anywhere, was going to care what kind of kid he'd been or what he might have done. It was a crime of Biblical proportions. I half expected sky to split apart and the Hand of God to come thundering down and sear me with the Mark of Cain.

But nothing happened. The honking of the geese faded in the distance. The sun set, shifting the colors of the landscape in a manner I might have, under other circumstances, found aesthetically intriguing.

I just lay there. My nephew lay beside me, his face smashed like a pumpkin, some of his teeth scattered on the floor in a pool of blood.

Mechanically, knowing full well the uselessness of what I was doing, I gathered Mark's remains into a burlap sack (like the kind you'd put potatoes in) and buried him behind the cabin, under some compost.

Then I went inside for Thanksgiving dinner, and that was when the real nightmare began. All else, I came to understand soon enough, was merely prologue.

It was porcine Tiffany who noted me first and said, "You look *bushed.*"

I mumbled something and took my place at the table. All the fixings and trimmings awaited, along with a turkey large enough to feed an army.

In the past, Markie always got the first drumstick. That's what he wanted. That's what he got.

Edward, doing the carving, put the drumstick on my plate.

"Are you all right?" Anne whispered. "You look a little pale."

I glared at her, and she drew away, startled, and I couldn't bring myself to say, *Of course I'm not all right, I'm a fucking child-murderer, and my life is over, and, you know, I can't bring myself to care right now because it was so, so satisfying—*

The girls smiled at me from across the table.

I forced a wink, in reply.

Our little secrets. But no, this latest one was mine alone.

And *everything* that followed from this point on, everything, is part of some impossible dream in which I am trapped, from which I cannot wake up, a torture of hope alternating with blackest despair—but why *will* you say that I am mad?—to coin a phrase—and—and—

Brace yourself for the horror, the horror.

The sky didn't open.

The hand of God didn't mark me.

I took a bite of the drumstick, and nobody said, "Isn't that supposed to be for Markie?" and I—alone it seemed—noted with amazement that there was no place set for Markie, as if he had never existed. Something was *gone*, ripped out of the fabric of reality. Either that, or I had to believe that everybody, brother, sister-in-law, Anne, both nieces, and even my wheel-chair-bound Momma knew perfectly well what I had done and were *pretending* to ignore it, goading me until I would scream out my guilt for all to hear.

Worst of all was Anne, whispering yet again, "Are you sure you're all right?"

"I'll tell you later," I said.

But *later* kept receding like a tide I was running after and could never catch. I forced my way through dinner, and the evening, and the mindless pleasantries that passed for conversation. I *almost* had a moment's reprieve when I took the girls out onto the lawn about 1 A.M. when, as does occasionally happen at such latitudes if you're far enough away from the city, the sky was patch-black and moonless and you could see the North Lights.

Shariann and Rowena's were so wide-eyed, so filled with wonder, that I thought, no, these are not little girls, but angels; and then it came to me that they must be fallen angels, beautiful as ever, but here to torment me by their very beauty and their constant, everlasting refusal to say, "Hey, where's Markie?"

I couldn't tell Anne any of this. I didn't want to hurt her. She never would have believed me.

And that same night, almost at dawn, I slipped out of the guest-room bed without awakening my wife and into my Mother's study. I clicked on a little lamp and started going through her things. I was looking for family photographs. I knew she kept whole albums of them. And I found them, and started paging through. Here, Christmas 1992. Then, Easter 1993, and Thanksgiving just last year, with regulation turkey with its first, steaming drumstick virtually taunting the camera. But nowhere in any of these pictures was any suggestion that my brother had a son at all. Above the desk, an the wall, were the carefully framed birth announcements for Rowena and Shariann, but nowhere, any, *any* sign of Markie.

I looked at my own fingernails and wondered if I hadn't washed well enough and still had blood on my hands.

There was a sound. I turned. Anne stood in the doorway.

"Hank? What are you doing?"

"I couldn't sleep. I was going through some old family things."

"Come back to bed."

I stepped toward her and winced. The pain in my groin was suddenly intense.

"Are you all right?"

"I think I pulled a muscle today. Kids can be quite demanding, you know."

She came into the room and kissed me gently on the cheek. "Yes, I know. You're a wonderful uncle. Now come back to bed."

I followed, and lay awake the rest of the night trying to convince myself that it all *had* been a dream and Markie had never existed, or that I had been inexplicably blessed and he had been erased from the universe like the horrible mistake he was. But no. I knew perfectly well that if I were to get up right now and go out behind the Log Cabin and opened that sack, there would be the dead, pale, bloody face of my nephew staring up at me, not accusing, not saying, *Look! I got you at last!* but instead doing nothing at all, because nothing is what dead people are good at; and well, in the end, we cannot deny, cannot delude ourselves, and must be rational about these things.

A *year* passed. I grew distant from Anne. I couldn't talk to her anymore. I know that hurt her.

More than once she reminded me, "You were going to tell me what's bothering you."

But I couldn't tell her and I couldn't lie, and I could only shrug and pretend to be preoccupied with my work. "The Muse is the other woman," I had warned her before we were married.

Sometimes I heard her sobbing.

Indeed, I *was* preoccupied. It was a very productive year, and a successful one, for all that critics soon noticed that my paint-ings had taken on a darker, more sinister cast, my verse sang of melancholy, and such fiction as I wrote tended to be populated by halfway-pathetic, but *angry* and sometimes monstrous pre-adolescent boys, all described with such passion and conviction that my writing career was actually starting to take off. So in a weird way I was blessed by and taking advantage of the fact that I had brutally murdered an eleven-year-old nephew no one else seemed to remember had ever existed.

Yes, a *year* went by, and another, in inexpressible agony for me, every *second* in expectation, like a five-inch hatpin jammed into some delicate part.

Anne started talking about divorce.

If only I could bury myself far enough, I told myself, in my work, in the compost heap, in the darkness apart from the world, I would be with Markie and he and I could have this out, man-to-man, at last.

Meanwhile Mother died and Edward and I settled the estate and sold the old place in the country. The new owners knocked down the crumbling shed in the back, and if they ever found anything behind it, they never complained.

Still, I was waiting. I have read that when a soldier is wounded in combat, sometimes, when the bullet goes through his gut and out the other side, he might glance down and see the blood spurting out, but his nervous system is so outraged by the injury that it *doesn't make sense* and for several seconds or even minutes the nerves don't report anything at all, and the soldier has a short grace period, knowing full well that the pain will soon begin and the wound may well be fatal.

It was like that for me, waiting for the pain to start.

And it started, *five years* later to the day. Thanksgiving, which I somehow thought of as Markie's birthday; and I said to myself, *He's sixteen now, and growing up big and strong.* I didn't get together with my brother's family on Thanksgiving anymore, though I still called his daughters on the phone and I missed them terribly. I was afraid to be around them, afraid of what I might say or do.

So, on that dark and melancholy evening in November, after Anne and I had finished our quite ordinary dinner without looking each other in the eye, she announced that she was taking the car to see her sister, who lived in Bryn Mawr, about twenty miles away. That she hadn't discussed such plans with me didn't surprise me. Off she went.

And she didn't come back.

And she didn't come back.

I fell asleep on the sofa, waiting up for her, trying to read, trying to screw up the courage to *finally* tell her what this was all about and ask her if she thought I was insane, or else a monster who had profited and taken gratification from the death of a child.

But it was a couple of policemen who came to the door at last. When I saw those uniforms I was ready to confess everything, demanding to know why they too were torturing me. *Villains! Dissemble no more!* But they spoke first and were trying to *comfort* me as they told me that Anne was dead, that she had been killed on the Roosevelt Boulevard in an accident which involved a tanker truck, the explosion of which almost completely incinerated her remains.

It was *just one more* outrage I hadn't begun to feel yet, another bullet through the gut, that the night went on and on and on, and somehow at dawn I was still on that sofa, still waiting and listening, when the front door opened and shut quickly.

"Anne? Is that you?"

I didn't question what was happening. Not now. If it had been a dream, I could still confess to her, and I dared to hope—

I lurched up and went to the door and found a cardboard box between the screen and inner door. There was no address on it. I rummaged through the packing material and drew out a greasy but empty bottle of automobile brake fluid and a Swiss army knife which had obviously been used to slash the bottle in several places.

I sat down on the sofa again, just staring at what I held, and then the phone rang.

It was a boy's voice. Not a child's. A teenager, now.

"Hi, Uncle Hank. Remember me?"

I slammed the phone down and said to myself no, no, no, this isn't happening, this isn't possible, no, not after all this time.

The phone rang again.

I didn't pick it up.

I went over to my brother's place in New Jersey. And again, an outrage, a dislocation. I never even managed to tell Ed and Tiffany that Anne was dead. I just mumbled her name and from their blank looks I *knew* that they, impossibly, conspiratorially, were *pretending* that she had never existed, that I had never been married; and my visit extended through painful small talk until my brother showed obvious signs of irritation (not to mention some puzzlement) that I had barged in unannounced for no discernible purpose. Tiffany said something characteristically tactless about my drinking too much. (Did I drink at all in this reality? I didn't know.)

I rose to go. On my way out I rummaged through my coat pocket and produced the Swiss army knife.

"This is yours," I said.

"Good God, where did you find that after all this time? I lost it at Mom's place years ago. Thanks."

"It's nothing."

I didn't see the girls. They were at boarding school. (On Thanksgiving? Did that make sense? Or had I slipped forward a couple days, in this other reality in which Anne didn't exist.)

When I got back home to Philadelphia, the phone rang.

"You and me gotta talk. We have things to settle between us," Mark said.

"The Hell we do," I said, and hung up again.

Somehow I had to fight him. I couldn't go down without a struggle, for all I knew I was going to go down. It was the difference between tragedy and pointless futility, between catharsis and bathos.

Even at such a time I could intellectualize about art. Maybe

Edward had been right and I had frittered my life away on useless things.

The next night Edward's house burned down. Both he and his wife Tiffany were killed.

I rushed over to New Jersey when the State Police called. The officers and firemen standing around the smoldering ruin were sympathetic. They took me on a little tour, but there wasn't much to see. They made it clear I wasn't required to identify the bodies.

Then I actually found the courage within myself to say, "What about their girls? What about Shariann and Rowena?"

A policeman looked startled. He flipped through some papers.

"Nobody said anything about kids. There were only two bodies."

I opened my mouth to explain, but saw the uselessness of it. I thought the cops were going to grab me, but they let me leave the scene, and when I got back home I found an empty gasoline can in the doorway, and the phone rang.

"Uncle Hank, this is Mark. There's a bar right behind your place, across the alley. I'm there. Come and talk with me *now*."

When the wounded soldier sees the blood gushing out of him and the pain begins, what does he do? What? What?

Here's what.

I took a shower. I made myself presentable. I deliberately forced Markie to wait, to reassure myself that I still had that much power over him.

The phone rang and rang.

I let it ring.

What more could he do to me?

At the very last, though, there was nothing more for me to do but go into that bar and slide into a booth opposite Markie.

He was a big kid. Maybe that was why he hadn't been carded. It was dark. I couldn't quite make out his face.

"Hi, Uncle Mark. Long time, no see, huh?"

"What in God's name do you *want*?"

He laughed. He wriggled in his seat, aping sexual delight.

"What I want is *you*, Uncle Hank. I want us to be pals. Remember we were gonna be pals?"

"We are not pals, Markie. You're not real. You're dead. I killed you. Now *you* remember."

And when I said this, faces turned to me and somebody said, "Hey—"

And Markie was eleven years old again, very pale and very dead, his face bashed in, his teeth scattered over the tabletop in pooling blood, and he did nothing at all, because nothing is what corpses do.

But no one stopped me when I got up and left.

It somehow didn't surprise me to discover, upon returning home, that in the few minutes I had been away, my house had been totally trashed, and everything which had meant anything to me had been methodically destroyed.

My life was over. I knew that. The wound was gushing. I could feel the pain now, getting worse, pain beyond any hope of healing.

The one phone which hadn't been ripped out of the wall rang.

"I left you a little something," said Markie. "On the coffee table."

It was more *through* the coffee table because the table's glass top had been stomped to shards, but there *was* an envelope there. Inside was a large photo of the Mayor of Philadelphia, himself a not entirely successful family man. A hole had been bored through his forehead with a red pen. There was a plastic rifle in the envelope, about two inches long, like the kind I had for G.I. Joe when I was a kid.

"What the fuck is this?" I said, still on the phone.

"I am glad you are speaking my language, Uncle Hank. We understand each other now. We are going to be such pals. I'm having so much fun. What the fuck this is, is a game we're playing, and the name of the game is *you can't stop me, you faggot*—"

"Wait and see," I said. "I can play too."

THE EMPEROR OF THE ANCIENT WORD | 199

The time he had to wait and see was about a week. During that time I managed to acquire a rifle. As I had—ha, ha, this is the funny part, you're supposed to laugh—*no criminal record*, such an upstanding citizen as myself had no particular trouble. Somehow nobody asked any questions even though the Mayor was due to make a speech, outside, in front of City Hall, where bleachers had been set up the way they are at New Year's for the Mummers' Parade.

Markie called me one more time, just to say we were pals.

And why will you say that I am mad? That spoils everything. This account is only of interest if it is fantastic but true, *extraordinary* and not a cheap, commonplace delusion, even as, in Poe's narrative, to which I have repeatedly alluded, the whole point is that the beating heart is *really there*, inexplicably, perversely, thumping away under the floorboards. Let Markie be taken for some kind of Fury or Imp of Conscience materialized out of my subconscious but quite solid, quite capable of interacting with the physical world, some Nemesis, *Doppelgänger*— anything less would have been unworthy of him, and of me, as stealthily, cleverly, precisely I positioned myself in my sniper's nest and saw his explosion of red hair so unmistakably in the crowd through my telescopic sight, and I, who had never fired a weapon before in my life, was actually doing it, actually doing it.

# SAXON MIDNIGHT

*In that time the Saxons strengthened in multitude
and grew in Britain.*

—Nennius

That time? I'll tell you about that time.

It was a time to curse God, despair and die, as Job was called upon to do, when he had lost sons, chattels, lands, and sat diseased atop his dung-heap.

A time to make an end to pain.

A time of a particular midnight, when I howled and ran on all fours through the woods in my madness, when I grubbed through the dirt and leaves like an animal, and unearthed an old, rusty helmet with a skull inside of it; and a voice spoke to me in the British tongue, which I had thought extinct, saying, "Set what you have found upon a high place, make it your idol, and fall down and worship."

This I willingly did, for I could no longer believe that God and Christ were alive in Britain. In Rome perhaps, or more distant Constantinople, or at the edge of the Earth, but no, no here.

It was a time for darkness, then, and for idols.

The dead thing filled with a ruddy light, and spoke like muted thunder, *"But worship me and all that you desire shall be restored unto you."*

That was the beginning of the terrible miracle.

* * * * * * *

I'd had a son once, when I was still a man, before I became a beast. My wife died, and my three daughters; but when the end came, Caradoc was small enough for me to carry him away in my arms. So he was saved that night when the thatched roofs went up with a roar and a whoosh, and women screamed, and silver-masked Saxons howled like devils.

I ran, like a helpless thing, and hid in the forest, and dwelt there, searching for nuts and roots like any other dumb creature; but I had one thing left to keep me human—my boy. Because of him, I could not allow my humanity to die.

I told him the stories of Arthur, of the Table Round, and of the glorious days that once were. I had the tales on the best authority, from my own father, who was a clerk in King Constantine's time; and my father had them from *his*, who actually beheld Camelot.

When he was very young, Caradoc would ask, "Are these funny stories, like Aesop?"

I never angered, but patiently explained that no, there may not have actually been a fox who hungered for grapes, or a tortoise who raced a hare, but there *was* an Arthur, as real as myself, and a Lancelot, and a Guinevere; and Arthur would come again.

Later, my son asked, wide-eyed, "Are these like the stories in the Bible?"

Very solemnly I said, "They are."

In winter's darkness, I cupped my boy's feet in my hands to keep them from freezing, and still told the tales with greatest reverence to distract him from his hunger. But then there came the sounds of horses and of underbrush trampled, and a gleaming helmet seemed to rise into view like the Moon.

Caradoc wriggled from my grasp. "Look father, knights!"

But there were no more knights left in Britain, and in an instant he realized his mistake, but it was too late.

The Saxon chief on horseback, who wore the masked, crested helmet, howled like a wolf. His fellows burst from the bushes all around. Someone grabbed me by the hair and thrust me to my knees before the chief. I heard Caradoc scream and looked up just in time to see the war-chief's axe descend.

Blood sprayed. Saxons laughed. I lunged at the chief, howling myself. I would have torn his throat out with my teeth if I could have reached him, but the others held me back, and, laughing, heaved from one to the other like a sack full of straw.

Then they held me fast once more, and the war-chief gestured with his bloody axe.

"You're not worth killing, old man. Not worth dirtying my blade. Therefore I grant you your life. Am I not merciful?"

All of them roared with laughter again, and beat their swords and axes on their shields; and I know that I became mad then, with rage and grief, for the next thing I knew I was running through the forest, naked and all fours, as has been known to happen to others—to Lancelot for instance, in the stories—and the island was filled with voices calling out for me to curse God, despair, and die.

* * * * * * *

Then the earth opened before the altar I had made, and there were exposed many bones; and I dug them up with my filthy hands, and joined them, bone unto each bone, sinew growing out of the muddy earth; and I placed the head upon the shoulders; and the rusted scraps of metal which clung to them were restored as armor; and with a clanking heave my knight stood before me, dripping and stinking of death, but a knight nonetheless, and his helmet was filled with fire.

"Let me serve you," I said, groveling at his feet.

"Be my squire and fetch my steed," said he.

And I fetched it, for the earth opened once more, and a black horse emerged, snorting fire from its nostrils like a furnace when the bellows blow on the coals.

Then the knight mounted and I got up behind him. I asked him his name, but he said nothing, and I knew him thereafter in my own mind as the Knight Unknown. We rode through the forest at full gallop, and it occurred to me that we were on a quest, just like in the old days, when there were hundreds or even thousands of knights sent out from Camelot, questing all over Britain; and I began to babble in my excitement, saying how the woods used to be thick with holy hermits, common as badgers, one behind every bush. A knight could not scratch himself or stop to squat without a holy hermit explaining to him the import and symbolic meaning of his quest thus far, as the knight struggled to come close to God.

But there were no holy hermits left, I said. And I wasn't so sure about badgers.

The Knight Unknown said nothing. We rode. The forest parted and we came to a field, and charged down a hillside; and it looked as if the knight would skewer the Moon with his lance before it set. We raced toward the horizon, faster, more steadily than Time. Perhaps it was a trick of the eye, but I think the Moon rose a little, back up from its setting.

Then a great white dragon reared up from over the corpse of a red dragon which it had slain. Its mouth was wide as the sky, its gleaming teeth the countless stars; and it roared with the wind of hurricanes.

My knight struck with his lance, then drew his sword and struck again, dealing mighty blows until the head parted from the body, and the dragon vanished with a shout, leaving only the bare hillside, the night sky, and the numberless stars.

\* \* \* \* \* \* \*

When I was a boy one of those innumerable holy hermits took me aside and said, "The doom of Camelot came because of the seven deadly sins, which are Pride, Wrath, Envy, Sloth, Lust, Gluttony, Avarice. These are the unsound foundations. It may not be rebuilt upon any of them."

I wanted to argue that nobody particularly overate at Camelot, which left six—

The badger scurried under his bush.

* * * * * *

What exactly was this quest for? I puzzled over it. I asked my knight but he would not answer. Still we rode, and the Moon did not set nor the Sun rise, and forever it was midnight.

A quest for vengeance. For Saxon blood.

And we came upon a great multitude of the enemy, all dressed and armed for war, with their helmets like silver masks, and their spearpoints gleaming in the moonlight.

Now my unknown knight caused his horse to rear up, and he called out a challenge, demanding a champion to fight him.

One came forth, and he slew him, and another, and a third. Then, seeing the fire within the knight's helmet, the Saxons took flight, and called out to their heathen gods; but to no avail, for the Knight Unknown rode among them and cut them down like wheat. I clung to his back, and snatched a spear from a falling man, and stabbed to right and to left.

And I rejoiced fiercely, certain that by this means the glory of Arthur would be restored.

We came to the stead of a Saxon chief called Wulfhere and caught him unawares. His masked helmet hung on the wall. We killed all his thanes, his carls, then his wife and children before him, then chopped him up a bit at a time, till he howled like a wordless beast in his pain, and when at last I plunged my spear into his throat, and his eyes met mine, and at the very end I said, "Am I not merciful?"

Again I rejoiced, laughing.

Then we passed into villages, and slew all who were there, even the laughing maidens, children at play, babies asleep in their mothers' arms. It made no difference.

We rode on and on, through the endless midnight, beneath the numberless stars, knee-deep in a sea of blood until the very land was hidden from us beneath its tide; and still I rejoiced, hearing the cries of despair from the Saxons. I called out for them to be damned, for them to curse their own gods and die.

The sea of blood stretched featureless from horizon to horizon, and yet we half-rode, half swam through it, until at last there was a speck on the horizon, which grew to become a mound, then a hill, then a great rise of land with a ruined castle atop it.

And when we emerged from out of the bloody sea onto the road which led up to the castle, the Knight Unknown spoke to me again, at last, saying, "Know you this place?"

I said that I did not.

"It is Camelot."

I let out a cry of amazement and, once more, of despair, for it was but a heap of stones, where only owls and wolves might live. Truly I already knew that all the cities of Britain were thus, Eboricum, Camulodunum, and the City of the Legions all burnt, Londinium itself left a hollow shell; but I wept to see Camelot.

"Weep not," said the knight. "Behold."

He touched the stones with his sword, and stone rose upon stone, and rooftops were restored, and light shone from windows, and before my very, unbelieving (or perhaps mad) eyes, the whole of Camelot, it seemed, was restored.

And again I felt justified in my rejoicing.

But when we rode into the great hall, I saw that this was not so, for within all was hollow, and a ruin, and the Round Table lay broken in a heap on the floor, and badgers and serpents lurked under it, and owls fluttered in the rafters.

Again my knight said, as if to reassure my faith in him, "Behold."

He dismounted, and I after him, and he strode to a certain seat, which alone of all that had been there was in no way damaged; but it was no ordinary chair, for I could not truly see more than the outline of it, as if it were a chair carved out of the very shadows of midnight.

"I have longed to sit in this place," said the knight, "for it is the Perilous Seat, where not even Arthur would dare to sit. But now I fear not him nor any other and shall sit there."

I cried out in alarm, and he sat there, his armor gleaming with blood and the corruption of death; and I beheld him in awe, and would have fallen down again, then and there, to worship him, but he merely waved his hand and said, "Look, look. It's all mine now."

I turned and looked, and all around me the feasting hall was filled with light, and the Round Table was whole again, and the knights feasted there.

But there was no place for me. When someone rose for some reason, I stole his place, and there was a silver plate before me, but it was empty.

I looked up, askance, and gazed into the face of King Arthur himself. No one else noticed me, or could see me, as if I were invisible, but I know that *he* could see me. His gaze was wise and sad. He nodded to me, then looked up, as if my eyes should follow.

A gasp arose from the assembled multitude, and suddenly a light suffused the hall, which was to me very faint, no more than a lessening of shadow; but to the others it was more intense than the rising sun, for they cried out and raised their hands to shield their eyes and were dazzled. Miraculously, on everyone's plate but mine was whatever meat that man desired most, and all of them ate, and were satisfied as they had never been satisfied before and never would be again. My own plate, however, was empty; but I was filled with an understanding, for this was a scene from the tales. I beheld that awful Pentecost, when the Holy Grail appeared before the knights at Camelot, and the Grail Quest was begun. Arthur wept in the tale, as he wept now, knowing that this was the beginning of the end, that God had set an impossible standard of moral excellence, for these knights were sinful men, proud, wrathful, envious, lustful, avaricious, even gluttonous just this once (but not, I think slothful; go argue that with a badger), and most of them would perish on the quest. Arthur knew that he would never see them together in fellowship again. Most of them he would never again see alive.

Then my Knight Unknown rose from the Perilous Seat and

shouted, "No, Father! *I* want it! Why can you all see it and not I? *I* shall have it for myself."

But he blundered about blindly through the ruins of the Round Table, for he could not see the Grail, but only knew that others saw it. He could not even see the light of it, which even I could see, though I could not make out the shape itself.

He stumbled and fell on his face with a clatter.

I stood up, and backed away from him, amazed and afraid.

Then a voice called out my own name, which is too insignificant to repeat—let me be called the Unnamed Teller—and said to me, "In the name of Christ, for the rescue of your immortal soul, you must challenge him."

And the miracle and the terror of this was that these words were in the *Saxon* tongue.

I looked and saw that we shared the ruined hall with one of those holy men you used to meet under every bush; and he held up a cross and read from a book and was performing the rites of exorcism. He was a *Saxon* and yet he was a man of God, and I could see the holiness in his eyes, even as I could see the fire of Hell between the slits in my Knight Unknown's visor.

Perhaps, I thought, I had never become insane until that point, but now, truly, I was mad. All that had gone before was mundane, ordinary, but *this* was impossible.

Yet, rather than froth or howl like a madman, I was ashamed, for I realized that I was naked and covered with filth, and I found a scrap of cloth among the ruins of the table, and tied it about myself to cover my nakedness.

The holy man said, "Before you is the great terror which comes in the night, which has haunted this place for many years. You must challenge him."

I stood helplessly.

"With what? I have no weapon."

"Take my staff."

He gave me a plain wooden staff, and it was strong and firm in my hands.

The Knight Unknown staggered to his feet, drew his sword

and came toward me.

"Tell me your name," I said, raising the staff.

"It is Mordred," said he. "Know you the place where you dug me up? It was Camlann, which was once a field is since overgrown. I should be grateful to you for showing me the road back from Camlann to Camelot. I could not have found it without you."

"Recreant traitor, it was you who destroyed Camelot and all of Britain."

He waved his sword toward the holy man. "I think his kind had something to do with it. I only tried to take what was mine. Now, I think, I shall kill all who live on this isle, and reign over a kingdom of ghosts, which shall serve me, even as you have served me."

But I knew that it could not be. The scales fell from my eyes.

I raised my staff and challenged him. He howled and rushed at me, striking mightily with his sword. But the staff held, and I who had no skill at weapons drove him back. I understood then that Camelot could not be rebuilt on unsound foundations. For righteousness could not be made out of sin, and it were better then that Camelot not be rebuilt at all than restored through treason and murder, like a ship floating on a sea of blood; for the kingdoms of this world are but transient things in any case. Nineveh and Tyre are gone. So, too, Camelot.

And if men had failed to meet God's standards, and therefore perished, it was the fault of men, not of God. This much was clear. The fault was mine.

Therefore I drove my knight back all the way to the Perilous Seat, and perhaps he stumbled at the last instant, or else he desired to sit, out of his pride, for that seat was reserved only for the perfect knight, who would achieve the Grail.

He sat, and there was a sucking sound, like a great wind blowing through a stone window, and then he was gone.

The Saxon monk finished his rite of exorcism, and I fell at his feet and wept like a child beaten, repenting my sin, in the full awareness that God is merciful. Even if I had despaired and cursed His name and called upon the darkness, all I had to do was turn again to the light, even as I had glimpsed that light dimly and from afar when the Grail appeared.

And the two of us were alone amid a heap of stones, atop a hill, while the sun rose and the world was filled with ordinary daylight.

\* \* \* \* \* \*

Later, the holy man explained to me the meaning of my quest, telling how a hundred years and more had passed while I sojourned among ghosts, and now the light of Christ had come even to the Saxons; for saints had journeyed from Rome to drive out heathenness as no British sword ever could. My Knight Unknown had been a demon, a terror, for generations, slayer of wicked and righteous alike, until at last, through God's mercy, he had been destroyed in the course of my own redemption.

It was both reward and curse, said the holy man, that I should not age or die for many more years, but go on, throughout the whole of this isle, as a witness to the wondrous things that God has done.

\* \* \* \* \* \*

I dwell under bushes like a badger. Listen! I have seen it all! I will tell you what it was like!

# THE EMPEROR OF
# THE ANCIENT WORD

*The most ancient word is remembered always, but
may never be spoken.*

—Apollonius Soter.

## I.

I cannot tell you where it was that I first met the Emperor
of the Ancient Word. In one of the former European capitals
perhaps, a city well off the usual tourist routes, where the script
was strange and the people spoke a language that sounded a
little like Greek or Italian, but a lot like neither. I know that the
Romans had been there once, because of their monuments, and
there were castles on the hilltops, so perhaps Crusaders passed
by, but the rest must remain vague as a dream, like the grey fog
that rolled up from the river and filled the narrow streets of the
walled town, thick as smoke. Yet it was not a dream, that night
when I was ten and my brother Christopher twelve, and I awoke
in our hotel room *from* a dream—something not quite a nightmare, about a burning mask—and saw my brother standing in
his pajamas, his face pressed to the window.

"*Don't* turn on the light, Alan, if you want to live, Goddamn
it," he whispered.

I dropped my hand away from the light switch. I got up and
stood beside him.

"*Look!*" he said, in tones of almost religious awe.

It took a while for me to figure out what we were looking at. Outside, the fog pooled in the streets, like dry ice fumes used for special effects in a movie, and the streetlights made it glow, so the back stone walls of the houses across the way were washed with a pale white. Above, the sky was beginning to clear. I caught a glimpse of the waning moon, blurry and indistinct.

*"There!"* said Christopher, pointing, and I followed his gaze and I saw it too.

Atop one of the rounded iron posts which lined the sidewalks—presumably to prevent trucks squeezing through those streets from knocking the corners off medieval buildings—was a *moth*, a blue moth, so brilliantly colored that it seemed almost iridescent even under such conditions, and tailed like the more mundane, pale green Luna Moth. It was huge by the standards of moths, nearly six inches in wingspan no doubt, and made even larger by that trick of the streetlight familiar to any night-time collector of insects. Both Christopher and I were dedicated naturalists, and I knew and I am sure he knew that among the giant silk moths of *anywhere*, not to mention Europe or America, a blue, tailed creature with very human-looking eyes on its hind wings was completely impossible. There *was* no such species.

This had to be, somehow, a dream into which we had both awakened.

"Get dressed," said Christopher. "I'm going to catch it."

"With what?"

"With your clothes, dummy!"

"I mean—"

We dressed quickly and in silence. Christopher searched around and found a plastic ice bucket and a guide book he could cover it with. This would have to do, for want of nets or killing jars.

I crept over to the door that adjoined our room with that of our grandfather and listened. Grandfather Septimus was awake in there. I could hear him moving about, and *chanting*, or perhaps praying, or even *conjuring*, whatever it was he did when he burned odd-smelling candles and wouldn't allow anyone to disturb him. Grandfather Septimus claimed to be a magician. He said that was why he was so rich, though I knew he'd made his fortune in business of some kind, but he did do such disconcerting things as go into cemeteries late at night and talk to the headstones. Where this might have counted as madness among more ordinary people, he was rich enough to be merely eccentric, and therefore fit to take his two grandsons, sons of his own son, our father, who had died along with our mother in some obscure way no one ever explained to us, on an amazing and decidedly eccentric tour of European backwaters.

"Are you *coming?*" Christopher said softly.

I followed him down the carpeted stairs. He hid around a corner until the clerk at the front desk was looking away, then darted across the lobby and out the door.

The air was almost cold. The low-lying mist, which sometimes came only chest-high to either of us, had an odd, sweet odor to it—rather like Grandfather's candles—and even a *flavor* which I cannot describe because there is nothing to compare it to.

The moth took off as soon as we came around the corner of the building beneath our window. I glanced up once. Candlelight flickered in Grandfather's window, but I don't think he was looking down at us. In any case, I hadn't the time to think about it, as Christopher and I both took off running after our prey. Our footsteps echoed in the empty streets. The moth flittered, then soared on, pausing again and again to rest on the iron posts at the curbsides, but always taking to the air again, as if it knew perfectly well what we were trying to do.

It *was* blue and it *was* tailed and it *did* have markings like human eyes, for all there was nothing like that in any of the books.

We followed, through the maze of streets, past countless empty windows, in the shadow of great leaning roofs which sometimes shut out the sky from overhead. In these dark places, the moth actually glowed with its own light, soft as that of a paper lantern, which was just one more impossibility, or one more picturesque detail in a dream, if it had been a dream.

And we suddenly emerged into a piazza, where there was a fountain shaped like a knight battling a dragon, and a crumbling arch beyond it.

There, before the fountain, stood a tall man wrapped in a purple robe streaked with gold brocade. He wore, too, a golden breastplate, rings on every finger, and a completely incongruous top hat, which made him look all the taller and somehow not ridiculous—just as impossible as the blue Luna Moth.

He held in his hand a paper mask mounted on a stick, a mask shaped like the very moth we had been chasing.

He put the mask to his face as we approached. The eyes in the hind wings opened. He bowed to us, and told us that he was the Emperor of the Ancient Word, who ruled all the lands, who was not, no, we should not even ask, at all like the mayor or a president, but the potentate of a *secret* empire, which had once been of this world but had now largely withdrawn from it.

He said that we were princes, and therefore welcome.

His voice was strangely accented, but clear. He spoke like an actor carefully mouthing lines he has learned syllable by syllable, in a language he doesn't know.

For an instant he seemed both familiar and indescribably strange.

Now all thoughts of moth-chasing were forgotten, and I was afraid, because none of this made any sense, but Christopher said nothing as the Emperor of the Ancient Word took his hand in his own free hand (the other still holding the mask to his face) and I stood beside them while the mist in the piazza beneath the indistinct moon seemed to take on shapes, which fluttered along the pavement, like countless moths. I saw paper masks and with streamers littered about, the aftermath of some a carnival.

Now these masks floated on the air, as if hundreds of people had been lying on the ground and suddenly stood up, wearing the masks. A great multitude saluted the majesty of the Emperor of the Ancient Word, but their voices were muted, like a distant, whispering wind and they sounded more sorrowful than glad.

I looked to my brother once, and saw that he was trembling, that tears streamed down his cheeks, that his gaze was fixed intently on something I could not see.

I had only the most fleeting sense of what he might be looking at, something glimpsed at the periphery of vision: huge, golden palaces and towers rising above the drab stone town like clouds at dawn gleaming above a ridge line, and, indeed, an ineffable *sense* that here was a place of great power, the center of an immense, perhaps infinite realm, whose borders could not be measured or population numbered by mere human beings.

Then I turned back to the crowd, and there was no crowd, only the darkened piazza strewn with paper, and the only sound was the trickling of water from the fountain. The waning moon had set, and now some *other* light gleamed on windows, like a soft fire just around the curve of one of those narrow streets, quite close at hand.

The gleaming shifted from one place to another, rippling as it moved along streets, just out of sight, momentarily eclipsed by some huge, ornate town hall with lions on the roof, and again flickering at the end of an alley, flowing, its motion almost liquid as it drew nearer.

This was not the light of the moon, I knew.

I heard something rumbling on great wheels.

And the apparition was before us, a huge car or chariot, all aflame, shooting sparks like constellations, its forepart shaped into an enormous mask of a human face. I wanted to run, but the Emperor of the Ancient Word dropped his mask and took hold of my wrist and held onto both Christopher and myself as the thing entered the piazza and came roaring upon us like an avalanche.

At the last instant, the golden eyes of the burning mask opened and its mouth spoke, thundering, *"Life and death to the Emperor of the Ancient Word!"*

It would be perfect, even archetypal, to say that I knew that voice, that I recognized in that instant my long-lost father; but I did not; it was only thunder and I was afraid and I pulled away from the Emperor's grasp and he let me go. More than that, he shoved me aside, hard, and I went sprawling over the paving stones.

I saw the thing run him down. He folded and fell like a crash-test dummy. His hat went flying.

I heard Christopher screaming.

Then there was nothing more until I was found in the morning by jabbering policemen in tall hats and uniforms like band costumes.

\* \* \* \* \* \* \*

It would be easy to say it had all been a dream, that perhaps I'd been sleepwalking to account for my being found quite some distance from our hotel, but it was not a dream, if only for the escapable fact that Christopher was gone, and no amount of police searches could turn up any trace of him.

He had not been kidnapped. There was no ransom note.

Of course any account I had to give was dismissed as hallucination by those psychiatrists and therapists who devoted so much time to me during my adolescence.

I was rich then, and could afford all that attention which my guardians lavished on me, because Grandfather Septimus began to die that very morning that I was found. I could see the vitality draining out of him, little by little, while he looked at me with deep, sad eyes. I could not get him to tell me whatever secret he must have been holding back, and I could not tell him mine, for whenever I spoke of the Emperor of the Ancient Word he waved his hands as if to say, "No! No! It's not true!" and he merely wept; except for the one time when he said something a great deal stranger, which was, "I tell you, Alan, upon my honor, that it wasn't me, but the spirit within me walks about by itself sometimes."

And his concentration seemed to drift, and he was far away

in his mind for several minutes, and again he wept and said, "But what good is the word of an old man anyway? Maybe I'm just in denial."

That summer when I was ten, we actually continued our tour for a little while yet, moving on to more conventional tourist locations. Often Grandfather sent me out with a guide. He said he was too tired, he who had once been able to walk the legs off both me and my brother. He spent a lot of time in hotel rooms with the door locked, praying or working his ineffectual magic. I can remember little of the rest of the trip, save that when we were in Istanbul I had a waking dream, or a vision if you want to call it that, of my brother inside the vast, domed expanse of the great church of Hagia Sophia. I saw him floating up by the ceiling, completely enveloped in flame, but not burning at all. He was transfigured, his arms spread wide to embrace blinding light. He wasn't aware of me at all, even when I disturbed the tour and drew unwelcome attention to myself by shouting his name.

It was all wrong, I somehow, obscurely, knew. I deserved it as much as he. But I was left behind.

When I was fifteen, Grandfather died of an unnamed, wasting illness appropriate for a wealthy recluse of sinister reputation. After all, it was whispered, hadn't he actually killed my father, mother, and older brother in some obscure cult ritual? Wasn't it some manic remorse which now consumed him?

After the will was read, one of the lawyers gave me a manila envelope and told me to open it in private. I did. Inside was the blue paper mask shaped like a moth, a gold coin, and a key. The coin showed an abstract figure in ornate robes and a top hat on one side, and on the other, in crude, bold letters, XPISTOFOROS BASILEVS.

The key was to a strongbox kept in the bedroom of his mansion, now my mansion, since I had inherited everything. Within were nearly a thousand more of the gold coins, and a note in Grandfather's hand, on hotel stationery, which said simply, "Alan, haven't you figured it all out by now?"

# II.

No, Grandfather, I haven't.

"Are you sure it wasn't the Byzantine Empire?" one of the therapists, who should have been a historian or even a poet, asked me once. "The name of the last dynasty was *Paleologos*, which, at least to my uneducated ear would seem to translate as *ancient word* or something very close to that. The empire was a long time dying. There is something irresistibly romantic about that pathetic, shabby realm of almost unimaginable antiquity, lingering, almost invisible in a world that has passed it by, Constantinople a ruined shell, the courtiers like players still on the stage after the audience has gone home. There was even a legend that the last emperor, just before the Turks took the city, vanished into the floor of the church of Hagia Sophia and sleeps there yet, in secret, one day to return. All this could have filtered into your dream—"

"It wasn't a dream," I said sharply.

The therapist shook his head sadly.

I fell asleep on his couch, at fifty dollars a minute, or whatever he charged.

About that time, in a French film about Molière, I saw an image which momentarily arrested me: revelers in the dark, pushing along between them a hay-wagon all aflame, the great wheels rumbling like thunder, the sparks trailing into the sky like stars, the marchers almost solemn in their step, not the slightest bit concerned with what they might set ablaze with this seventeenth century equivalent of fireworks.

But no, it wasn't like that. The image only held me for a moment.

I suppose that I, too, was rich enough to be judged eccentric and not crazy, and so was allowed to attend various universities as I chose, to travel around the world, consulting esoterica in some of the great libraries.

At one point I immersed myself in the study of entomology,

the science of insects, but I already knew that there were no blue Luna Moths, not even in Graustark or Scythia-Pannonia-Transbalkania, or wherever we'd been.

From my occasional hobby of numismatics, I learned that the design on the gold coins superficially resembled a middle Byzantine *solidus* from about the year 800 or so. XPISTOFOROS was typically muddled, Latinate, Byzantine Greek, but I never suspected the piece of any particular antiquity, and the top hat on the obverse figure was a giveaway anyhow.

From a jeweler I learned that the gold was of the highest quality. Each of those coins was worth nearly five hundred dollars apiece for the metal alone, and if there proved to be more stashes of them around the house or grounds, they might indeed have been the source of my grandfather's wealth.

But to the Empire of the Ancient Word I could find no reference, save a hint that Borges had once begun an essay on the subject, then put it aside. Yet there was no trace of it in his papers, which I travelled to Buenos Aires to examine, after having taught myself Spanish for the purpose.

I grew up, not as an international playboy, which might have been expected of the heir to such a fortune as my grandfather's, but as a mysterious figure, I think, a recognized scholar of considerable accomplishment, but someone people shied away from, someone hovering right on the boundary of rich people's eccentricity and madness by any standard. By the time I was twenty I should have been the most eligible bachelor in the world, but I didn't have time for that sort of thing, and I was left alone with my obsessions.

I dreamed of my brother, floating up under the enormous domed ceiling of Hagia Sophia in Istanbul, all in flames but not burning.

I called out to him. He did not answer me, nor did he even look down.

I wanted to be where he was.

# III.

Grandfather, this is what I did to figure it all out:

Occult lore, strange books purchased by my agents at auctions, even initiations into secret societies did nothing for me. The *Necronomicon* proved so much expensive rubbish. The self-proclaimed sages of the esoteric world might have as well have been gibbering apes.

But one of them said something that, incidentally, mattered: The way to travel is to stand still. The way to remember is to cease trying to remember. The way to find is to seek nothing.

I let my fate come to me.

I dreamed my dreams.

But waking, to pass some idle time, I chanced to be at a coin fair in London's Marble Arch, happily rooting through an unsorted box dirty and sometimes encrusted *folles* of the likes of Theophilus, Nicephorus the First, and Michael the Drunkard. The dealers didn't recognize me here, or else they'd be vying to show me the rarest and choicest, and I certainly would not have accomplished what I actually did accomplish.

It wasn't much to look at, a dirty piece about the size of a United States quarter, only thinner, its designs smeared from a bad strike, the concavities filled in with hardened soil. But I could make out enough of the legend: XPRISTOFO.

I scraped the obverse with my fingernail. The crudely rendered figure was wearing an impossible top hat.

That was how it started. In Amsterdam, at the Rijksmuseum, I was the only person, I am sure, who was able to see that some of the figures in Rembrandt's *The Night Watch* wore the purple and gold brocaded robes of the courtiers of the Emperor of the Ancient Word. In Venice, during the carnival, of course, I saw the masks. I thought back on the French *Life of Molière*. Here too, I understood, the Empire of the Ancient Word peered through, from out of some submerged realm, into the "real" world.

It was not to be searched out geographically. It was anywhere and everywhere.

Therefore I went home to the family estate in New York, overlooking the Hudson, and merely waited. Rummaging about I found my grandfather's various ritual candles and such—even the secret panel which slid back to reveal his conjuring room, with its golden masks on the walls and pentagram on the floor—all that useless Halloween stuff. How close to the truth my grandfather had come, and how far away he remained.

He had only to wait as I did. The evidence was all around me, whenever it wished to reveal itself. In a story in a popular magazine, I found an eerily precise description, but cast as a fantasy, amid a ridiculous plot about rival brothers, like a perfect diamond set in the middle of a child's mud sculpture without any comprehension of its worth.

I waited on my pillared porch in the evening, gazing down over the river. I had time to contemplate the exact meaning of the phrase "Ancient Word," and to wonder what that word was, and I concluded, as had some ancient writer I couldn't quite call to mind, that the most ancient word is the one that no one can speak. It is sacred, like the Hebrew names of God.

I waited, until the blue Luna Moth came to me of its own accord, fluttering on my outstretched hand, certain now that I had no intention of dropping it into a killing jar or impaling it on a pin.

I waited, with the old, tattered paper mask held before my face, a dozen gold coins in my pocket, and I saw the light in the distance, hovering in the air; no, rushing toward me across the level plain of another world which had superimposed itself on the Hudson Valley. The earth shook as the flaming carriage approached on its massive wheels, as my brother's golden face opened startled eyes and called out, *Life and death to the Emperor of the Ancient Word!*

I did not flinch or turn away, but hurled myself into the flames, into his gaping mouth.

And I landed with a thump, tumbling, in the throne room

of a vast golden palace where a flame-crowned emperor sat amid countless purple-and-gold robed courtiers. A palace I saw, though it swayed and shook like the car of a railroad train that's going much too fast.

I knew what I had to do.

All that while I had contemplated this moment.

I pushed my way through the startled courtiers as if through a field of wheat. I mounted the steps before the throne. The Emperor, who was a child, who was my brother Christopher still twelve years old, stirred as if out of a deep sleep and blearily said, "Alan? Is that you?"

I seized him. I tore off his golden robes. I told him I'd come to save him, to give him his life back.

"Just think. You get to be a kid again," I said. "Isn't that great?"

But even he knew I didn't mean a word of it and he began to struggle. Never mind. I swiftly overpowered him and *heaved* him *out* through some opening or angle in the air that only I could perceive. And he was gone, and I, I, sat down on the throne, clad in gold and in fire, and I, I, placed the burning crown on my head, I, I, motivated not by any petty jealousy, but by certain destiny, the knowledge that I, I, and I alone was destined to rule the Empyrean Realm forever and ever, that I, I, and I alone was the last and true Emperor of the Ancient Word—

Milton's Satan, if he had somehow managed to steal the throne of Heaven, would have understood. So the burning carriage of the Emperor of the Ancient Word passed through all the hidden lands, to receive the tribute of subjects, to shower, in turn, largesse upon them in the form of golden coins bearing *my* name and likeness; and when I addressed the people I wore, not the burning crown of the court, but the slightly ridiculous, if traditional top hat, which made me seem as one of them, first among equals, a regular guy looking out for their welfare.

But most of the time I wore the *crown*, and then I soared in dreams like an impossible moth through all the minds and memories of men; and I knew all pleasures and all pain; and

I heard the Ancient Word itself echoing among the stars; and I think a thousand years passed; and I came to know that the Empire I ruled over was populated entirely by ghosts, that once, long ago, it had actually existed in the real world and could be found on a map, and had decayed away to nothing more than a shabby court living out meaningless rituals in the ruined shell of a capital while barbarians pounded at the gates—and then, *then* it happened, long ago and just yesterday, for the act suspended time—and then the Emperor in desperation *uttered* the Ancient Word aloud, folding space and time over himself like a cloak, until he sank beneath and *behind* the empirical world—what a strange choice of words—ha! ha!—and he and his court and his domain vanished from history, from time, and slowly, imperceptibly the memories of him faded from the minds of men, and books written about him either disappeared or came to be about something else; allusions in poetry drifted away, until the meaning was no longer clear; those few coins of the various emperors which might still be found were either corroded and illegible, or inexplicable novelties.

So I understood, and so I reigned, in the fulfillment of my ambitions and desires, for a day, a century, an thousand years, wearing the crown of fire.

But then Grandfather Septimus, who had died, came to me, wearing his robe and his top hat, and he said, "Alan, you haven't figured it out at all."

"How's that?" I asked.

"You haven't understood the *cost* of the Emperor's action."

"What cost?"

He held out his hands, and the blue moth drank blood from out of his palm, for his hands had been pierced; and I saw that he was barefoot, and his feet and been pierced, and he left bloody footprints on the floor; and his robe clung to him, soaked in blood; and blood streamed down his face as if he wore a crown of thorns beneath his absurd top hat.

"Oh yes," he said. "We had all that imagery first, before the other fellow."

There was a nimbus of light around his head. His face glowed, like a paper lantern.

He explained to me how the Emperor of the Ancient Word died and was resurrected countless times, in the person of each of his heirs, who are *himself* repeated again and again down the centuries, like reflections in a house of mirrors.

I saw my brother Christopher crucified, dying, in terrible pain, but clad in the robes of priest and emperor, and at the same time triumphant, transcendent, because he, too, was the Emperor of the Ancient Word.

And I saw Grandfather Septimus thus, and I saw him rise from his grave.

I was told that my father, the real coward in our line, had tried to escape. He fell on a sword, in the antique manner.

But it didn't matter, for I met my father there in the court, and he was bleeding from but one more wound, and he said to me, *"This is Hell, nor am I out of it; but it is also Heaven, nor am I out of it."*

And I saw that he, like all the courtiers, was barefoot and wading ankle-deep in his own blood.

His face burned softly.

Christopher came down from his cross, floating in the air, and he spoke to me, revealing that everyone here, everyone in the entire empire where echoed the Ancient Word was but a reflection of the first and only Emperor, and this was our legacy and our family curse, that the first-born of each generation of our family should *be* the Emperor of the Ancient Word, even as my brother, father, and grandfather were not separate individuals, but the *same*.

"It takes some getting used to," said Christopher.

"Well what about *me?*" I demanded.

"You could have escaped. You are a *second* son, of no importance, unless the first fails to produce an heir, which never happens, of course—"

"But sometimes," Grandfather said, "when we are on Earth or when we journey back there, we forget all this, and the truth has to be discovered all over again. Out of fear, I denied it for a long time."

"This is crazy!" I shouted. "I rule here! *I* am Emperor of the Ancient Word! I command you to bow down before me!"

I had no idea what I was saying, of course. I surely *was* insane just then, if I thought to be the first *usurper* of the Ancient Word.

Instead of bowing down before me, they all as one, because they all *were* one, spoke the Ancient Word aloud, and I heard it echoing through the stars; and I tried to repeat it, but my lips could not form the shape, and my tongue burst into flame; and I was falling, falling as someone stripped off crown and robes and hurled me down from the throne, down through the darkness and the stars, through the invisible realm of the invisible sovereigns of whom I was not one; and in some dark place I was scourged and nailed to a cross, but without priestly robes, naked, and I felt only the pain, not any transcendence, not any hope of resurrection as I saw my rightful kingdom draw away from me like a golden tide across flat sand.

## IV.

It takes some getting used to.

I think it is because I have the blood of the emperors in me that I did not die, that I cannot die.

I was found, naked and horribly wounded, lying by a roadside in upstate New York. The police called it ritual torture and pressed me at length about Satanic cults, and when I told them the truth they thought I was delirious, and when I even told them who I was in *this* world they dismissed it, telling me that my family had died out twenty-five years ago when the last heir mysteriously disappeared, and I could not be he, because he'd be about fifty by now and I was half that age.

But I told them that in the Empire of the Ancient Word times moves differently, and these things get mixed up.

In the end my wounds healed, but I had no identity and

nowhere to go, and so was placed in an asylum, where I came to understand my true self, that I am *not* the Emperor of the Ancient Word, but his adversary, his dark brother, the rival, the usurper, who will cause war in the Empyrean Realm *behind* the spaces men know, who will tear down Heaven and rebuild it to his own liking.

I have only to gather followers around myself, to work dark miracles, to wait until the blue moth rests upon my scarred hand and the very air opens up for me.

# ACKNOWLEDGMENTS

"At the Top of the Black Stairs" first appeared in *Realms of Fantasy*, October 2005. Copyright © 2005 by Sovereign Media.

"The Hero Spoke" first appeared in *Realms of Fantasy*, August 2006 as *The Hero*. Copyright © 2006 by Sovereign Media.

"Tom O'Bedlam and the Mystery of Love" first appeared in *The Enchanter Completed* edited by Harry Turtledove, Baen Books, 2005. Copyright © 2005 by Darrell Schweitzer.

"The Fire Eggs" first appeared in *Interzone* #153, March 2000. Copyright © 2000 by Interzone. It has also appeared in *The Year's Best SF #6* (2001) edited by David G. Hartwell.

"The Dead Kid" first appeared in *The Book of More Flesh* edited by James Lowder, published by Eden Studios, 2002. Copyright © 2002 by Darrell Schweitzer.

"Fighting the Zeppelin Gang" first appeared in *Postscripts* #8, Autumn 2006. Copyright © 2006 by Darrell Schweitzer.

"Sweep Me to My Revenge!" first appeared in *Talesbones* #35, Summer 2007. Copyright © 2007 by Talebones Magazine.

"A Lost City of the Jungle" first appeared in *Astounding Hero Tales* edited by James Lowder, published by Hero Games, 2007. Copyright© 2007 by Darrell Schweitzer.

"Our Father Down Below" first appeared in *Cemetery Dance* #35, August 2001. Copyright © 2001 by Cemetery Dance Publications.

"The Messenger" first appeared in *Weird Tales* #347, November/December 2007. Copyright © 2007 by Wildside

# ABOUT THE AUTHOR

Four-time World Fantasy Award nominee (and one-time winner) **Darrell Schweitzer** has been has been publishing short fiction in various fantastic modes—heroic fantasy, horror, surrealism, science fiction—for forty years now and is one of the more prolific writers in the field, with over three hundred published stories to his credit. The present volume is his seventh collection of unrelated stories. He has also the author of the story-cycles, *We Are All Legends, Sekenre: The Book of the Sorcerer, Living With the Dead*, and *Echoes of the Goddess*—and three novels, *The White Isle, The Shattered Goddess*, and *The Mask of the Sorcerer*. He is additionally a noted scholar and critic, the author of books on H. P. Lovecraft and Lord Dunsany, a poet, and anthologist—and he served as co-editor of the legendary *Weird Tales* for nineteen years.

CPSIA information can be obtained at www.ICGtesting.com
Printed in the USA
LVOW12s1032130414

381490LV00007B/431/P